LAVA

A Historical Novel of Haunted Hawaii

DAVID D. ALLEE

Email: ddallee@att.net
Website: http://www.davidallee.net

For my parents, James and Frances, whose life-long dedication and support has made all the difference over the years…

And to my Hawaiian *ohana*, a group of caring folks from Kurtistown A/G (…you know who you are…) whose love, acceptance, and forgiveness remains embedded in my soul to this day…

This story is for you.

"Oh, honest Americans, as Christians hear me for my downtrodden people! Their form of government is as dear to them as yours is precious to you. Quite warmly as you love your country, so they love theirs. With all your goodly possessions, covering a territory so immense that there yet remains parts unexplored, possessing islands that, although new at hand, had to be neutral ground in time of war, do not covet the little vineyard of Naboth's, so far from your shores, lest the punishment of Ahab fall upon you, if not in your day, in that of your children, for "be not deceived, God is not mocked." The people to whom your fathers told of the living God, and taught to call "Father," and now whom the sons seek to despoil and destroy, are crying aloud to Him in their time of trouble; and He will keep His promise, and will listen to the voices of His Hawaiian children lamenting for their homes."

- *Lili uokalani, Last Queen of Hawaii*

I Kings, Chapter 21, verses 1-19, 23:

"And it came to pass…*that* Naboth the Jez'reelite had a vineyard, which *was* in Jezreel, next to the palace of Ahab king of Samaria. And Ahab spake unto Naboth, saying, Give me thy vineyard, that I may have it for a garden of herbs, because it *is* near unto my house: and I will give thee for it a better vineyard than it;

or, if it seem good to thee, I will give thee the worth of it in money.

And Naboth said to Ahab, The LORD forbid it me, that I should give the inheritance of my fathers unto thee. And Ahab came into his house heavy and displeased because of the word which Naboth the Jez'reelite had spoken to him: for he had said, I will not give thee the inheritance of my fathers. And he laid him down upon his bed, and turned away his face, and would eat no bread.

But Jez'ebel his wife came to him, and said unto him, Why is thy spirit so sad, that thou eatest no bread? And he said unto her, Because I spake unto Naboth the Jez'reelite, and said unto him, Give me thy vineyard for money; or else, if it please thee, I will give thee *another* vineyard for it: and he answered, I will not give thee my vineyard.

And Jez'ebel his wife said unto him, Dost thou now govern the kingdom of Israel? Arise, *and* eat bread, and let thine heart be merry: I will give thee the vineyard of Naboth the Jez'reelite.

So she wrote letters in Ahab's name, and sealed *them* with his seal, and sent the letters unto the elders and to the nobles that *were* in his city, dwelling with Naboth.

And she wrote in the letters, saying, Proclaim a fast, and set Naboth on high among the people and set two men, sons of Be'li-al, before him, to bear witness against him, saying, Thou didst blaspheme God and the king. And *then* carry him out, and stone him, that he may die. And the men of his city, *even* the elders and the nobles who were the inhabitants in his city, did as Jez'ebel had sent unto them, *and* as it *was* written in the letters which she had sent unto them. They proclaimed a fast, and set Naboth on high among the people.

And there came in two men, children of Be'li-al, and sat before him; and the men of Be'li-al witnessed against him, *even* against Naboth, in the presence of the people, saying, Naboth did blaspheme God and the king. Then they carried him forth out of the city, and stoned him with stones, that he died.

Then they sent to Jez'ebel, saying, Naboth is stoned, and is dead. And it came to pass, when Jez'ebel heard that Naboth was stoned, and was dead, that Jez'ebel said to Ahab, Arise, take possession of the vineyard of Naboth the Jez'reelite, which he refused to give thee for money: for Naboth is not alive, but dead.

And it came to pass, when Ahab heard that Naboth was dead, that Ahab rose up to go down to the vineyard of Naboth the Jez'reelite, to take possession of it.

And the word of the LORD came to Eli'jah, saying, Arise, go down to meet Ahab king of Israel, which *is* in Samaria: behold, *he is* in the vineyard of Naboth, whither he is gone down to possess it.

And thou shalt speak unto him, saying, Thus saith the LORD, Hast thou killed, and also taken possession? And thou shalt speak unto him, saying, Thus saith the LORD, In the place where dogs licked the blood of Naboth shall dogs lick thy blood, even thine…And of Jez'ebel also spake the LORD, saying, The dogs shall eat Jez'ebel by the wall of Jezreel."

Chapter One

November, 1780 A.D. – The Big Island of Hawaii

Moisture-laden sea breezes blew softly across his face, gently parting the curly locks of hair which fell across his burnt forehead. Standing this close to the ocean, he could actually smell and taste the salt in the air as he licked his lips. The roaring crash of turquoise-green surf against the sharp cliffs sent forth leaping fountains of foam; the outermost edges of the spray dappled him and the young Hawaiian girl standing at his side.

The savage serenity of this moment contrasted sharply with the unrelenting terror which had pursued them for the past four hours. Chased through thick forests of ohia trees and then out on the lava flats of Kau, the tiny refugee group finally paused. Breathlessly panting, the two lovers stood hand-in-hand, bare feet bloodied by the exhaustive trek. He glanced down into her face, staring into those large, dark eyes – eyes which neither blamed him nor held him to account for that which was about to come upon them. *My God,* he thought inwardly, *has it all come down to this? Is this going to be the end of it?*

Another mournful, low-pitched tone wafted across the horizon – the alarm call of the conch shell. When blown by an expert, its somber note could be heard for well over two miles away. Jonah Pessoa knew its meaning all too well. They would be closing in now. Based on the volume of the call, they were perhaps no more than a couple of hundred yards distant, just where the Hawaiian woodland yielded to the undulating tables of broken lava which fringed the bay where the two of them now stood. He and Lilena would not make it to the City of Refuge. They would be caught, caught and punished. He knew the fate that awaited him. He would be kept alive, his bones systematically broken – *Lua*, as the Hawaiians called it – carefully, one at a time, until his entire body could be literally folded over. They would carry him back to Hilo where he would be sacrificed, still alive, in a make-shift temple of the war-god Ku. He had seen the bone-breaking done so many times to so many others and had actually studied the art himself. It was a gruesome thing. He determined right then and there that he would not be taken alive.

Lilena's fate was uncertain. After all, she was *ali'i*, Hawaiian royalty, and, as such, could not be harmed by the soldiers of Kamehameha's armies. But, then again, she had violated his wishes, deliberately and willfully, and Kamehameha was not known to forgive those who disobeyed him. He was an unmerciful leader and his single-minded determination to rule over the Island had brought a level of fighting and bloodshed to the royal family that was unprecedented in the history of their people. Jonah Pessoa hated him for that.

A piercing groan escaped from the lips of the young girl as she doubled over in pain, grasping her swollen belly just below the waistline. "Is it going to happen now?" asked Jonah, speaking flawlessly in the native tongue.

"Yes," she whispered back in-between painful gasping breaths, desperately trying to suppress the scream that was building within her. Hawaiian women did not cry out in pain, lest they be shamed. Another pang seized the young girl and she whimpered, buckling over and falling down onto one knee.

"The child is coming now. We must get her to a safe place. There is a small cave back over there," said Jonah to the eldest of the three who had fled with him and Lilena as they escaped from the volcano. Two were personal guardsmen, assigned for life to the care and keeping of the young Lilena, daughter to Keoua, the only remaining rival to Kamehameha for rule of the Island and rightful heir to the throne of his deceased father, King Kuahuula, ruler over all Hawaii. The other one among them, an old woman – he actually had no knowledge of whatsoever.

The Hawaiians had spied the small cave as well, and the two guardsmen feared it. The signs of *kapu*, meaning forbidden, were clearly posted — small piles of rocks stacked up in vertical columns on either side of the cave's mouth, a universally recognized signal. "It is kapu," said one of the Hawaiian soldiers, half-heartedly, his protest a mild submission. He waited nervously for the first voice, any voice, to overrule his weak objection. "We have no choice," said Jonah somberly.

"She comes. The baby — she comes now!" whispered Lilena, grimacing in pain.

Jonah grasped her by the arm, cradling the scorched .69 caliber British musket in the crook of his elbow just as she collapsed. The two younger guardsmen picked up her limp form and carried her over to the cave, stooping down to enter into its darkness. Jonah and the old woman followed behind. The shade of the grotto provided a welcome respite from the intense heat of the tropical sun; the floor of the cave was smooth, sandy, and free of debris. It was the best place they were going to find.

Once inside, Lilena kneeled to the ground with her knees apart. The elder, white-haired Hawaiian woman took charge. She reached into her grass-woven basket and brought forth morning glory leaves. She inserted these into Lilena's mouth, instructing her to chew them as she knelt in front of Lilena, positioning herself.

In one massive push, the young Hawaiian girl delivered a child. With a quickness which belied her age, the old crone wiped down the infant with banyan leaves and expertly cut the umbilical cord with a koa-wood knife. One very large banyan leaf, brought forth from her woven basket, provided the only covering that was needed as the silent infant was laid gingerly into the center and then wrapped tightly in the broad, green material. Both sides of the leaf covered the newborn; only her face peered out from the soft wrapping. The disheveled old woman carefully massaged the child as she gazed lovingly into the infant's eyes – a depth of emotion coming from her that Jonah Pessoa found intriguing, curious…and just a little bit out of place, given the very short time she had been among their company.

Shadows fell across the grotto's opening as the sunlight streaming into the mouth of the cave was interrupted, broken up by the sinister forms of men. Each one blotted out a portion of the sun, throwing the inhabitants of the small cave into an even deeper darkness. The warriors stood silently at the mouth of the cave, the occasional shuffling of feet the only sound that was heard. Every second it appeared another one had joined their ranks until the entire opening was filled with warriors, standing two and three deep, perhaps forty men or more in total. Jonah slowly cocked the hammer back on the flintlock musket. Its audible click resonated throughout the cave like a thunderclap in the midst of an otherwise eerie silence which had enveloped them all. The ancient looking crone, holding the newborn child, faded back, deeper into the darker recesses of the grotto.

"King Kamehameha demands you be killed. No one is to be spared, but Lilena. The King demands his betrothed be returned to him," proclaimed the leader of the troop, a wide man with a thick neck and expansive chest. Framed by the sunlight, the figure standing at the front of the cave mouth cast an intimidating shadow. Atop his head sat a red feathered skullcap; a central crest of bright yellow feathers rose high above it, culminating in a pompadour which protruded forward. A feathered cape, emblazoned with the same vivid red and yellow feathers as his headdress, lay across one shoulder and dropped down no further than the belly. A simple tapa loincloth draped down the front of his waist. His feet were shod with reed-woven sandals, a luxury his intended victims did not enjoy. In his hand he held a shark-toothed war club, a vicious slashing weapon with over thirty teeth surrounding its oblong outer edge. Dried blood encrusted the edges of those jagged shark-teeth.

"Kamehameha is no King to us," replied Jonah Pessoa, his voice dripping with resentment. "Keoua is the rightful King of Hawaii. We serve him and him alone." Jonah paused before adding, "Why do you persecute your own brethren?"

There was a moment of silence before the warrior chief answered back. "It was foretold you might answer in this manner. Keoua is already defeated. His armies died at the hands of Ku, god of war. The goddess Pele herself has cast her lot in with Kamehameha, no?"

"Liar!" screamed out Lilena, exhausted from the childbirth but spirited enough to defend her father's honor.

"It is destined that Kamehameha reign. It has been prophesied," continued the war chief.

"I have heard things such as this before," replied Jonah, "but I have come to one conclusion. It is not the gods we worship which ordain the affairs of men but men which ordain the affairs of our gods. Which god among us would not even have a temple, had not the hand of man built it for him? Which god among us would have not even a totem, or an altar, had not the hand of man carved it from the wood of the tree or the stone of the earth? Who are these gods, who seem unable to create anything of worship by themselves, requiring the hand of man to build it for them? They are no gods whatsoever. That which we do, we do of our own accord. Let us not prescribe our actions to the will of a god. Either for good or for evil, our actions are ours and ours alone."

Jonah Pessoa remained silent, taken aback by the very words he himself had just uttered. It was almost as if another were speaking through him, words he had not planned nor intended to speak – and he was unconvinced by his own diatribe. No matter how much he tried, he could not shake himself from an underlying faith in divine Providence. No matter how many times he had cursed God, had paid homage to the local Hawaiian deities, then become angry with them and cursed them as well, in times of danger he always found himself defaulting back to a belief in the ultimate Being – a single god above all others, one Supreme Deity, as he had been taught from childhood. He was a hopeless monotheist, despite his blustering.

"It was foretold you might say these words as well. Is this the belief of each of you, or only that of the light-skinned stranger?" asked the war chief. No one answered.

"And you, daughter of Keoua, betrothed of King Kamehameha? Are these your beliefs as well? Have you forsaken the goddess Pele, and refuse to honor Ku? And you two, her guardians – have you forsaken the beliefs of your ancestors as well?"

His questions were met with silence and the stone cold glares of the young daughter of Keoua and her lover along with her two guardsmen. The white-haired old woman and the newborn child had silently disappeared deeper into the cave and were not heard from.

The war chief turned to his men and somberly ordered, "All are to be killed. Spare no one, not even the daughter of Keoua. Save the white man for last. These are the orders of King Kamehameha, given their response."

Slowly, one step at a time, the warriors entered the cave mouth, their long spears now hoisted at ear level, ready to be hurled in an instant. The two royal guardsmen arose from their kneeling position and stood in front of the young girl, crossing their own spears against one another, forming an X.

Jonah Pessoa raised the scarred and burnt musket to eye level, planting the butt stock firmly against his shoulder as he sighted down the barrel, the pewter front blade fixed squarely upon the war chief's wide chest. If the damned thing still worked, then that man would be the first to go down. After his one and only shot, he would try to kill as many as he could before they overcame him. Death was inevitable.

He cast a quick glance over at his beloved, their eyes making contact with each other in the dark, communicating his deepest love and sorrow for the circumstances he had brought upon them. His eyes apologized, desperately seeking her forgiveness, for the situation he had put her in, put all of them in. But there was no fear or remorse in her dark, youthful eyes. Only love – and a resolute determination. It was as if, without saying the words, she was communicating back to him, somehow telling him that she would not have wanted it to be any other way, that she had no regrets, and that she was ready and willing to face what lie directly in front of them...and that, at some deeper, unfathomable level, this was the way it was supposed to be.

Then he spied a face, a face above the crowd, taller than any man standing there, the only white one among an entirely bronzed-face gathering. The face made its way from the back of the group of warriors, walking in an awkward gait, until it appeared directly in front of the war-chief, assuming the position of command. It was a face Jonah recognized. A face that had once been a friend to him, one of only two friends he had left aboard the *Fair American*, before he was tossed overboard, a face that had helped to save his life when the others would have seen him dead. It was the face of Isaac Davis!

Jonah's eyes lit up at the presence of one who had long ago befriended him. But the look of friendship and assurance was not returned in the sorrowful gaze of Isaac Davis. He watched as his one-time savior slowly raised a British musket at him, its gleaming silver barrel bands catching the sunlight which streamed into the cave. This time there would be no rescue. This time they were on opposite sides of a war – a war neither one of them belonged in, a war that Jonah had earlier convinced himself had everything to do with which God or gods would prove themselves true when, in fact, it had nothing to do with the gods. It was pure simple lust for power. Men, killing and being killed, all of it for the right to reign over one's brother – for the right to be called King over an island. There could be nothing more base, more human, than that. *How could I have been so naive as to believe God would care or even want to be involved in affairs such as these?,* thought Jonah Pessoa to himself.

"I guess this is going to be the end of it?" asked Jonah, deliberately speaking in the English tongue. None but they two recognized the language.

"You are on the wrong side of a war, my friend," answered Isaac Davis… in English. "I fight for the King, King Kamehameha. You have taken one of his betrothed. And he has ordered you dead. I see you have cheated death once already?"

"Only because of your intervention, my friend. Without you, I would not have survived it," replied Jonah.

"Then I am truly sorry to have to do this."

Jonah changed languages, shifting to the Portuguese tongue. "Helped save a life once…only to have to take it again, by those very same hands?"

questioned Jonah, seeking some small semblance of guilt or hesitation in the eyes of Isaac Davis. Then, mockingly, he repeated that too familiar refrain – "Is it all you can do, Mr. Davis?"

"Forgive me, *again*, Jonah," rasped out the Englishman in broken Portuguese as he cocked back the flint-jawed hammer on his .69 caliber Brown Bess musket.

"Only God can do that," Jonah replied, his own rifle still cocked and aimed directly at the Hawaiian war chief who stood beside Isaac Davis.

In spite of the imminent threat, Jonah Pessoa's thoughts began to drift, drift back to the beginning of all this, just two years ago. Had it really only been that short of a time? Was it only two years past when his otherwise undisturbed and tranquil young life took such a dramatic turn, setting in motion a spiraling series of events, events which had brought it all to this moment.......?

Chapter Two

November, 1778 A.D. – The Port Village of Horta, on the Island of Faial, The Azore Islands, 900 miles to the west of Portugal.

From the first time that Jonah Pessoa had laid eyes upon it, the lush sub-tropical landscape of Faial had cast a spell over him. From the sea, it shone a brilliant blue in color, thousands upon thousands of hydrangeas casting their azure hue over the land. The abundant blue flower prospered throughout the island, climbing up and down every little river valley and cresting over each hilly ridge. The tillable lands of Faial were sprinkled with small farms, orchards, vineyards, and gardens dotting the landscape, criss-crossing the rich vegetation and rustic laurel forests with their hedgerows and stone walled fencing. The small vineyard Jonah had cultivated on a patch of unclaimed land, less than a mile from their tiny stone cottage, sat just outside the reaches of the village of Horta, a small port community protected by a massive stone fortress, built in the 16th century.

Jonah and his mother had resettled here less than six months ago, migrating from the Douro region of Portugal. It was there that the original Pessoa family heritage had been built with the production of some of the finest grapes ever used in port wine. The Pessoa ancestors had long ago planted vineyards into terraces that they had hand-carved, built into the steep slopes which surrounded the river Douro. Young Jonah held many a fond memory of long voyages down the lazy waterway with his father, their banana-shaped flat-bottom boat loaded to the brim with Tinta Barroca grapes which they offloaded in Vila Nova de Gaia, just across the river from Oporto. There, the large port houses – which clung to the steep hillsides much the same way the Pessoa family vineyards did along the steep mountainsides miles upriver – purchased the Pessoa grapes as well as wine from other local growers. Here the grapes and finished wines were blended, aging in barrels and giant wooden casks which lay deep in underground cellars until they were shipped out on British vessels, providing a prosperous trade for all the parties involved. It was a happy time, the kind of simple, earthy life a fifteen-year old vintner like Jonah was proud to live. That was before his father had died – before he and his mother had come to Faial.

Manuel Pessoa was a good man, a strong man. Although not tall, his square cut features and broad shoulders gave him a powerful look, the look of a man that demanded respect. His high broad forehead was topped by a straight line of sandy colored hair, curly and thick; his dark eyes were deep set, crested by thick eyebrows. A full mustache framed his upper lip and a broad, square chin gave his face a chiseled look. A lifetime of hard labor in the fields and vineyards had made him strong as an ox. Without warning, he had often delighted in lifting his wife up onto one arm while scooping up Jonah in the other, literally lifting the weight of his family onto his shoulders. Despite her shrieks of protest, the show of strength had always impressed Jonah's mother, evidenced by the grin on her face. What had also been just as evident to young Jonah was the fact that his father worshipped his mother.

Being the only child meant Jonah was close to his father. Young Jonah had looked forward to a lifetime of harvesting the family vineyards alongside his father, perhaps even producing their own port wine some day, as so many of the other growers along the Douro River had done. Simple dreams, simple hopes, yet the whole of it came to a devastating halt that balmy summer evening young Jonah would forever remember.

"Papa! Papa! Dinner is ready. Come to eat!" Jonah had shouted from their cottage high atop the hillside, but to no avail. Usually, his father would have ceased tending the vines by now, making his way back up the steep terraced hillsides in time for supper. It was not like him to be late for Mama's supper.

"Go and find your father. Hurry, now, before the soup gets cold," she ordered him, half annoyed, half worried. She had been married to the man for sixteen years and not once had he been late for her famous kale soup.

Not yet thirty years of age, Maria Pessoa was still a striking figure. Long coal black hair, shiny and straight, was knotted at the back of her head other than at bedtime when she would let it down, the length of it falling below her knees. She was as tall as her husband, though much thinner, petite of frame. Soft olive-green colored eyes set off a face that was heart-shaped, rounded at the top with a defined widow's peak then narrowing down at the chin, with a complexion that was just one shade lighter than her husband's. Her voice was sweet, almost musical in tone, and Jonah had often wondered why she did not sing fados when their small village held its annual festivals, something his father never missed an opportunity to do.

Manuel Pessoa was famous for bringing both his strong baritone voice and his twelve string cittern to every festival and celebration in the village, singing fados well into the night to the delight of everyone, including the village women – especially the women. The sad mournful lyrics, which Jonah's father could string together in a melodic prose unlike any other, conveyed pain, sadness, happiness, and love, blended together in a complexity of emotion that was impossible to contest or mimic. Whenever Manuel Pessoa strummed the cittern and sang fado, everyone and everything else would fall silent until he finished. It was a strange magical spell, unlike anything young Jonah had ever witnessed. It further bolstered his boyish belief that his father could do anything, be anybody – yet he chose to stay and work the vineyards, the vineyards his ancestors had left to him, the vineyards Jonah imagined himself working as far out into the future as childhood imagination could carry him.

Jonah sprinted down through the terraces, driven, in part, by his own hunger. No matter how famished they may have been, no one was seated for supper until Papa was seated. Carefully, Jonah made his way through the succeeding lower terraces, calling and calling for his father. Winding down one level after another, Jonah continued to call until he reached the river's edge. That is when he first saw him, lying face down in a slow circular moving jetty of the river.

"Papa! Papa!" he cried out, but there was no stirring, no movement of the body.

He raced towards his father, splashing into the river with wild abandon. Grasping him by the thick leather belt which surrounded his mid-section, Jonah pulled with all of his might. Manuel Pessoa was a heavy man and, despite the buoyancy of the water, young Jonah barely managed to drag his father's body out onto the steep bank. As he carefully cradled the head of his father between his wet hands, the waterlogged face inadvertently turned toward him. It bore little resemblance to the broad, smiling face he had come to love and admire. Deep purple contusions marked the cheeks, disfiguring his countenance. The lips were cracked and split open. Teeth were missing and a broad gash striped across his thick neck, carved from ear to ear. Although still just a boy, Jonah knew all too well the look of death. His father was dead, murdered.

Overwhelming despair engulfed his young heart. An immediate sense of loss and aloneness was suddenly upon him. Although Jonah had never before known the feeling of abandonment that comes with the death of a parent, its presence was instantly a part of him – the feeling was never to leave him.

A choking sensation arose from deep within Jonah's chest. It forced its way up through his lungs and involuntarily escaped out through his open mouth. It was a scream of agony, pain, and loss, a bitter scream whose volume echoed up through the steep vine-cloaked terraces and around the bend of the river.

Drawn by the gut-wrenching wails, the surrounding cottages quickly emptied. The men rushed toward the sound, down to the river and then across to the Pessoa vineyard where they found the young boy, crying and clutching the dead body of Manuel Pessoa.

The confusing emotions within the young heart of the boy quickly morphed from shock, to grief, then to anger – anger at God.

"Why? Why did God let this happen? Why did God let my father die?" he demanded of those who quickly surrounded the gruesome scene, including his mother and the other men. It remained a question no one dared answer.

Things happened quickly after that. A jealous uncle moved swiftly, taking over the entire vineyard operation and cutting out his brother's widow and child. Jonah Pessoa's dream of a life spent working the family vineyards disappeared in a moment. Maria Pessoa suddenly found herself homeless and without any visible means of support, despite young Jonah's protestations that he could support them. A hastily arranged second marriage to a distant cousin found the relatively still-young widow and her son aboard a stinking whaling ship, out in the Atlantic Ocean, headed for the island of Faial, one of the nine Azore Islands.

Disembarking in Horta, upon the island of Faial, the desperate family soon discovered the cold, hard truth. The promise of land and a means of support for them quickly evaporated as the drunken old man appeared on the beachhead. A reluctant and obviously frightened young Franciscan priest performed the marriage ceremony right there on the waterfront, the sailors and the townspeople silent witnesses to an unbefitting circumstance. *Why weren't they waiting to be married in the Church?* Jonah wondered to himself.

Anton Soto was a bald headed, grizzled old sailor who had served a lifetime in the Portuguese Navy. After more than forty years at sea, he wrangled a land grant out of Jose I, King of Portugal, in the year of our Lord 1768.

The faithful sailor was ceded over 80 acres of land in Castelo Branco, a quiet rural area six miles west of the little seaport village of Horta. Over the next ten years, the always drunken, never married loner, managed to gamble away all of his holdings until he found himself dispossessed, bereft of anything of value. One final land swap moved him off of the last few acres he held in Castelo Branco and onto a meager lot with a crumbling stone cottage, just outside of Horta. It was this poor hovel that the new Mrs. Soto and her son moved into. Within weeks, the hellishness of their predicament was evident.

"Goddamm it, where's my god-damn boots! I thought I told you yesterday to clean them and put them by the door, ready for me when I go out. Maria! Where the hell are you, woman?" hollered the unshaven old man, arising from a drunken stupor which had kept him in bed until mid-day.

The battered Maria Soto appeared from out of the kitchen, her face and hands covered with flour, her head downcast. She hastily wiped the sweat from her brow, grasping the white apron which surrounded her black woolen floor-length skirt, dobbing it across her forehead. In her other hand, she held the polished leather boots.

"Give those to me, damn you!" shouted the old man.

Maria Soto handed the pair of boots out to him, her head still downcast. He yanked them violently out of her hands.

"And look up at me when I'm talking to you!"

Her head remained downcast, chin buried to her chest.

Maria recoiled at the slap, the imprint of his hand burning across her cheek. Her head snapped backwards from the force of the blow. She reached out to steady herself from falling but there was nothing to hold on to, nothing but the thin, wiry arms of Anton Soto.

His legs tiring under the weight, Jonah finally returned to the broken down cottage yet again. With a single heave, he offloaded another full tray of grapes, hoisting the shallow wooden pallet off his shoulder and into both arms. The repeated weight of carrying fully loaded grape-trays upon his shoulder carved a deep red impression into the flesh above his collar bone; Jonah massaged it gently, rubbing his fingers across the crimson wound. He drew in a ragged breath and then sighed. It was the only source of income they had. Selling fresh grapes in the town square every morning brought in enough *reals* to sustain the three of them, allowing them to eat. But beyond that, there was nothing. Their clothing was thread-bare and every time a few extra reals came in, the old man managed to drink it away.

Their home, if it could be called that, was an ancient stone cottage that was weathering away with each passing day. The miserable little room Jonah was abandoned to was hardly anything more than a lean-to, the crumbling stones barely held together. In spite of the abject poverty, Jonah honestly searched for ways to try and find happiness. He was impressed with the island. There was plenty of room for a young man to roam and abandoned farms were everywhere.

One of these plots actually served as his own private little vineyard. Young Jonah had pirated aboard the whaling vessel a small wooden barrel of packed earth and vines, clipped from the Pessoa family vineyards. In no time, the volcanic rich soil of Faial had yielded a first crop – the large, thin-skinned purple grapes flourished in the sub-tropical climate. The growth of the vines and the appearance of the grapes brought a smile to the young man's face. It often led him to think upon his father. He pondered what his father might think of him now, planting his own vines and growing his very own first crop, keeping the Pessoa family vineyard alive, in another place, far away from their Douro River home. Would he be proud? Would he be pleased how his one and only son had turned out? Was he looking down from Heaven, even at this moment?

He missed his father, missed him in an unfathomable way, a way only a son and a father can know. A profound depression suddenly overtook him and, again, Jonah felt hot tears rolling down his face. He had tried his best to conceal it before, confident that his mother had not seen nor heard him weeping in the dark of the hull of the ship on their passage over from the mainland. And he had managed to keep a dry face even as the priest performed the marriage ceremony, less than an hour after the two of them had disembarked in Horta, forever changing his mother's name to Soto. It sounded so strange… Maria Soto – her name was Maria Pessoa! And his name would forever be Pessoa! – there would be no changing of his name. He was born a Pessoa, and he would die a Pessoa. No drunken, old man was going to ever change that.

But why had God allowed all this? he raged inwardly, even as he wiped the hot tears from off of his cheeks. Then he spoke aloud, assured there was no one else around. "Why, God. Why? Why did my father have to die? What sin have I committed against you, that you punish me so? Why don't you answer me? Speak, so I can hear you! Tell me why!"

The sound of her soft whimpering cry snapped Jonah out of his self-indulgent musings. He entered the courtyard, stooped down and then stepped through the stone shaped archway which framed the back exterior of their undersized dwelling.

Anton Soto grasped Maria about the shoulders, even as her frail thin arms clutched onto his, trying to break the lock he had upon her. He shook her violently, her head snapping back and forth with each forceful shove.

"I said you look at me, bitch, when I'm talking to you! You hear me? Look at me!"

She tried to turn her face away from his hate-filled glare even as he slapped her once again, both sides of her cheeks bearing the bright red marks left by the palm of his hand. She cried out, this time more of a brief yell than a whimper, tears gushing forth from her panic-filled eyes.

"Leave her alone!"

Anton Soto swiveled his head to the left, without loosening the death grip he held on his young wife.

"You? Boy! Shut your mouth."

The old man turned his head back around to the victim of his rage. Her eyes were widened in shock, fixed upon her son even as she shook her head negatively. "Jonah, no!" she pleaded.

"I said, leave her alone!"

Suddenly, the young man rushed at Anton Soto, hitting him broadside with his shoulder, both arms wrapped around the older man's body. Crashing to the cracked tile floor, both rolled over one another, each grasping for a hand-hold on the other. The older man ended upright, sitting astride Jonah's chest.

"You little son of a bitch," he roared, landing a crushing blow to young Jonah's face, a right hand fist to the jaw. Blood flowed freely from Jonah's mouth as he struggled to overpower the wiry old man, a man who was manifesting more strength than the youthful Jonah would have imagined.

"Not ready to take on a full grown man, are you, pup?" the elder man mocked, his teeth clenched together in hate. Lying prone on his back, Jonah could not manage a forward punch but youthful legs were more limber than the elder man would have expected. With a single heave, Jonah swung both legs up and wrapped his ankles around Anton Soto's neck. A massive pull back down with his strong thighs and the elder man was thrown off, rolling over to one side.

A deep growl escaped the old man's throat as he righted himself and then rushed at his young opponent. Both of them went crashing into the stone wall, Jonah driven back by the force of the onslaught. A sharp crack resounded as his skull made contact with the aged rock. He slumped to the ground in a heap, still bleeding from the mouth.

Anton Soto backed away, his breath coming in heaving gasps, his chest and lungs expanding and contracting with each painful inhale and exhale.

"Little…son of a bitch. That'll teach you…to take on a man…before you're ready to…even an old man."

Maria Soto rushed to her son's side, collapsing to the ground and cradling his face in her hands.

"You goddamn bitch," Anton cursed, kicking her once in the side. She howled, yelping out in pain.

"To hell with both of you. I'm going to the inn for a drink."

The exhausted old man, still breathing heavily, rummaged through the leather pouch which lay folded upon the worn wooden shelf, mounted into the stone wall. Leisurely pocketing the few silver reals he found there, he limped out the wooden door, leaving it open as he sauntered off.

Maria Soto clutched the hem of her apron, using it to dab the blood away from the corner of Jonah's mouth. He groaned once before opening his eyes.

"Are you alright?" he asked her, surveying the damage that was done to her face, her cheeks still beet red from the scorching blows.

"Yes, I'm fine. Don't ever do that again, Jonah. He could have really hurt you," she pleaded, her hands still stroking the top of his head.

"But he was hurting *you*," he replied, simply, honestly.

"Don't worry about me. What I am worried about is you. How does your head feel? Are you alright?"

"Mama, don't let him treat you that way. Papa would have never treated you that way."

"Well, your papa is not with us any more, is he? Went and got himself killed, did he not? Probably by some jealous husband, no doubt."

Jonah had never heard her talk about his father in this way and it surprised him, silenced him. He did not know how to reply back to her, or even if he should.

"Oh, Jesus!" she exclaimed, clasping the palm of her hand against her forehead. "I'm so sorry, Jonah. I don't know what has come over me," she blurted out before breaking down, heaving deep sobs erupting from her soul. Her shoulders rocked violently as she wept, burying her face into his chest, clutching his shirt with her clenched fists. They held on to one another until it was over, both of them weeping. After a few moments, she withdrew herself from him, patting him gently upon the chest, her eyes all but dry now.

"Go and gather some more grapes. I'll clean up in here. You go, now. You know we need those grapes."

"Yes, mama," he replied, obediently.

Jonah arose from the floor and straightened his shirt and trousers. Maria Soto was already on her feet, patting down her white apron, dotted on the corners with bright red blood.

"You go on now, and bring in those grapes. I'll be in the kitchen."

He smiled at her, weakly, his face cringing at the pain still throbbing in his swollen jaw. She smiled back, bright pink handprints still evident across both her cheeks. It was a smile of understanding, a smile that communicated, at some deeper level, that they would both get through this. They were in this together and they would survive it together. Jonah had no inkling it would be the last time he would ever see his mother.

He retreated to the small vineyard, his vineyard, crating an empty grape tray upon his shoulder. Though in pain, Jonah's spirits lifted as the long walk ended and he approached the sloping vines. This was his making. Here, he was the boss. He carefully raised the wide sticky leaves, examining the loosely knit clusters of grapes. Color and texture were important and he discriminately picked out just the right clusters for harvest while leaving the others surrounding it on the vine, allowing them to ripen for just one more day, or perhaps more than that. It was an art form, an art his father had taught him at a very early age and Jonah was proud of it – proud of what he knew and what he could accomplish, given just a little bit of land. Table grapes for another season, two at the most, and then the vines would begin producing wine-ready fruit.

Jonah grinned crookedly, even as the pain in his jaw screamed out, forcing him to keep the grin almost wholly to one side of his face.

Then the strangeness began. Jonah Pessoa felt the undulating rolling beneath his feet, as if the ground itself were mimicking the gentle rising and falling of the ocean waves – it was the first indication that something was amiss. Although Jonah had never before experienced such an occurrence, the oddity of the sensation below his feet struck him as wrong, incredibly wrong. He immediately threw the heavily laden tray off his shoulder and onto the ground, spilling its bounty. Jonah raced across the sloped vineyard even as the earth shifted beneath him, casting him violently to the ground.

Clawing and scratching his fingers into the crumbling terrain, young Jonah tried desperately to stand upright on the rapidly moving landscape. Gaining a small foothold, he rose to one knee, even as the peal of booming thunder reached his ears. He instinctively turned his eyes to the highest peak on the island, the Cabeço Gordo, rising over 3,400 feet from the sea. The mountain caldera was covered in a dense cloud of ash-laden gas which had exploded from the crater and arced high into the sky. Steaming hot ash formed a whitish cloud near the top of the cone. Then, suddenly, it billowed downward, tumbling over itself again and again in roiling clouds of death, racing its way across the slopes and towards the village, incinerating everything in its path and leaving behind a thick blanket of gray colored soot. *The village!* Jonah's thoughts raced wildly.

Without realizing it, he screamed aloud, "Mama! Mama!" His heart quickened as he scrambled across the broken terrain, falling time and time again before righting himself, managing a few more paces. A foul, odorous smell completely filled the air – a strong sulfurous stench. The air molecules themselves actually thickened and Jonah began choking; every inhale brought hot, burning gases into his lungs. He gasped desperately for oxygen, but there was none to be found. Jonah spit and coughed, afraid to even suck in another breath. Suddenly, he was pelted with white-hot projectiles, traveling faster than musket balls fired from a rifle. All around him, stones of every shape and size were bombarding the earth in a shower of death. Within seconds, Jonah was struck, his skull fractured. Laying prone upon the ground, with the final fleeting moments of consciousness left to him, Jonah was oddly cognizant of three distinct things: his shirt was on fire, his head was bleeding, and the stone cottage where his mother remained was completely overwhelmed by the rolling gaseous white-grey cloud. He opened his mouth to scream, but nothing came out. Then everything became dark and he lost all consciousness.

Chapter Three

Darkness utterly surrounded him. A strange light pressure completely enveloped him, encasing his entire body from head to toe – then, slowly, he recognized it, sensed that it was…wool; a blanket. It lay taut across his face and, at first, he did not know what to think. With each exhale, his breath caused the cover to rise slightly. With each inhale, it would fall again, literally coating his nostrils and covering his open mouth as he sucked in oxygen. Convinced he would suffocate if it remained over him, Jonah reached up with one hand and in a single fluid motion, tore the covering away.

The dank, unlit stone carved room was strange, unfamiliar to him, and Jonah panicked upon first viewing his surroundings. The cold stone bench he lay upon was hard, despite the woolen blanket which separated his naked torso from the chiseled rock. As self-cognizance slowly came to him, Jonah sat up, wincing in pain as he did so. His back was sore, blistered, and he instinctively reached a hand back around to the source of the pain, rubbing at the throbbing agitation. Jonah was suddenly aware of something different about his head, a weight and a bulkiness that was not natural. Slowly, he reached a hand up to his scalp, cautiously feeling around the layers of cloth bandages which surrounded and wrapped his entire skull.

One at a time, the visual pictures of his last conscious moments came flooding back to him:

gathering the grapes from the vineyard; the earth trembling and breaking up; Cabeço Gordo exploding in a thunderous blast of smoke and gas; the hot stones pelting the earth, one or more of them striking him to the ground; and the hot grey ash cloud, roiling over and over, down the side of the mountain and straight towards the village and their cottage…

Instantly, that familiar foreboding of incalculable loss was with him again, as it had been when he found his father on the bank of the Douro River. A deep painful chill began somewhere within him and enveloped him, starting from his innermost being and rapidly working its way throughout his entire body, terminating in a numbing coldness at his fingertips and toes.

Mama! Oh God, what has happened to Mama? he screamed in silence. Jonah cringed in a vague dread, then took wildly to flight. A wave of terror passed through him as he bolted out of the tiny square room and began running, running blindly, racing through the gloomy maze of stone carved corridors and dank hallways.

Panicked and confused, clothed in nothing more than a linen breechcloth, Jonah sought only to escape, searching desperately, turning down every passageway and peering through every portal, seeking to find some answer to his whereabouts and the fate of his mother.

The dark, confusing labyrinth he found himself in only heightened his mania. The entire edifice appeared to be carved completely out of stone, as if it were dug into the bowels of the earth itself. The walls were moist and water dripped occasionally from the arched stone roof over his head. His skin prickled with the cold and the dampness. At that moment, Jonah became aware of how little clothing he had upon his body. His bare feet made no sound as he sprinted across the rough hewn floors, itself nothing more than chiseled rock. Room after room was filled with large and small oak barrels, containing what he believed were wine, wheat, barley, or whale oil, based on their odors. He wandered for what felt like an eternity before something froze him in his tracks.

He smelled it, at first. A faint wisp, a scent that was somehow familiar although Jonah could not place it initially. Slowly, the sweet pungent aroma intensified, growing stronger with each step he took. He inhaled deeply, scanning his mind for any sense of recognition. Where had he smelled this before?

Following the scent, he turned left at yet another, but narrower, passageway. Its small chiseled steps led upwards. He climbed the rising stairway, over forty steps in all, before they ended. Yawning out before him was a grand opening in the rock lit by torches and just beyond that, a large pair of wooden doors. They were immense, straight grained oak, and carved to match the vaulted ceiling of the rough-hewn stone. Giant brass hasps and pins, already turning green from the moisture, bolstered the thick wooden planks.

From just the opposite side of the heavy wooden portals, Jonah could hear rumbling, the low murmuring of voices. People, at last! Perhaps his mother was there! He ran for the two portals, pulling with all his might on the twisted bronze handles which protruded from the center planks. The heavy oak doors moaned loudly on their hinges as they slowly parted; soft light from the immense room flooded into the torch-lit cavern.

Everything stopped, including the voices, as he entered the magnificent space. Its ceiling vaulted up into the heavens, higher than any building Jonah had ever been in, instantly drawing his eyes upward. Massive white marble columns, each one fluted and rimmed, rose from the polished tiled floor to embrace the white domed interior, their uppermost tiers fanning out in octagonal ribs. The entirety of the concave ceiling was filled with ribs, each symmetrical web spanning over 20 feet in diameter before adjoining its fellow – the whole of it an intricate design of perfectly proportioned architecture. Frescos adorned the ceiling and in the center of each octagon sat brilliantly painted blue and gold starbursts. The great columns also served to create archways and in each arch, high above ground level, stood a stained glass window. They were over six feet tall, narrow and rounded at the top. Their brilliantly colored sections captured the light and transfused it into the sanctuary with a soft, delicate glow. Adding to the hue in the great room was the flicker of hundreds of candles set on pedestals throughout the sanctum. Rows of plain wooden pews filled the space and incense burned from a gold plated censer, the familiar aroma Jonah had detected back deep in the caverns. A small collection of black robed monks, no more than five, stood at the front of the altar, their devotional prayers interrupted by the presence of what some would later describe as a miracle – and others, the work of the devil.

The littlest monk, the one holding the censer by its chain, unceremoniously dropped it to the ground, fear and shock overcoming him. The clamor of the clanging censer, rolling on its side as the burning contents spilled forth upon the floor, broke the silence of a moment that was otherwise galvanized by sheer awe – and fear.

"My God! He's alive," whispered one of them.

"No. It cannot be. It is his ghost," said another, recoiling in fear.

"It is him. God has seen fit to grant him life," said yet another monk, smiling. He was a young man, close to Jonah's age, with darkened skin and jet black hair. His eyes were dark and his face wide. When he smiled, a row of bright white teeth gleamed across a still boyish-looking face.

"No. He was given the last of the sacraments. The Church has had its final say with his soul. He was dead. If he returns, it is because God has rejected him. His only path now is that of the damned. May God help us all," replied the eldest one amongst them, chief of the Jesuits who maintained the monastery.

"Do you know where my mother is?" queried Jonah as he tentatively stepped into the light filled sanctuary. His eyes worked hard to adjust to the new level of brightness after wandering so long in the darkened caverns. He squinted as he raised his hand to his brow, shielding his eyes from the light. The half-clothed young man, head still wound by white cloth bandages, stumbled as he shuffled across the tile floor, collapsing to the ground in a heap. Immediately, the smiling young monk ran to his aid.

"Stop! Do not go near him!" barked out the senior monk, his orders freezing the young apprentice in his tracks.

"Monsignor, he is a man in need," pleaded the boyish-faced monk, leaning over the fallen Jonah Pessoa.

"He is of the devil now. Show him no aid and escort him out of here."

"Monsignor – would God have us to cast out this one, the only poor soul we know of who stood in the path of the mountain's eruption and survived it? Did not Jesus himself teach us to be as the Samaritan, binding up the wounds of those whom evil has befallen?"

"Do not teach me the scriptures, Israel. It is you who are the student and I who am the teacher."

"Yes, Monsignor."

There was a momentary pause as all eyes remained on the Monsignor, the monk above all others, both in age as well as in years of service to the Church. He was an ancient man, as far as all the other monks knew. Years of servitude to the Church had taken its toll on the old man; he walked with a perpetual stoop, never quite standing straight up. He was a short man, with a small frame and tiny features yet the aura surrounding him was one of utmost deference, the title of Monsignor conferred upon him directly from the Pope. His wrinkled head was surrounded with just a wisp of hair, thin and grey, which circled around his skull, leaving the crown uncovered and exposed. Tired looking eyes, steel grey in color, peered out from a diminutive face cragged with the lines of years and years of worry, angst, and un-fulfillment. A heavy black woolen cowl lay gathered in bunches around his neck and shoulders, almost swallowing him up, and the black cassock he wore underneath draped down to his feet.

"I will not be responsible for an anomaly such as this in my monastery. He dies? He lives? This is surely the work of the devil."

"Let us see if we can bring him back to health. If he lives, he may be a servant for the Lord. Who knows why *God* has chosen to spare this one?"

answered the ever smiling Israel, coyly emphasizing the word *God* in his response.

The Monsignor's hard steely gaze held the younger monk's eyes in a vise-like grip before they softened, ever so slightly. But the change, however minor, was enough; enough that young Israel de Silva took note of it. It was all the permission he would need. Quickly wrapping his arms under the unconscious body of Jonah Pessoa, he motioned for the other monks to join him, which they did but with the greatest of reluctance, all under the watchful eye of the master.

With help, a semi-conscious Jonah was carried to the monk's quarters. They were plain and unadorned rooms but much more hospitable than the cold, dank stone underground quarters the monks used for their storage…and for the bodies of the dead.

Jonah awoke to the broad, grinning face of Israel de Silva immediately above him. The young monk was rewrapping the bandages that surrounded Jonah's skull, carefully tending to the aching wound that throbbed from the back of his head. He attempted to sit up. The quick motion of his torso bending forward caused blackness to surround his vision and, instinctively, he fell back upon the feathered cot, collapsing into the arms of his caretaker.

"Whoa there, friend. Lie back and be still. You're in no condition to be running the corridors of Saint Salvador. I do have to admit that you've caused quite a stir. Appears that God still has plans for you – otherwise, you would be gone, as all of us suspected you were. Still can't quite figure that one out. Even put a mirror glass to your lips but there was no breath, no condensation whatsoever. Sorry about placing you down there but that's where we placed all of the bodies."

Silence passed between them as Israel de Silva continued to wrap, cautiously tucking in the tail of the last linen dressing into the front lower wrap.

"All of the…bodies?" Jonah Pessoa responded, belatedly, timidly.

"Yes, over two hundred in all," answered Brother Israel, matter-of-factly. "The volcanic explosion wiped out over forty homes on the south slope. The cinder and ash buried most everything this side of Castelo Branco. We've had our hands full with the dead these past couple of weeks. God have mercy on their souls," he added, making the sign of the cross over his face and body, a tone of somberness and finality in his voice as it trailed off.

Another moment of silence followed.

"The Soto cottage?" Jonah asked, pensively.

"The little stone cottage just east of town? Where the old drunk man with the new young bride and kid live? Afraid it's gone, completely buried. Just on the outermost edge of the hot…cinder……flow."

The words trailed off in increments as realization dawned upon Brother Israel. It was a small island, Horta being the only community, per se, on the entire land mass. The Jesuit college and monastery was just outside the heart of the village but privy to everything that occurred and central to the religious and social life of Horta. Jesuit monks, like himself, knew everybody and everything that occurred. He remembered clearly the day the young woman and her son from the mainland offloaded in Horta, a marriage ceremony performed immediately thereafter. He remembered the look of the young man who attended that ceremony, stone-faced and emotionless. Transplants from the mainland tended to have a different look about them, a look that set them apart from the native Faialese.

Mainlanders were often a lighter skin color than those of Faial. And their hair and eyes tended to be lighter in color than the dark eyes, hair, and skin of the islanders. He remembered the light-skinned face of the boy, about his age, who disembarked that day, suffered through a wedding ceremony he obviously was not in favor of, and then disappeared. It was rumored he had started his own vineyard. He was sometimes seen in the marketplace on Saturday mornings, selling the thickest bunches of purple grapes anyone on the island had ever seen. It was that same face that looked up from the cot at him now, eyes brimming with moisture, lips quivering.

Brother Israel was instantly aware, aware that this young man, who had been found all but dead on the eastern slope of the hot cinder flow, was that selfsame boy. And any kin that he had in the cottage that day were dead, although that knowledge was just now sinking in for Jonah Pessoa.

"I'm sorry. I'm so very, very sorry. There were so many bodies. And so many that we did not find. The hot cinder flow was up to twelve feet in height, in some places. The Soto cottage was completely consumed. There is no way anyone could have survived it. You barely did, and we found your body over a mile away from there. I'm sorry but I'm sure they're gone."

For the second time in less than six months, Jonah felt the cold hard sting of the loss of a parent. It was a numbing, bitter feeling and it swept over his entire body like a cold wash, icing his heart and deadening his emotions. It was as if Jonah could feel nothing, nothing at all – save hate.

Brother Israel de Silva's eyes were closed and his head bowed. He clutched the simple wooden cross, which lay draped around his neck, in both hands, hovering over the prone Jonah Pessoa.

"Our Father who art in heaven, hallowed be thy name, thy kingdom come, thy will be done, on earth…."

His prayer was cut short. The strong calloused hand of Jonah Pessoa reached out and clutched his soft hands, crushing them around the wooden crucifix so tightly they began to hurt. Instinctively, Israel attempted to pull away, the strong grip of Jonah holding his hands in place, painfully surrounding the cross. Brother Israel's eyes widened in fear as he stared into the cold hard gaze of Jonah Pessoa.

"Don't ever pray that horseshit around me!" ordered Jonah through clenched teeth.

"Let go," pleaded the young monk in a half-whisper.

Jonah's strong grip did not lessen. "I never want to hear that again, ever! If there is a God, he most certainly does not care one iota about me."

"Friend, the ways of God are mysterious, beyond the scope of our understanding…" continued the anxious monk, his two hands turning red under the intense grip, an anger fueled clasp that troubled the young Jesuit who was still trying to pry his hands free even as he continued the exchange.

"First my father. Then my mother! What kind of hateful God is that?" cried Jonah Pessoa, his voice cracking with emotion.

"Only God knows the reasons why such things are allowed. It is not for us to question…"

"Not to question? Not to question!? I have no one now! And I am not even allowed to question God about it? To hell with Him! Who needs Him? Why would anyone want to serve a God like that!" he shouted, the anger in his voice intensifying with each syllable.

"I understand your anger, my friend…"

"No! No you do not understand! Have you lost a mother *and* father?" screamed the injured young man, collapsing onto the cot as he released his grip on the monk's hands.

Israel de Silva sighed in relief, rubbing his two chaffed hands together, each one turning over the other again and again as he responded solemnly, "Yes. Yes I have. I, too, know this pain. Know it all too well," he whispered, even as his eyes drifted, a distant far-off look clouding his otherwise bright eyes and constant smile. "The Church will be your mother and father now. Just as it has been for me."

Chapter Four

Israel de Silva and Jonah Pessoa rapidly became friends. Jonah was drawn to the young monk, in part, because of his eternal optimism and joyful disposition, knowing that they both shared a common tragedy – orphans, neither one having a mother or father. For his part, Israel de Silva was drawn to the young vintner because of the mystery surrounding him – his improbable return from the brink of death, a divine work of God if Israel had ever witnessed one and a thing which both amazed and troubled Brother Israel. From the moment he had witnessed the young man wobbling into the chapel, he had determined within himself that he would watch this one, follow him; it was obvious to the young mind of Israel de Silva that the hand of God was upon this young man but for what purpose? What strange, mighty, or tragic things were bound to follow him? Israel de Silva wanted to be around to witness those things when they occurred. Yes, they were going to be friends for life.

Monastic life was a good fit for Jonah Pessoa, at first. The young vintner was no stranger to hard work, and life in the Jesuit Monastery was hard physical work. There were the ten hour days of labor, the afternoons spent in the field tilling and planting the ground and the still-dark cold mornings spent in the windowless barn, endlessly milking the smallish Holstein cows which dotted the grounds.

Sitting upon a low wooden stool, Jonah spent hours upon hours grasping and pulling the multiple teats of one cow after another, squeezing his fingers from the udder to the tip of the nipple, swapping one hand for another with every pull. The monotony of the daily exercise, done alone in the grey darkness of the early dawn, left the young man with ample time to think…and to further alienate himself from the cruel world which had dealt with him so harshly at such a young age. Often, his thoughts wandered to things not of this earth; his mother and father and their whereabouts. Was there really a life after death? Were his parents in heaven, even at this moment? Were they happy there or were they somewhere else?...the hell he had so often heard the monks discuss amongst themselves, when they were alone in the night, in their beds, assured the Monsignor was not listening to their spiritual doubts and ruminations. And, for Jonah, always the same enduring question, the question without an answer – why? Why had a God, whom his parents, the Church, and now these Jesuit monks, assured him was an all-knowing, all-seeing, benevolent God allowed such evil to befall him? What had he done to deserve such treatment from a God such as this?

The daily exercise of milking the cows continued until Jonah had built up the largest forearms and wrist muscles he had ever possessed; he marveled at how quickly his own recovery was coming. He could feel himself growing stronger every day and often would stop to examine his aching wrists and arms, thicker, fuller, and more robust than ever. How he wished he could have had one more opportunity to face off against that son-of-a-bitch Anton Soto. Things would be different now, no doubt. One solid blow from either of his now-much stronger fists would crush the wrinkled balding head of that old worthless drunk.

Often, Jonah's mind wandered as he milked the cows and he imagined himself back in the cottage again, facing off against the old man as he had done that fateful morning when the volcano erupted. He imagined how different their battle would have gone, if he had the forearm and muscle strength then that he possessed now. His mind's eye re-created the scene, Jonah landing one solid punch after another, strong powerful blows delivered from stronger, robust arms, blows which crumpled the old man over and left him doubled up, collapsed onto the floor in utter defeat. Too bad that would never happen. The explosion had no doubt taken the life of that useless wretch as well as nearly one-fourth of the villagers in Horta, according to the monks, including every soul who lived to the west of the little port community.

Wooden slat buckets filled quickly to the brim with the bovine's warm creamy liquid, each squirt making the same distinctive hiss as it streamed into the cedar timber pail. Jonah rushed the buckets, milk slopping over the lip, to Israel de Silva who transferred the milk into larger wooden casks. The two work-partners heaved the heavy casks onto the creaky wooden ox-drawn cart. Brother Israel alone then led the cart into the village every morning where the milk was sold fresh. The town's folk were a people whom young Jonah was increasingly being alienated from – but he did not seem to mind it. Always a gregarious spirit, not unlike his father in that way, the tragic and devastating loss of both a father and mother changed him somehow, altered his personality. He found himself quite comfortable with being alone. He withdrew deeper into himself with every passing day.

The rigorous scholarship, on the other hand, was challenging and, at first, Jonah did not believe he was capable of it. Attending school was a luxury young Jonah had never been afforded before. He was completely and wholly illiterate; he did not even know how to write his own name. Studying Latin, along with the Portuguese language, was hard work and yet, strangely, Jonah grasped the linguistics more rapidly than any of them would have imagined.

"He learns with a quickness that is amazing for one never educated, no, Monsignor?" asked Israel de Silva, provocatively.

"With a quickness that comes from the devil," replied the Monsignor, dismissively.

Prayers were said six times between sunrise and sunset. There were no lay brothers at the Faial monastery; it was the monks who did all of the physical labor in the fields, barns, and workshops, in addition to their obligations in prayer and learning. The Jesuit monks were by far the best educated members of this small island – in fact, they were among an elite few who were literate members of Faialese society. Throughout the island chain, and even on the mainland of Portugal, it was the Catholic monasteries which acted as libraries for learning. Astronomy, geometry, mathematics, and languages were the purview of an educated few and that number included the religious orders, chief among them, the Jesuits. An order to which Jonah Pessoa found himself enmeshed in, without ever intending to become one. And then there was the secret training. The training the monks knew the Monsignor would never approve of…the arts of the ancient Chinese. Israel de Silva had first introduced him late one night, when the brothers were assured the Monsignor was asleep.

"Now we learn what Brother Chin has to teach," he whispered.

Led by torchlight down into one of the lower chambers beneath the sanctuary, Jonah Pessoa followed until he and Israel found themselves in a single large stone carved chamber with an earthen floor, covered in hay and reeking of man sweat. All of the other monks were gathered in a lateral row. Brother Chin was the only one opposite them, facing them as they all bowed in unison; a gesture Brother Chin returned. Not a word was uttered. Stripped down to nothing but their underclothes, Jonah was initially unnerved. Israel de Silva took note of the look in his eyes then whispered reassuringly, "We learn to fight, nothing else. Chinese boxing, the closest way Chin can translate it into the Portuguese tongue, but there is so much more to it than the boxing. It is all about balance…it is…spiritual."

"But I thought the purpose of a monk was peaceful…" Jonah began.

"Sometimes that peace can only be achieved through strength," Israel responded, repeating the mantra that had been drilled into him by Chin.

"But what of the ways of God?"

"Who is to say that this is not one of the ways of God?" responded Brother de Silva. "Brother Chin says it is part of the training monks receive in his home country; before he was forced to flee. He learned with the other monks in the Temple of Shaolin. And, at the core of its philosophy, is the principle - do no harm."

He stopped there before adding with a grin, "If that is possible. If it is not, then one must learn to defend oneself and to protect others. But the arts of the Boddhidharma must never be used in anger or to attack another without cause or for selfish purposes. The eighteen hand movements of the enlightened one can be powerful but the true strength comes from within, not without. Inner strength…'*chi'* is what Brother Chin calls it. I don't know the Portuguese translation for that word exactly but I understand what he means," said the smiling young monk as he dropped his cassock to the ground and took his place in the line with the others.

Jonah copied his actions and moved into the formation as well, although not nearly as comfortable with it as his mentor.

"Then why do we learn in secret?" whispered Jonah, deftly changing the subject.

"Because the Monsignor would not approve," replied Israel, cutting his friend off gruffly, his countenance falling. "Not everything the Monsignor disapproves of means that it is disfavored by God. The arts of the Boddhidharma, for example, are one. You are another," said Israel de Silva matter-of-factly.

The stretching, leg kicks, hand strikes, and throws, all done in absolute silence, were strange and new to Jonah Pessoa but he took to these as well as the others and better than most. Brother Chin recognized this, devoting extra time to the one among them who seemed driven to learn. However, it was the words Brother Chin had shared that very first night of training, more than anything else, which remained forever etched in his memory, words which found their way deep into his consciousness, words that he would never be able to escape from.

"Remember my young friend…those who are skilled in combat do not become angered, those who are skilled at winning do not become afraid. Thus the wise man wins before the fight has even commenced, whereas the ignorant man commences fighting, hoping to win."

Stances and postures which seemed awkward and bizarre soon became comfortable for Jonah as his muscles and tendons adjusted to the painstaking exercises. The one-legged positions, the wide arm movements, the clawing fingers, the spinning kicks, the stabbing hand motions, all of them new and strange yet Jonah couldn't get enough. Fighting styles known as the Tiger, the Dragon, the Snake, the Leopard, and the Crane were all taught by Brother Chin and eagerly absorbed by the keen young man who found the philosophy and the physical training of the Chinese monk something which ignited his passion. In a very short time, Jonah Pessoa was as gifted at the art of Chinese boxing as any of the other monks, actually preferring to spend his free time practicing the kicks and the punches, when not required to spend his time milking cows or copying texts.

The monastery's cramped scriptorium contained over twenty oak-carved desks, although no more than one was ever occupied at a time. It was a single small rectangle, built off of the library wing, with walls of unadorned stone and plaster. There was no source of heat anywhere in the room – something which the Monsignor took particular delight in, when assigning his monks to their writing. A single whale-oil lamp flickered above the desk, providing the only light and heat Jonah would have. Its rancid-smelling stench only added to the unpleasantness of the task before him and yet Jonah found the work engaging and stimulating. He drew his feet in tighter underneath of him and bundled the black wool robe over himself, guarding against the ever present chill in this dark, small space. The oval wooden inkwell, which had been filled with the sluggish black ooze when he started, was almost empty by now. Multiple quills, their sharp hollow tips worn down smooth by his furious writing, lay abandoned, littering the floor around him. He had been sitting at his assigned workstation, feverishly copying script for over three hours. Jonah presented the carefully written parchment to his closest companion and confidant who studied it carefully before returning it to its eager author.

"You have learned well, my friend," said Israel de Silva, encouragingly.

"It all seems to be related, somehow, in some deeper way," responded Jonah.

"It is. Latin is the root from which the Portuguese tongue springs, as well as the tongue of the French, the Spanish, and the Romans. You have a deductive mind, my friend."

Jonah smiled; something he did not do very often these days. His mind was reeling with the possibilities as the spark of knowledge grew within him. The difficulty of his earlier attempts at study were beginning to fade, replaced by a hunger to know, to know more, to somehow put all of the pieces of the puzzle together, to synthesize the knowledge he felt was bursting inside of him, ready to explode at any moment. It was his only defense against the heart-numbing sadness that was a constant shadow in his soul, awaiting its turn to take over and remind him, yet again, of the loss of both mother and father.

"It's not just the languages. It's everything. The mathematics, the geometry, the astronomy, the Chinese boxing…they all seem strangely connected, somehow. I don't know how to explain it, but it's there. Right on the edge of my thinking. Somehow, someway, all these are connected."

The broad-faced young monk smiled. "It is as Sir Isaac Newton and Sir William Herschel proclaim in their writings. It is God. All knowledge comes from God and He is the source of it all. There is no surprise that a bright young mind, such as yours, would see this ultimate connection. Everything that we learn, all that we know, eventually points back to Him."

Jonah frowned at the response of his mentor and friend, the only friend he had in this stoic palace of stern discipline and self-denial. "You mean the same God who allowed my father to be murdered and my mother killed when the volcano erupted? You mean *that* God?"

"Jonah – we've covered this phase of theology a hundred times or more…"

"And we'll cover it a hundred times again until you see - see what I see. Those things cannot be the work of God. And if it is, then He is an appalling bastard whom I have no interest in serving…"

Brother de Silva gasped, visibly recoiling at the anger, the blasphemy being uttered by his protégé, cursing God in that fashion and uttering things that ought never to be said in a monastery, let alone from the lips of a Christian.

"You go too far, Jonah. You are my friend. Perhaps the closest friend I have ever had but even I will not stand idly by while you curse God and defile the Church."

"Then perhaps my time here is done?"

Israel de Silva's face dropped at the startling revelation. It was a response he had hoped would never come and, in his mind, it had come far too soon. Israel de Silva was an orphan too, and had longed for a true friend within the brotherhood, someone who understood where he was coming from, who knew what it was like to be without father or mother, trusting wholly and utterly alone upon God for sustenance and survival. Although well liked by the brothers, and by the Monsignor, Brother de Silva knew he was different, knew he was never fully accepted by them, knew he would never advance within their ranks. He did not come from a famed or wealthy family, as all of the other initiates did, other than Brother Chin. For them, the Church was nothing more than a path towards a superior education; the vows of the Church meant nothing to them. Too often he had watched from the shadows as his less-zealous brothers had their dalliances with the young girls or women of the village, defiling themselves in the eyes of the Church. It disgusted him and yet he was powerless to do anything about it. Who would believe him? He was just an abandoned infant who had been left on the door of the Monastery, or so the Monsignor had told him. He was a nobody, a man without a name, without a lineage and who, but for the Monsignor and the Church, would have certainly died before his life had ever really begun. He owed the Monsignor everything and loved him as a father but there was always still that void – that empty feeling, that lack of companionship. Given his vows of chastity, accepting he would never know the love of a woman, he had resigned himself to a life of devotion, hoping only to find the fellowship of brothers, such as himself, to help stave off the loneliness. But even that had eluded the friendly, broad-faced youth with the perfect smile. The others had always referred to him as the "bastard," avoiding and alienating him, in part because he refused to partake of their hypocrisy, their late night sexual forays into Horta. The other part remained hidden from him, obscure but ever present, just that hint of something different that caused the others to shun him, treat him differently, excluding him from their inner circle. He was never able to determine exactly what that was but its presence was visceral and undeniable. It only added to the loneliness and abandonment he felt.

Then Jonah Pessoa's body was brought into the monastery, with all the others who had been killed when Cabeço Gordo exploded. The only difference was that Jonah returned from the dead, so to speak, after three days of lying in the underground cellars, cold enough to freeze a body, if it were not already dead. But this one was not dead. And he was an orphan like himself, without father or mother, wholly dependent upon the Church, just like Israel. How overjoyed Brother de Silva had been when the Monsignor agreed, albeit reluctantly, to allow Jonah to stay and be mentored by Israel. And how readily the young mainlander from Douro had learned, learned faster than anyone would have imagined, including the Monsignor. Israel de Silva had finally found a friend, someone like himself. How he had imagined them growing together in the priesthood, serving side by side, friends to the end. It was obvious Jonah had his doubts about the faith but God's ways were not to be challenged. He himself was abandoned by parents; people whom he had no knowledge of, including whether they were alive or dead. The Church, and the Monsignor, had become his family. Jonah would come to understand and accept this as well, in time. And then there was that spark about him, that un-identifiable quality that Jonah Pessoa had about him. It was hard to define it but it was present nonetheless.

Now…none of that was going to happen.

"Are you sure, Jonah?" asked Israel de Silva, heart-broken by his friend's declaration. He wanted desperately to stop the next words from coming out of Jonah's mouth, words he feared would spell the end to his relationship with the young vintner. It was a relationship he treasured and valued, in part because he was really the only friend Israel had come to have in this lonely place and in part because Jonah was someone much like himself in so many ways and yet always so different, so unique…God-ordained, Israel had come to call it.

"I'm no priest, Israel. This is not the place for me," Jonah replied.

"But who will take care of you?" pleaded Brother DeSilva, appealing to his young friend's sense of aloneness, a sense he himself knew all too well. He knew it was a ploy that would not work.

"I can take care of myself. I'm stronger now, in so many ways…thanks to you," Jonah responded, instinctively reaching his fingers up to massage the scar that lay buried just beneath his hair line. The coarse sandy hair which lay across his scalp covered it now, but it was there, always present. Anytime Jonah Pessoa needed a reminder of that fateful day, he would reach up and comb back his hair, feeling the scarred dermal ridge line where his head had been split open by volcanic rocks, showering down around him. Strangely, Jonah felt comforted by the presence of the scar; just knowing it was there, somehow, made him feel connected to that time and place, serving as a reminder of how things had once been – when at least he still had his mother.

Israel de Silva grinned slightly; a twinge of regret showed in his smile.

"It's never been about me. It's always been about you. God has something unique in store for your life, my friend. This has been obvious from the start. I've just been trying to tag along for the journey…see how far it would take me, see how far I could go and what amazing or wondrous things I'd be able to see before I would have to take my leave from you. I guess it has just come earlier than I thought it would."

"Your training is not yet complete," interjected a voice from the darkness, a voice that both Jonah and Israel recognized instantly. He emerged from out of the night, standing beside Israel de Silva now.

"Brother Chin, I can't thank you enough. I've learned so much from the both of you. You've done so much for me. I wouldn't have made it, if it wasn't for you," replied an apologetic Jonah, genuine affection rising up through his voice.

"You are not yet prepared to fight the world out there that will oppose you. And oppose you it shall. Your skills are under-developed, both fighting…and otherwise," he added, almost as an afterthought.

"There is much more for you to learn. I fear you will not survive," said the elder Chinese monk solemnly. It wasn't meant as a psychological ploy to keep the young man in the monastery. It was a conviction, a firm belief.

A moment of silence lingered between the two good friends and their Chinese mentor before Israel de Silva spoke again.

"It is a small island. Where will you go? And what will you do?"

"Don't know. All is know is…I'm not going to make a very good priest," remarked Jonah, smiling at his two mentors and friends. The mutual respect and admiration between Israel and Jonah remained, despite the obvious rift in their views and feelings about God.

"You take the knowledge of the Jesuits with you, my friend. Wherever you go, remember this," remarked Israel, as he slung a leather rucksack around the shoulder of his short-lived companion. The weight of the content told Jonah they were books, texts from the Monastery which Israel had presumed Jonah would not, could not, live without.

"Thank you, Israel," said Jonah simply, honestly, extending one hand; it was embraced by the young monk who gripped it tightly.

"No, thank you. It has been my privilege to know you, Jonah Pessoa. God be with you."

Brother Chin only nodded, the time honored Chinese equivalent of the handshake.

Jonah, unsure of how to react to his friend's determined salute to Divinity, simply spun around and walked off, out the side door of the scriptorium and down the worn foot path towards the port village of Horta. The moon was already sinking below the horizon as he began; if he kept up his pace, he would make it to the village before dawn.

"He will not make it," whispered the elder Chinese monk to his younger protégé, eyes fixed on the darkness which swallowed up the foot path to the village.

“He has God on his side,” responded Israel de Silva, his eyes also fixed forward, neither man willing to break the spell which held them in that moment.

“We shall see,” answered the elder monk.

Chapter Five

A salty ocean mist permeated the lower stratums of the forlorn seaport village. Each edifice at the waters edge was coated with a fine, wet spray. It covered everything with an eerie, slick glow which shone in the emerging sunlight – and the look of it made him uneasy. The harbor was enveloped in silence. An acrid stench hung in the air, a new smell he did not recognize. Not one gull or tern was heard screeching and even the lapping of the waves against the shore appeared muted, as though the ocean itself was paralyzed, in shock.

Nothing was as he had remembered it. The volcanic explosion had inexorably altered the landscape, including the bay of Horta. The cream colored fine-grained sand which had comprised the smooth beach at the waters edge was replaced by a rocky, tumultuous flow of jagged lava, as if the blackest bowels of hell itself had vomited up onto the beachfront.

Surreal images greeted him as he made his way down the avenue which formerly fronted the stone fortress wall. Only angled portions of white lodges, buildings, and inns stuck out defiantly against a thick charcoal cloak which smothered them, some of the structures actually bending over slightly as if the heat had melted them, turning their sandstone exteriors into something soft and pliable. Dark grey ash rose as high as the second story windows, in some cases. The smooth dark powder lay over rooftops, sides, and streets as if it had been deliberately ladled out by a careful hand. *The hand of God* thought Jonah to himself, contemptuously. *How many people lost their lives in this 'act of God'?* he wondered to himself.

Another step and Jonah Pessoa was struck by the brightness of the sun in his face. Shielding his eyes from the glare, he quickly brought his hand up to his forehead, forming a shade over his brow. Squinted eyes quickly readjusted, bringing into focus the reason behind the dazzling reflection. It was more than the glare of the sun upon the waters which had blinded him; it was the brilliant glimmer of a brightly painted…ship.

A large, two-masted brig lay in port, less than a hundred yards out into the waters. Jonah marveled at the sight of it, unlike any he had ever beheld. Nothing like the clumsy, stinking whaling ship he had endured on the way over from the mainland to Faial, the large elegant brig in the bay of Horta rose stately from the waters like a gleaming citadel, her bow sprit piercing the morning sky like a spear of fortune. He was struck by the size and the grace of the large vessel. She appeared to be well over 100 feet from bow to stern yet rested comfortably upon the placid waters as if she were a queen sitting atop her throne. Her bright white sails were furled, leaving the masts with a bare but crisp look. Ropes and riggings were tight and appeared fresh, new even. Men bustled around her deck, busy with their respective chores.

He hadn't realized he was standing in the middle of the road, staring, until he was startled by the harsh commanding voice, spoken in the tongue Jonah recognized as English.

"What are you looking at?" growled the gnarled old seaman, hacking coarsely as he spoke. His voice was gravelly, as if it were forced out through lungs which had long ago been scarred by some unknown cause.

Jonah Pessoa eyed him cautiously at first, taking careful note of the man. He was obviously a sailor. There was that distinctive look about him, as if he did not belong on land, a man ill at ease without the sea underneath him. A black tarpaulin hat crowned his head, set low over one side. Faded blue eyes pierced out from underneath thick brows of white bristly hair. A thin pinkish scar rose above one of those brows, drawing a conspicuous vertical line across a brow otherwise filled with horizontal creases and crinkled with years of salt and sun-bake. The scar continued down across his eye then ran the length of his cheek; an obvious slice of the sword intended to take his head off. He had managed to avoid its deadly cut but it had taken its toll in his face. A stubby nose and thin lips were set amidst a face crowded with coarse white hair, thick but well trimmed. Despite his advanced age and a coarsened voice, the old man moved agilely, stepping lively out into the street, blocking the path of Jonah.

"She's full up of crew, now. Don't need no priest aboard 'er, you hear? Go on about yer business now but don't be thinkin' to board 'er. Kain't take on anymore a-wantin' to get off this here island, as bad as things may be here."

His voice declined with the last few words, dropping in their intensity as his worried eyes scanned the disfigured landscape. He appeared to be looking for something, or somebody. Impatience showed in his eyes.

Abandoned homes and storefronts protruded from the suffocating gray ash in every direction. Those structures not buried stood stark against the undulating grey silt, their black-charred door and window frames marring their otherwise white appearance. In some instances, only a blackened skeletal frame remained. Not a single pane of glass was left intact; the heat of the explosion had either melted or cracked every one, giving the small community the look of a once-again sacked village, despoiled and weary worn. Horta had been smothered, her life blood all but choked out by the volcanic explosion. There was little left to hold anyone there and many had abandoned their buried homesteads and dingy storefronts for life elsewhere, boarding any and all ships which pulled in to port. A hearty few had remained behind, determined to rebuild.

He spied them here and there, methodically plodding their way through mounds of granular cinders, their feet sinking into the dreary ash, their faces solemn but resolute. It made sense to Jonah now - these were the poor souls who so readily consumed the fresh milk the monastery cows produced each morning. The hours upon hours of lonesome pre-dawn milking Jonah had so faithfully completed now seemed not quite so mundane, so meaningless. For some of them, it was most likely the only sustenance they had in a day. Jonah felt proud of that task now, as if it had been more than just milking cows. He had helped to keep a village alive, in his own small way, and had never even known about it. *Another one of Israel de Silva's secrets*, he mused silently as a small grin came to the corners of his mouth – he had underestimated his friend.

Jonah quickly surveyed the remainder of his surroundings. A deep, forlorn melancholy settled upon him and in that instant, he knew – knew utterly, as if it had been foreordained, as if it were a thing always true, just waiting there for him to come along and discover it in due time – he was not to spend his life on Faial. There was nothing left for him on the tiny island. And once gone, he would never return. Some would remain and rebuild; it was their legacy, their generational heritage. Horta would, without a doubt, rise again from the ash heap of Cabeço Gordo. But this was not his legacy, his heritage. His future, whatever it may be, lay elsewhere. But where? And how was he to get there? His eyes inadvertently turned back to the gleaming brig, sitting proudly in the bay, giant masts standing naked against the breeze, a breeze so slight it was not even felt on the waterfront where they two stood.

"I said she ain't a-taking on any more! Don't need another landsman on deck. Already gots more sods than salts aboard her now, God help us all. Now, hove off with ya."

The grizzled old sailor slowly turned around at the sound of someone grunting, as if he were expecting it. A figure stumbled from out of the nearest abandoned establishment, an inn or tavern, before the lava came.

The man was stooped over, smallish wine casks supported on each shoulder. The two equal burdens weighed down on him and he struggled underneath the load, his legs wobbling at the knees. His weight shifted as he fought to keep his balance, one leg shuffling forward to steady himself. His head and neck remained down, keenly focused on the path his bare feet were maneuvering through; the importance he attached to his cargo was evident. He did not lift his head until he reached the spot where Jonah and the white bearded old sailor stood.

"Only two…wine…left there," the man stated emphatically in halting English, his eyes fixed on his sailing companion. "Look like…abandoned …she no even…" his words trailed off as he made eye contact with Jonah, the cognizance coming slowly but oh so perceptibly. There was a flash in his eyes, a flicker of recognition, then fear…or was it guilt? Before the stooped old man could drop the two casks from off his shoulders, Jonah was on him.

In a blur, the young orphan from the Jesuit monastery rushed his victim. Both wine casks fell to the ground, cracking open and spilling forth their bright red contents. Jonah and the other tumbled over one another, falling to the ground in a flurry of violence. Both combatants arose, although Jonah was much quicker to it than his adversary. The rolling throws taught by Brother Chin were automatic now – Jonah did it without even thinking consciously. As the other gained his feet and steadied himself for yet another charge, his eyes wide with disbelief, Jonah rushed forward again. His lips were pressed together in a silent scowl as he leapt high into the air, his body tucked in tight with one exception – the left leg. It was fully extended, foot turned perpendicular, exactly as he had been taught by the Shaolin priest. The powerful kick hit his surprised opponent square in the face and the older man collapsed to the ground in a heap. But it was not over.

Amazingly, the bloodied and crumpled old man arose, slowly, his broken jaw dangling slack from his face. He wiped the blood from his mouth. His eyes held a fire that was not evident before he had been attacked. It was about self-preservation now; without saying a word, each man knew this was to be a fight to the death.

The older man rushed Jonah Pessoa with a quickness that caught him off guard. Jonah was incredulous – how could this old man take a blow like that and keep on coming? It was this moment of introspection that caused him to lose focus…the focus a trained, disciplined practitioner of the arts of the Boddhidharma would never lose. It cost him dearly. An overwhelming blow rounded up from a clenched fist, even as Jonah snapped his head back to avoid it. The young man's agile movement avoided full contact with a punch that otherwise would have shattered his jaw as well; as it was, the strike managed to glance off of his neck, severely bruising his thorax. Jonah choked for a split second before falling over backwards, the older man on top of him, raining blows down around his face and neck.

How did I let it happen? Jonah berated himself, even as he gripped his attacker around the wrists. *How did I let him get this close to me? Master Chin would be so disappointed,* he continued, conversing inwardly. *This needs to end now!* Jonah Pessoa raised his head up with one quick strike, crashing his own forehead into that of his attacker. The sudden unexpected move stunned his opponent, causing his eyes to roll upwards into their sockets. Jonah felt the strength in those wiry arms fade for just a moment. In that instant, Jonah made his move. With his adversary still straddling over his chest, Jonah simultaneously struck the man on both sides of his ribs. The chopping motion, made with the hands open but fingers held against each other tight, formed an axe-like movement. Jonah actually heard the elder man's ribs break, the unique cracking sound unlike any other noise in nature. A low roar escaped the still-dazed man as fresh blood and bile oozed from out of his mouth.

The young monk shoved the elder man off of his chest with a mighty thrust. Rolling over, he sprang to his feet, poised and ready, both hands held high. Amazingly, the old fighter was also righting himself, but much more slowly than Jonah. His bent frame was still bowed at the waist as the man steadied himself, balancing on all fours, both palms still planted on the ground. He rose precariously, one hand still fixed on the blackened earth, shaking violently. His face was covered in the charcoal soot and darkened blood oozed freely from his ears, nostrils, and mouth. He stood eventually, his breath coming in heaving gasps, and slowly raised his head until his face made contact with his foe. As their two eyes met, Jonah sensed something different this time, something slightly askew, unexpected. It was a look of resignation, an acknowledgement that the end was coming…and there was also a glimmer of…contrition? Was the old man trying to say he was sorry? Jonah was incensed by the thought of it and rushed to the man, chopping and kicking as he flew into the body of the other. A flurry of blows, completely undefended by the other, and it was over.

A heaving Jonah Pessoa stood back from the unmoving body of Anton Soto. He felt nothing; no sense of justice, no sense of regret, no feeling whatsoever. He was cold, blank, and utterly devoid of emotion. It was if he was standing outside of himself, watching the events unfold, as if he were just a spectator of the scene which had just occurred and not the doer of the deed. And that is what startled him the most.

.

"By God, boy, I believe you've killed 'em. One of the few true sailors we'd managed to find in these here islands. And one tough son-of-bitch, too! Small fella and yet he whipped damn near every man I've ever seen 'em fight. Hellfire and damnation! Should have never let 'em come back here, even for a supply run."

The bearded old man turned his gaze from the collapsed body of Anton Soto to the lithe figure of the young man clothed in a monk's black cassock. His chest heaved in and out with breath, sweat drenching his body, eyes still ablaze with hate – the most intense hatred Elihu Smith had ever seen in the eyes of one so young.

Jonah did not speak. He continued to stare at the still body of Anton Soto lying there on the ground. He had dreamed of this moment, had pre-lived it again and again in his mind – and it was nothing like he had imagined. He wanted more; felt cheated somehow. He shouted, in Portuguese, at the prone figure lying face down on the cobblestone pathway.

"Get up! Get up you miserable son-of-a-bitch! I'm not finished with you yet! I said get up!" Jonah screamed through tear filled eyes as he kicked the body lying in the soot. Anton Soto did not move.

Elihu Smith slowly backpedaled, moving away from the conflagration in front of him. Suddenly, having some extra wine aboard the *Fair American* didn't seem like such a great idea after all. Soto was an old Portuguese sailor, known to many seamen in the Atlantic. Picked up on the isle of Terceira, he had come ashore here to scour for rope and other supplies, claiming he knew the isle well. The Captain had allowed it but with great reluctance. Every ship which pulled into port at Horta quickly found herself overloaded with refugees attempting to flee the island.

But Soto was adamant. He knew this village, had lived on this particular island for years, and assured the Captain he could put off and be back in no time, fresh ropes and other supplies scavenged from the abandoned homes and inns without any additional boarders. When he suggested to Elihu that they check out the old abandoned tavern for liquor, it seemed like a good idea; there was always room aboard a ship for more liquor. Now Elihu would have to report that Soto was not coming back, that he had been killed in a fight – by a priest! It seemed so unreal. Would he be believed? He was a seasoned veteran, a true salt-of-the-sea, but crews and Captains were a distrustful lot, given to superstitions. He gathered up the coiled hemp ropes that lay piled on the ground next to the stone paved pathway and headed back towards the bay.

"Reckon his own can see to a proper burial. He's from here; no doubt's gots family here to see to a good Christian burial, although I always kinda figgered he'd be one that ended up buried to the sea."

Jonah Pessoa responded in broken English. "He have…no one here; no family." Jonah was solemn, head downcast, eyes still fixed on the form lying in the path. Oddly enough, no one else had taken any notice of what had transpired and not one of the town's people had come to the scene of the combat between the two men. It was as if the sorrow and devastation of the volcanic explosion had numbed the survivors; no one cared about a brawl between two men on the edge of the bay.

"Reckon the Church can take care of 'em, then. You know somethin' bout that, don't ya? I reckon from the cut of your clothes your'n a priest?"

Jonah lifted his head and looked Elihu Smith directly in the eyes. Long moments passed before Jonah answered in English, the response startling the old sailor, the look of surprise evident in his weary eyes.

"No, I'm not…I'm not a priest."

An ashamed and confused Jonah sat on the beachhead, alone, feet submerged in the cool waters. No longer feeling the victor, he was immune to the world around him, lost in his own thoughts…and self-judgment. *How could I have done it? How could I have lost it so easily, so quickly? I'm not worthy to have sat at the knee of one such as Brother Chin! Oh God, what have I done?*

He was only vaguely aware of the bustle and commotion far behind him, back on the cobblestone street where he had left the body of Anton Soto. Murmurs and voices he could not discern carried on in whispers and muted conversations. Were they pointing at him? He wondered, without glancing back to see for himself. Would they be coming for him now, to haul him away before the magistrate? He did not care. Let them do to him as they saw fit. At this moment, he could feel no further than his regret and self-loathing. What a failure he had been at the sacred philosophy of the Boddhidharma!

What seemed like hours passed before he noticed the grizzled old sailor climbing into the small dinghy alone. He watched solemnly as Elihu Smith rowed the little craft back out across the bay water and up to the great ship. Not once had the old salt taken his eyes off Jonah Pessoa, not until he had reached the masted vessel and climbed aboard, empty handed. Jonah's head remained downcast, his thoughts absorbed by his own future, now in serious doubt. The King of

Portugal put to death those among his servants who killed without provocation. He would be sentenced by the magistrate and be taken back to the mainland where he would face the gallows. There did not appear to be any other outcome. His life, as short as it had been, was effectively over – all because he could not, would not, control his temper. He would not run nor hide; he would face his judgment and die like a man.

Engrossed in his thoughts, Jonah did not hear the rhythmic slapping of the oars through the bay waters, nor the creaking of the dinghy until its wooden bow was thrust upon him, the sea-battered hull literally sliding between his feet. Still seated upon the sand, he raised his head, surprised and confused at the sight before him.

"Well, climb aboard. Don't intend to wait fer ya all day. I said git in!" shouted Elihu Smith, his scar covered eye squinting with a loathsome look. Another man, dark skinned and shirtless, remained in the rear of the dinghy. A curved scimitar gleamed out from beneath his fine silk trousers.

Jonah Pessoa, frozen by the bizarre turn of events, did not move. Internally, his instincts screamed at him to be ready to defend himself – but his soul was tired and overruled those instincts. *Let them kill me here and now, if they wish,* he thought to himself.

"Well, damn it all to hell, t'werent my idea a'tall. I'd just as soon leave you here on this god-forsaken spit and let them do whatever they wish with 'ya. Was his dyin' wish, though, and the Captain agreed. Seems we're one man short now that ole' Soto won't be a-sailin wit us."

"I no understand," replied Jonah, pensively, keeping the conversation to the English language.

"Me neither. I thought for sure you'd killed 'em dead. Was dead, too, but for one last little spark of life left in 'em. Last words he said afore we buried 'em, a-knowin' they would be his last in this life. Said…*put the boy on the ship*…don't make no sense to me but he repeats it one last time…*put the boy on the ship. Let them be together – they're all each other has…now.*

Yessir, that thems his dying words. Then he sucked in his last breath and it was over, finally over. Yep, we buried 'em while you was a-runnin' off. Didn't figger I'd see you here right on the beachhead, though. Ain't none of the village a-calling for your head but they don't want you here on the island neither, so I guess the sea is yer fate after all. Checked with the Captain first, though, just to be sure. He has his reservations too but if it was Soto's dyin' wish, then it otter be honored, he figgers. None of that fancy Chinese kickin' or punchin' though, ya hear? You bring trouble aboard the ship and you'll be punished, that's fer sure. Brought the Turk here, just in case you get any ideas about starting a fight wit me. He's a killer, fer sure. Over ten men have tasted his blade and he's still alive to tell the story; they are not. Well, let's stop jawing away here; are you comin' or not?"

Jonah Pessoa paused for what felt like an eternity. He dropped the leather rucksack filled with books. He gazed, emotionless, as the multiple scripts, leather parcels, and bounded scrolls, containing the most advanced wisdom and teaching of his generation, fluttered in the slight breeze and then tumbled into the bay waters, slowly sinking below the waves. He rose up and stepped into the small dinghy – it would be a step he would later come to regret.

Chapter Six

Jonah marveled at how effortlessly the old sailor wielded the wooden oars, dipping their paddle shaped tips into the foamy sea water then pulling and rising them up again at just the right moment, gaining an efficiency of movement that would have been invisible to most other eyes.

He knew what it was like to have to repeat the same laborious motion again and again, pulling on one udder after another until the cows had provided all that they were capable of. Endless hours spent milking had taught Jonah, eventually leading him to master the nuances of just how far up on the teat one's fingers should be before beginning the downward stroke and how just the right amount of pressure should be applied before releasing it and moving on to another. Gaining the maximum result for the most efficient effort was a skill one learned when milking cows a thousand times over; a skill Jonah never dreamed would come in handy until his muscle hardened fingers and chapped palms subsequently became instruments of strength under the tutelage of Brother Chin.

Then the wisdom of the elder man became amazingly apparent. He now understood why, in the earliest days of his stay at the monastery, the elder Chinese monk had insisted to the Monsignor that Jonah be the one assigned to milking the cows every morning and evening. God, it made so much sense after the fact!

It was that same efficiency, the same economy of movement that Elihu Smith employed every time the old man flexed his back, pulling the two oars together in perfect tandem and re-inserting them at exactly the same moment, at exactly the same depth and angle, while never once taking his eyes off of his cargo.

Efficiency; experience; Jonah was impressed. The Turk, hand still held to his dagger, also kept his eyes on the black robed stranger sitting in the bow of the dinghy. Nothing changed amongst them – each of the three remained in silence, the Turk staring at their passenger, the old sailor rowing, and the black robed Jesuit staring back. Only occasionally did Jonah glance beyond them to the bright masted vessel they were approaching unerringly, despite the fact that Elihu Smith's back was turned toward the great ship, utilizing only the geography on shore as his mark.

The polished vessel they rowed up to was a sight beyond Jonah's imaginings. Unlike the cramped and dirty whaling vessel he had come over from the mainland in, the *Fair American* appeared expansive and immaculate. The two masted ship bobbed stately upon the waves. Her hull appeared freshly scraped; not a barnacle could be seen clinging to her crème-colored wood. Shiny black paint striped down the length of her hull, forming an intimidating gunwale. A complement of eight cannon lined her port side with an equal number on the starboard. Her canvases were still furled and knotted tightly but Jonah was now close enough to see the cotton ducking itself, crisp and white as the snow in the Serra da Estrela. He had never been on board anything of her caliber in all of his short life and the thought of serving aboard such a vessel impressed him.

A gathering of curious sailors had gathered at the port side, gawking down at the trio in the approaching dinghy. A knotted rope was thrown over the side of the ship, its last tie reaching just to the point where a standing man could grasp it and begin pulling. Elihu Smith nodded in silence to the Turk before beginning to climb. Only after Smith was aboard did the silent swordsman nod for Jonah to begin climbing, leaving the ever vigilant Turk in the dinghy as the last man. Jonah grasped the knotted hemp and began pulling himself up, hand over hand, with a quickness which astonished the sailors. Before anyone could so much as extend a hand, Jonah Pessoa was over the side and threw himself onto the deck, the Turk fast behind him.

Unused to being at sea, he promptly lost his footing with the roll of the waves and sprawled onto the deck, face first. As he righted himself, the crowd roared with laughter. Suddenly and mysteriously, they instantly grew silent and then backed away, giving the stranger some space. Jonah did not know what to expect next.

"Well, give 'em more room than that, men. I said back away, the lot of you!"

The raised, cackling voice was obeyed by all, although reluctantly. The air of authority in it was forced, artificial; as if volume alone could make up for the lack of ease in wielding power. Before Jonah even turned to face him, he knew it must be the ship's captain.

The steely eyed man, youthful in appearance, short of stature and thin framed, strode up to the black robed stranger. The Captain looked him directly in the eye, his hands clasped behind his back. Jonah was wary but unimpressed; he simply looked too young to be a ship's Captain.

A spotlessly clean coat draped over the man's scrawny frame, outlining him in dark indigo. Gold epaulets draped down from the coat collars, capped by a fringed round pad which crowned both shoulders. The jacket front was pleated with a white vestment, trimmed in gold. Eighteen gold buttons lined the vestment, nine on each side. White cotton breeches were tucked into knee-high boots of black polished leather, shiny and crisp. A high necked collar, also trimmed in gold, rose stately to his chin, adding to the air of superiority which he worked so hard at to convey. Locks of fine white powdered hair, a wig unlike anything Jonah had ever seen, peeked out from beneath the gold-trimmed bicorn which sat atop his head, crowning his entire outfit with a regality unknown to the humble vintner whose entire life had been spent with farmers…or black robed monks.

"Well, what have we here? Let's take a look. A Jesuit? Yes, well well, story is you killed one of my best sailors. Yes, cut him down with those odd Chinese boxing moves. Strange fighting, that…yes? Stranger yet coming from a priest."

"I am no priest," retorted Jonah in the English language.

"Well now, not a priest? Looks like a priest. Dresses like a priest. And speaks English, as well. How is that?"

"The monastery…they take me in; when the volcano…she…erupts. They nurse me back…healthy. Teach me many things…teach me languages. Give me these robes…the only clothes I have. Make me work, too, to earn my keep. Like I plan to do here…to work …to earn my keep."

"Well, well, you certainly shall do that! There are no loafers or slackers aboard my ship, by God. You shall *earn your keep*, as you say, very well, then. We'll make a sailor out of you, yes? Doubt you can replace the likes of old man Soto and another greenhorn is the last thing I wanted but I need a set of hands to replace his, by God. Learn the rules. There'll be no fighting board my ship, you hear? I'll stripe you good if you start that nonsense. The crew works in shifts. First meal is at sunrise, with the others at mid-day and sunset, seven days a week."

"Yes, sir," answered the young man, familiar with responding to authority but bristling under the pretentious yoke of it, coming from one so young.

"Very well, then. Mr. Davis! – See this man below."

"Aye, Captain," replied Isaac Davis, first mate aboard the *Fair American.*

Jonah Pessoa watched the tall, muscular man cautiously. He was well over six feet, taller than any man Jonah had ever seen. A small tail of flaxen hair was knotted at the back of his neck, tied in a ribbon bow of finest black silk. His large frame and bony structure made him appear awkward. When he walked, it was as if his torso fought against his legs, the upper and lower parts of his body locked in a contest of wills, an awkward gait of sorts, yet he moved across the deck swiftly, never once grasping a handhold. For all of his Shaolin training in balance and body posture, Jonah struggled to keep his feet underneath him, constantly shifting his weight back and forth with each wave of the sea.

"It'll take a while," said Isaac Davis, smiling "but you'll get your sea legs underneath of you, eventually. First time on a ship?"

“No,” replied Jonah honestly. “Come over… from mainland…in whaling ship. Nothing like…this,” he replied, his admiration for the war brig evident.

Jonah stood in awe at the cleanliness and tidiness of the deck, longer than the 100 feet he had earlier guessed. Not a plank was out of place. Fresh ropes, perfectly coiled, hung from over sixty wooden tongues along her sides. Twenty or more wooden tongues surrounded the base of the two giant masts, a complement of fifteen or more were symmetrically placed along the gunwales of the deck. Tight riggings, tarred black, draped down from the four cross beams of each mast, casting a canopy of rope over the entire ship, although her deck face was clean and unencumbered. Two wooden platforms surrounded the midpoint of each mast, large enough for two men to stand upon and keep watch. A graceful statuette crowned the bow of the ship, a finely carved figure of a woman warrior, complete with shield and helmet. She faced the sea, her proud breasts exposed, jutting into the wind as it swept back the hair from her face. Directly above her head, the bow sprit stretched out to the sea, her jib boom protruding from the ship’s front like the mythical horn of the unicorn.

Glancing down her stern, Jonah Pessoa noted the captain’s helm, a magnificently carved wheel of darkened-stained wood, ten spokes emanating from her core, each one with a corresponding handhold on the outer circumference. It stood on the quarter deck, encircled by a railing, a porch of finely carved wood. The last one-third of the stern also housed what appeared to be the finest section of the ship: the captain’s quarters. It rose from the quarter deck, a gracefully rounded edifice. Each side boasted a complement of three six-paned windows, elegantly painted beams and cornices surrounding them. The rear face of the captain's quarters sported an upward curved row of seven windows, each one supporting nine panes of glass. These were surrounded by finely chiseled cornices and columns, painted in shades of black and copper. A graceful bow of scalloped wood rose stately above the windows, crowning the rear of the vessel with distinction. In-between the rear windows and the peak of the bow sat a brass figured emblem, Neptune and his bride, cavorting in an undersea embrace. It was the most magnificent vessel Jonah Pessoa had ever been aboard and it mesmerized him…temporarily.

"Not up that way, bub. Those quarters are off-limits to you, and everyone else, for that matter. Only for the Captain. And me, when I'm called there; and *only* when I'm called. Let's go below," Isaac Davis said.

He led them to a hold in the middle of the deck, parting the gawking sailors as they walked.

"Get to work, all of you. Don't just stand there, by God. There's much to be done and no time to be wasted, so get on about your tasks."

"Aye aye, Mr. Davis," retorted the sailors, one by one. The men quickly scattered, each one running to various parts of the ship, coiling rope yet again or buckling the riggings.

"So you speak English?" quizzed the first mate, leading Jonah down into the hold, taking the wooden steps two at a time; the younger Jonah struggled to keep up, finding himself lurched from side to side.

"Yes, a little," he replied.

"Just a little? And a little of some other tongues, no doubt?"

"Yes."

“What else?”

“Latin, mostly. I…talk…Spanish, French, and… some words, how you say? – a smattering?...of a few others; as well as fluent Portuguese, of course.”

“Well now, that could come in handy. We intend to put into port off the coast of Brazil, and then around the Horn to the Sandwich Isles. Always helps to have someone aboard who can speak the language, you know what I mean?”

Jonah Pessoa did not answer. A nod of his head was sufficient for the both of them.

The bright clean look of the upper deck rapidly gave way to a cluttered, darkened gun deck. Jonah’s eyes quickly adjusted to the shadows, taking in the sights. Fresh water barrels were located immediately to his right. Black powder kegs were dispersed along the length of both sides of the deck. Barrels of rum were stacked in-between the cannon stations. As the two stepped off of the steps and onto the gun deck, a squawking hen scurried across their feet, flapping her clipped wings. Chasing behind her was the ship’s cook, a thin, African man, old and balding. He swore at the chicken as he pursued her. The crew laughed, including Isaac Davis.

“Don’t let her get away from you, Stewart. It’d be a hard life at sea without fresh eggs every morning,” joked the first mate.

Once caught, the precious egg-layer was carefully placed into the top layer of a brightly painted wooden pen, tucked in just underneath the steps. Below the hen was another set of pen boxes, containing three turtles. Ignoring the stares of the men, Jonah followed the first mate as he walked along the gun deck. Spaced apart every six feet or so were short, squatty canons.

Each iron cast gun had three bands encircling its circumference. They sat on wooden carriages, each one sporting solid wooden wheels, facing a square portal. Heavy duty ropes lashed them all to the ship's hull.

"Sixteen cannon, eight to a side. We can take on any challenge on the high seas. Ever fire a cannon?" asked Isaac Davis.

"No sir," replied Jonah.

"Well, you certainly shall, then. Yes, you shall learn," smiled the ship's mate.

They continued down the long deck, Jonah's eyes taking in the sights. There was not an inch of space that was not occupied for one purpose or another. Hammocks, some with sailors still sleeping in them, were suspended from every nook and cranny available, tucked in between barrels of black powder and pyramids of stacked cannon balls. In some cases, the men slept, suspended over one another, in a maze of canvas and webbing. The odor of unwashed man-sweat, urine, and excrement was overwhelming.

"Get used to it, lad. This is not a monastery; there are no bathing tubs aboard her. This is a ship. A British ship of the Royal Navy, by God and the King!"

Jonah Pessoa did not answer; his face communicated all that the first mate needed to know – he would try.

Another hold slid open in the gun deck floor and Isaac Davis led young Jonah down lower, into the very bowels of the vessel, the orlop deck. Here there was no natural light whatsoever. Lanterns hung from various points along the roof beams, casting an eerie faint glow. The strong smell of pickled cabbage flooded his nostrils. This was both the galley and the ship's store hold. More barrels of fresh water were stacked atop one another; then kegs of beer, and barrels marked salt beef, salt pork, oatmeal, butter, biscuits, and sugar. Wheels of cheese hung suspended from the roof beams, tiny ropes encircling them.

"Stewart is the ship's cook. Does a fine job with what he has, too. Prepares three meals a day. You'll get salt pork or beef on Tuesday, Thursday, Saturday, and Sunday. On Monday, Wednesday, and Friday, you'll get two ounces of butter and four ounces of cheese. If he runs out of cheese, then you'll get a double issue of butter. When we're in port, you can usually expect fresh meat twice a week – each man gets four pounds of fresh beef and three pounds of fresh pork; that's true measure, without the purser's cut."

Jonah nodded his head in silence. Although more meat than he was used to, it would have to do in lieu of vegetables. He would be without the fresh greens, tomatoes, and peppers the monks tended to so faithfully, in the gardens of the monastery. Other than the barrels of vinegar soaked cabbage, there did not appear to be a vegetable or herb anywhere on the vessel and fresh milk was out of the question.

Jonah glanced to the left just long enough to see bottles and casks of wine stacked behind a gated cabinet, locked by a key.

"Captain's private store. Don't be eyeing anything in there, lad. It'll cost you dearly if you take from the Captain's reserve," warned the ship's mate. "Not even Stewart holds the key to that. Purser only, Mr. Winscott. Captain's private chef, among other roles he has. Some of the finest port in the world, though. He got it in Oporto," remarked Isaac Davis.

Probably some of my family's wine, though Jonah Pessoa to himself.

They continued down a dank path towards the bow of the ship. With each step they took, the wooden hull and the planking became damper and damper. Moisture condensed on the walls of the hull, as if the sea herself were trying to seep through the wood. It was colder, darker, in this deepest part of the ship, below the waterline. The smell of tar was overpowering. Coils of rigging, spare sails, boxes of unknown content, and miscellaneous ship stores were crowded into the curving bow, stacked haphazardly. There were no hammocks here; odd collections of rolled up blankets appeared to be nested in-between crates, boxes, and every other square foot that was not wet.

"Well, here you be, lad. The other greenhorn, like you, sleeps here. There's no room on the gun deck; can't possibly squeeze in another hammock anywhere. If a spot does open up, it's up to men on the gun deck which one of you gets to hang a hammock up there, so make friends and get along or you'll end up down here for a long time. Find yourself a dry spot, if you can, and set up."

"Didn't appear that you brought anything with you, other than the robe on your back. I'm sure there is a blanket or two that can be found down here, or shared amongst you and you can always find an outfit or two in the slop chest, just over there. You'll want to change; that long robe won't do for a sailor working the deck. You'll be caught up in some rigging real fast and liable to lose a hand or a foot. Don't drive any nails in her hull – that's an order. Get some shuteye because you'll do watch tonight. I'll send someone down for you when it's your turn. Welcome aboard the *Fair American*. Your name?"

"Pessoa. My name…Jonah Pessoa."

"Jonah Pessoa, it is," replied the first mate.

A quick pat on the back, and Isaac Davis was gone. Left alone in the dark, Jonah quickly assessed his situation. No family, no friends, alone in the bottom of the coldest, wettest portion of a ship, answerable to a group of men he did not know nor trust, speaking in a language he was not fluent in. And not a clue how long he would be in this circumstance.

From out of nowhere, the pain of the loss of his father rushed over him again, suddenly crushing his spirit. He fought the urge to cry, steeling over his emotions with the power of his *chi*, just as Brother Chin had taught him. It was a struggle but he managed to control it. This was going to be his home now, at least for a while and he needed to make the best of it. He knew, somehow, his destiny lay beyond this present circumstance. He was not to be a sailor for the rest of his life. This, too, would pass in time.

He reached up to his scalp, fingering the thick scar that lay just beneath his hairline. He had not slept in over two days. He stared at the black woolen robe which covered his body. He had not had the opportunity to bathe for more than three days. He stunk. *But not nearly as bad as the men up on the gun deck,* he thought to himself, smiling.

The ship lurched suddenly, throwing Jonah against the starboard side. Crates, blankets, and riggings slid across the damp floor. They crashed into one another, rolling then piling on top of him as he struggled to gain his footing. He was covered in wet rope and fought to keep the weight of the wooden crates from crushing him. A barrel rolled across the deck, crashing next to his head. Broken pieces of hard tack biscuits spilled out from the cracks in its wooden ribs; they were moldy and infested with weevils. The ship righted herself and everything began sliding back across the deck, in the opposite direction. Jonah sat up amidst a nest of coiled rope and laughed. He climbed out of the rigging. Sheer exhaustion suddenly overcame him and he lay down on a folded sheet of canvas sail, closing his eyes. Within moments, he was in a deep slumber.

Two figures entered the orlop deck, stealthily making their way to the bow where Jonah Pessoa was fast asleep.

"Is that him?" whispered the larger one of the two.

"Yes. That's him," the skinny one with the pock-marked face replied.

"Well?"

"I'll kill that son-of-bitch right now." The figure pulled a shiny knife blade from the back of his waist wrap.

"Wait. You'll be hung for sure if you do that here and now."

"You suggesting something else?"

"Don't be a fool. There's a better way to get this done. And it'll look proper, too."

"What is your plan?"

Chapter Seven

Isaac Davis bounded back to his cramped quarters, his thoughts racing. The strange, young priest – or was he not a priest? – was going to be a problem. Why had the Captain allowed it? As first mate, it was his job to know the men aboard and to listen to their rumblings. He had heard the talk; about the fear the men had, bringing on board the very one that had killed Anton Soto in a fight. Or was it murder as the thin, pock-marked faced Eusebio had so vehemently claimed? Only a fool would have allowed that trouble on board. The ongoing impetuousness and inexperience of their too-young Captain, Thomas Metcalf, was straining the crew. He recalled vividly the shock and trepidation he felt, the moment it was discovered that Simon Metcalf would not be serving as Captain on the *Fair American.*

"Sir, I signed up as mate with the understanding that you would be Captain aboard her. Not someone else," he had replied, masking his anger carefully.

"Mr. Davis, I understand your concern and I appreciate your commitment to me personally. But I cannot be two places at once, can I now?"

"Where will you be, sir?"

"Captain aboard the Eleanor," he replied.

"Then I shall serve as first mate aboard her, sir."

"Sorry, Mr. Davis. I appreciate your willingness to accompany me and provide your services; it is an offer I shall yet call upon you for. But the Eleanor already has a first-mate."

"A fact that was unknown to you, sir?"

"Of course, man! Good God, what kind of scoundrel do you take me for, Mr. Davis?"

"My apologies, sir."

"I planned to captain the *Fair American* and take you on as first mate, just as we discussed. Seems the Eleanor's captain took deathly ill, poor fellow. And the Crown asked me to step in."

"And you agreed, sir?"

"Good God, man, what else was I to do? I am a servant of the Crown, just like everyone else aboard His Majesty's ships. I take my orders from the King, now don't I?"

"I understand, sir."

"Do you, now? Well, we shall see about that."

"Meaning what, sir?"

"Well, well, now. Just because I'll not be at the helm of the *Fair American* does not mean she does not require your services."

"Sir?"

"I mean, Mr. Davis, that your role as first mate aboard her is still needed and required. Perhaps, now more than ever," he said, his voice trailing off perceptibly at the last few words.

"I don't understand, sir. I agreed to serve as mate because of you."

"And I thank you for that. If you believe in my leadership, sir, then I shall take the opportunity to ask for your services as first mate aboard the *Fair American*, as a *personal favor*."

"A *personal favor*, sir?"

"I have been asked by the Crown to choose a Captain for the *Fair American*. And I have made my choice. I now need you, kind sir, to provide that level of dedication, discipline, and order you would have provided me to the one whom I have hand-chosen to captain her. Can you do that, Mr. Davis?"

"Sir, I shall try."

"Not good enough, Mr. Davis. I need to know that you will do it. That you will serve her crew, and especially her Captain, as if I myself were the one at the helm. Again, I shall ask you, sir. Can you do that? Do I have your word, as a gentleman?"

There was a momentary pause before Isaac Davis replied, quietly.

"Yes, sir."

"Very well, then. That's what I needed to hear. I knew I could count on you. Count on you to provide the same level of service to her present Captain as you would to me, if I were her Captain. Thank you, Mr. Davis. Allow me to introduce you to your Captain."

Simon Metcalf retreated behind the rich oak paneled doors to the Royal Naval Academy's Offices. Within moments, he returned with a young lad, no more than eighteen years old, following him, bedecked with all the regalia of a Royal Navy Captain.

"Mr. Davis, meet my son, Captain Thomas Metcalf. Thomas, allow me to introduce you to your first mate, Mr. Isaac Davis."

The veteran seaman was visibly stunned. The young man before him was barely of adult age. The royal costume he wore, fitted with all the proper regalia, seemed to be out of place, somehow. The lad appeared ill-at-ease, standing beside his father. The newfound authority he wielded was unbecoming for one his age but he quickly covered for his lack of experience with a false bravado.

"Well, well. A Welshman for a mate? Couldn't find a proper Englishman for the job, I see."

The remark was a stinging indictment, bringing up hurtful memories of wars fought long ago and countless lives lost in the bitter history between Mother England and the isle of Wales.

"Now, now, let's have none of that," replied Simon Metcalf, his eyes still fixed solidly upon Isaac Davis. He had seen the flash of anger that flared there momentarily and he moved quickly to ameliorate the damage.

"Mr. Davis is the finest first mate I've ever had. He'll do you a fine job, lad, and you'll do well to learn from him. Yes, you'll do well to learn from him."

The younger Metcalf chaffed under his father's words; they were a veiled reprimand but a reprimand nonetheless. He spun around, quickly leaving the room, his costume sword clumsily banging against the desk as he retreated.

The silence was deafening. Neither man spoke a word, each one staring into the eyes of the other before Simon Metcalf finally broke.

"I need you on this Mr. Davis. The lad won't make it without a seasoned mate aboard and you're the best that's ever served me. And I need you to serve my son, just as you have served me. You gave your word, as a gentleman." It was more of a plea than a command.

"The men won't trust him, sir. He'll never get their respect. For the love of God, sir, he's still just a boy!"

"He's not a boy!" shouted Simon Metcalf, slamming his clenched fist into the mahogany desk between them. His face was red and distorted with angst. "He's a man, by God! When I was his age, I had already served more than two years before the mast!"

His voice calmed appreciably as he continued, "I need to get him exposed to the world, get him out there, learn the discipline of a ship…"

Isaac Davis cut off his friend's remarks, interjecting with an insolence of tone the elder Captain Metcalf had never heard before. "He'll not learn discipline by serving as Captain…*sir*." The emphasis upon the last word was evident in both its pause and the inflection of his voice. He continued, "That's a recipe for disaster. Putting a young lad in command who has never even been to sea before is…"

Simon Metcalf interjected, "…something which you're going to help me with, now is it not? You gave your word…as a gentleman."

The hellish predicament Isaac Davis found himself in was evident in no time. There was more to being first mate than just keeping the ship's log and ensuring a watch was kept. It was his duty to convey the orders of the Captain and ensure that those orders were followed. And, if not followed, to administer the discipline, acting on behalf of the ship's Captain. And it was soon apparent that every concern he had expressed to the senior Metcalf, about his young son, was well-founded. The passage from London was an exercise in futility, the irascible and harsh young Captain making one mistake after another.

"The fresh water is gone, sir," reported Isaac Davis.

"Well, what do you want me to do about that!" exclaimed Captain Thomas Metcalf, exasperated by the duties of command and inexperienced in dealing with the burden of caring for a crew of men aboard a ship.

"Well, sir. The rations you allotted were double the amount normally let."

"You've already told me that, Mr. Davis; on more than one occasion. I wanted to make an impression. Let the men know that I was interested in their welfare," the young Captain replied, the tone of desperation in his voice growing with each syllable.

"Yes, well sir. There is no more water now and the meat is all gone, as well. On account of the double portions you let, sir."

"Damn it, man! What do you expect me to do!" shouted Thomas Metcalf, his fist slamming into the desk where his maps and papers lay scattered.

"I'd suggest we head toward the Azores, sir. We can pick up some fresh stores there. We'll never make it to the Brazilian coast on the stores we have left…*sir*." Emphasizing the last word was Isaac Davis's only way of expressing his disrespect for the irascible young man, a man he was subject to only because of a promise made to the elder Captain Metcalf; a promise he now realized was made in haste.

"Very well, then. Set course for the Azore Islands. Well, go on about it, man! You have your orders!" screamed out the inexperienced Captain, dismissing his first mate with a petulant wave of his hand.

"Aye, Captain," replied Isaac Davis, leaving the opulence of the Captain's quarters to the impudent young dolt who occupied it alone, for the most part.

Thomas Metcalf rarely came out to face the men, preferring the privacy of his cabin. It was uncommon for Isaac Davis to accompany the Captain at a meal, although this was not true of the lad's father, who insisted on his first mate sharing every dinner with him, when possible.

The *Fair American* boasted a Captain's quarter that was second to none. Dinner served in that luxurious setting, which always included the ship's purser, Mr. Winscott, and the ship's surgeon, Mr. Carlisle, was an extravagance which the seamen aboard would never know. Finest china, delicately rimmed and scalloped, with prints of roses emblazoned upon them, were routine. Silverware, intricately forged and exquisitely decorated, was set out upon tablecloths of whitest silk, embroidered throughout. Special meals, prepared by Mr. Winscott in the ship's galley, were presented, including delicacies which the men on deck never consumed, among them turtle soup, fresh eggs, and select cuts of the beef and pork, set aside at the privilege of the purser. And then there were the wines, bottles and casks of it. Rum or beer never appeared at the table of the Captain. The privileged few drank Madeira, Port, and Brandy out of elegantly chiseled glasses, rimmed with gold. Although not averse to the privileges of being counted among the officers of a ship, there was something about this particular Captain and his way that made Isaac Davis uneasy. He felt guilty every time he dined there. He found himself wishing he was not invited, as rare as those invitations were; and that in and of itself bothered him.

The unplanned stop in the Azores had saved the ship. Without the stores they were able to pick up there, the crew would have most certainly mutinied. Fresh water was obtained from the isle Terceira. Fresh beef, oranges by the crate load, and more wine was purchased from the isle São Miguel. And now, they were pulling up anchor from Faial, one experienced seaman dead and one greenhorn aboard, a strange young man from the Jesuit monastery whom some said was a murderer. Yet one who possessed a skill with languages and the superior knowledge of the Jesuits – making him the most educated man aboard, absent the nautical wisdom one gains while at sea – and a fighting style, or so he was told, unlike any man he had ever known. Isaac Davis pondered for a moment before coming to a conclusion, one he was reticent to admit: he actually envied the young man.

Chapter Eight

Jonah Pessoa awoke to the heavy sounds of raindrops falling on deck, thick and fast. Even this far below, he could hear the methodic plopping of the heavy drops. He had no idea how long he had been asleep. His rousing came with a sinking sense of guilt, a feeling of shame. Had he missed the first mate's call?

The place where he had lain was in complete disarray. The canvas had folded down on top of him and he was surrounded by wooden crates and tangled rope. He wasn't even sure he was still on the starboard side of the ship. The load had shifted yet again but he must have slept through it all. He slowly picked up on loud and repeated voices, men's voices, barking out and responding to orders. He heard the trampling of feet up and down the length of her deck and the creaking of blocks. He knew there was a storm coming; and that he should be on deck, helping out somehow, in some way. The slide of the hatch was suddenly thrown back. The noise and tumult of all that was occurring topside abruptly became much louder.

"All hands, ahoy!"

Jonah jumped to his feet. He understood the command – he grinned slightly, impressed with his understanding of the English tongue. Scrambling up the wooden steps, he collided with another young greenhorn, about his age, already dressed in the wide-legged duck trousers and checked shirt most of the men wore. The young man gave Jonah a curious look. It was only then that he realized he was still clad in the black robes of a Jesuit monk; it must have been a bizarre sight and he instantly understood the awkward stare of his berth companion. Silently, they climbed up through the gun deck, noting the absence of any sailors whatsoever, before sliding open the closed hatch and clamoring onto the top deck.

The angry sea was beating against the ship. The force of it was not unlike the volcanic tremor Jonah had lived through, the ship lolling back and forth underneath of him – it was difficult to keep one's footing and Jonah fell to one knee more than once on the slickened deck. Everything and everyone was soaking wet. The fierce wind whistled through the rigging. Heavy rain assaulted the crew, drenching the sailors in an unrelenting deluge. The topsail halyards were loose and the great sails began to fill out; they slapped back against the masts with a strident clap.

Suddenly, Jonah was violently sick. His knees wobbled beneath him; he was unable to stand. Stumbling his way to starboard, he gripped the rail with all his might before leaning over to retch; then retch again. His empty stomach fiercely tried to expel everything that was within him – but he had not eaten in over a day and there was nothing to vomit up.

He felt childish and worthless, his inexperience at sea making him all but useless as the sailors around him scurried to and fro, taking and following orders, pulling and knotting the ropes and rigging. He wiped his mouth and turned around, just in time.

"Pull! Pull!"

Jonah watched as a rain-drenched sailor slid past him on the deck, the force of the wind dragging the man and the rope he was grappling with. Jonah grabbed a section immediately behind his skidding companion and pulled with all his might, weak as he was. The sideways momentum was finally halted as both men strained against the power of the gale force wind. As soon as Jonah had a steady grip, the veteran seaman let go, shocking young Jonah. *He's going to leave me alone to hold it steady*, he inwardly questioned? Immediately, the veteran fell in behind Jonah, looping the end of the rope into a knot with an expert flick of his wrist and quickly wrapping it around the nearest wooden tongue. Despite the unrelenting tug of the wind, the rope held. The danger was past, thanks to the veteran seaman.

"She tight now!" he shouted over the howl of the wind and rain, a grin breaking across his wide, wet face. Jonah Pessoa stood in the downpour, staring at the man. He was short of stature but thick, wide in both the chest and belly. He wore no shirt, unlike any other sailor aboard, but did not seem to mind it, despite the torrent of rain. His skin was dark bronze and his hair a wiry black in color, tied in the back, a bushy ponytail draping down his neck. Strange geometric tattoos encircled his biceps and neck. A splash of tattoo spread across his chin, rows of dotted marks draping down from his lower lip then splaying out across his jaw line. His broad faced grin never ceased. Rows of square set teeth were framed by thick lips.

Jonah, still seasick, leaned over the gunwale once again, retching forcefully but in vain. After yet another round of gut-wrenching spasms, he turned back to the deck, empty, drained, exhausted, and soaking wet. The bronze-skinned man still stood there in the rain, still grinning.

"You priest?" inquired the peculiar looking sailor.

Jonah was reminded once again of his monastic garb and how it instantly, and wrongly, classified him, giving him an identity he was desperately ready to shed. He acted on an impulse.

"No. No priest," replied Jonah. He pulled the rain soaked black robe from off his shoulders and let the heavy garment collapse to the ground in a pile around his feet. Gathering it up, he tossed it overboard in an act of revolt against all that the monastery had stood for; in his mind, he was crossing a line he was sure he would never come back to...he could not have been more wrong.

He stood on deck, stark against the wind and rain, wearing nothing more than yarn spun underwear and leather sandals. He was instantly chilled to the bone, every pore in his body soaked through. The kanaka, somehow standing fixed on the rolling deck, each fist pressed to his waist, laughed aloud.

"Ho, now! You look like sailor!" he exclaimed, shouting above the roar of the wind.

"Manu – get him below," barked out Isaac Davis, running past the two men. "The worst of it is over and we'll get calm weather in no time…and get some decent garb on him, for God's sake."

"Aye, Mr. Davis," responded the tattooed man. He motioned for Jonah to follow him and they readily climbed below, happy to leave the rain splattered upper deck for the relative calm of the ship's hold.

The stranger led Jonah to a wooden chest, stored in the bow. It lay next to the folded up sail he had slept on the day before; or had he slept longer than that? Opening it up, the stranger drew forth some garments, patched here and there with bits of cloth or canvas, but still serviceable. They were a pair of wide-legged trousers and a plain white shirt. He held them out to Jonah, who began shivering, his body finally reaching its limit of cold, wet, and sea-sickness.

"You wear. Then, you eat. Feel better after."

"Thank you," he replied, truly grateful for the kindness of this stranger.

"You speak English?" asked Jonah, keenly aware that the man before him was not of European origin.

"Yes. Some," he replied.

Jonah waited for more to come, but there was none. He proceeded to don the clothes he was given. The shirt was long but he tucked it into his waist. The pants were loose in the waist but a piece of cut rope, also taken from the chest, served as an adequate belt; Jonah cinched it tightly into a knot. He suddenly felt better, as if the simple changing of his clothes, from that of a Jesuit priest to a sailor's cut, had wrought a change within him, somehow. His companion smiled at the look of him dressed out in a seaman's outfit, worn and patched as it was. Jonah ventured further with his new-found fellow sailor.

"Where you learn…English?" he asked.

"From men…on ship," replied the kanaka, the overt smile on his face disappearing at the thought. His eyes seemed to glaze over, his mind wandering, as if a far away memory had seized him.

The response was inadequate, leaving out the many details Jonah was interested in knowing, such as how, why, and when. But his friend remained mute on that. The clanging of bells, seven in number, immediately brought the tattooed man back into the moment. He was grinning broadly again as he proclaimed, “We go eat.”

A crowd of men, still wet from the storm that had recently drenched the ship, clamored to the orlop deck below, readily finding every nook and cranny upon which one could sit. The ship’s cook methodically dispensed the provisions for their evening meal with the precision of an assayer, carefully weighing and measuring out equal rations. The food was readily consumed by each man, silently gnawing away on each item apportioned them. The hold was in relative silence, other than the sound of chewing and swallowing – an occasional grunt every now and then.

A single battered stein, carefully measured and filled with fresh water from one of the barrels, made its rounds. Each man drank from it before passing to the next. Jonah and Manu fell in, clearing a space near the end of the line of men which looped about the hold adjacent to the galley in a strange, curling fashion. The thought of eating something, anything, excited Jonah. Strong hunger suddenly overcame him and he found himself eagerly anticipating whatever the cook would dish his way.

The old African grinned crookedly as he approached Jonah, a row of blackened teeth showing out through his parted lips.

“Lad, you’s look well cleaned out by now; mebbe you’s no have any land gut left in you? Is good, is good! Start here - eat sea bread and salt beef. Will cover your ribs good. You be as strong as others by the time we reach the Horn.”

The extra large cut of cold salt beef and the two biscuits, which Jonah checked carefully for weevils, tasted glorious. He never imagined how strong just a little bit of sustenance could make one feel, particularly one who has nothing left within him. Manu and he ate in silence with the rest, although the young vintner turned monk turned sailor could not help but notice all eyes were upon him.

One set of eyes in particular appeared to be fixed upon him with an intense gaze, a gaze which Jonah tried hard to ignore. With his brow crinkled and his head still downcast, the cold steely glare of Eusebio bore like a dagger into the soul of Jonah Pessoa. The last thing Jonah needed aboard this ship was trouble. The stare remained unbroken until the meal was finished.

"Him make… eyes of hate…for you," whispered Manu.

"Why?" asked Jonah of his new found friend. "What have I done to him?"

"Him say…you make big trouble…come on ship."

Jonah pondered this thought for a moment. He had no answer and would not try to respond. What else was there to say?

"We go watch now. I help you. Ship more calm, now. Rain all gone. Wind all gone. Easy for you, now."

Jonah Pessoa smiled at his friend. Then it struck him – he hadn't actually smiled in a long, long time. His face widened even further at the thought of it and Manu, who seemed to be smiling perpetually, laughed aloud.

"Come. I show you what to do on deck."

Chapter Nine

The unlikely duo stood watch until sunrise. The upper deck they re-appeared on was a scene vastly different from the one they had fled from two hours earlier. Gone were the pelting rains and the howling winds which tore so violently at the sails and the rigging. Everything appeared quiet, serene, and dark. The deck, although still damp, was steadier and Jonah found himself adjusting to the gentler pitch and roll. With a little bit of practice, he was soon holding his own, balanced as well as any other man on a surface which was in constant motion. The sea was calm. Only a faint breeze whispered across the star-studded night sky.

Another sailor, unknown to Jonah, was already at the helm, lazily adjusting her giant spoked wheel every so often. Manu posted himself mid-ship, careful to stay off of the quarter deck while Jonah took watch in the forecastle.

The monotonous crest and fall of the cold dark waves, stretching out into infinity, soon cast a mesmerizing spell over the young man. The gentle sloshing sound of water, lapping against the wooden keel in a rhythmic tempo, dulled the attention of Jonah; he found himself transfixed by the beauty and sound of it. The vastness of it, the majesty of it, and the mysterious beauty of it stirred within him emotions and thoughts of the Divine. How could there not be a God out there, somewhere? One who had put all this together…yet certainly it could not be the same God the

Church had tried to convince him of, a God who capriciously made orphans out of the innocent and who punished the guiltless with scorching lava, taking the lives of saints such as his mother but sparing the life of the likes of Anton Soto? No – there had to be another answer out there, somewhere, other than that. If there was a God out there, somewhere, it certainly was not the God he had been taught about all of his life.

Manu suddenly appeared in the forecastle, surprising Jonah with his stealth. The young vintner turned monk turned sailor jumped, leading Manu to laugh.

"No be afraid. Only Manu," he whispered.

"Did not even hear you come up behind me. You are sneaky," replied Jonah, utilizing the English tongue, the language expected to be spoken aboard an English vessel.

Manu put his forefinger to his lips in the universal sign of silence. "Shhhhh. Captain and first mate no happy when sailor make talk. Think talk mean no work. Think we lazy. Give more work. So we whisper…when talk. When Captain or Mr. Davis come by, we no talk. Wait until they gone. Then we whisper again."

Jonah nodded his head in silent acknowledgement of this universal sailor's agreement. They both continued whispering, Manu turning back to keep an eye on the helmsman.

"Manu answer your question now. You like know where I learn English. But, me think you like know more than that. You like know where I come from. You like know what happen me. You like know how Manu come to be on English ship."

"Yes," answered Jonah truthfully, cautiously, amazed at the insight of his new found companion.

Manu smiled wide. "It good. Because…Manu like know what happen you, too. How you learn English so well, but…you Portuguese? How you learn fight, like they say you fight. How you learn so many thing, like others say you know." There was a distinct pause before the young kanaka finished. "And what you know about the heavens. And the white Father God. The one God above all the other gods."

"Well," continued Jonah almost inaudibly, "perhaps we can learn from one another. I would like that. But you'll get no theology from me."

"The…olo…gy?" questioned Manu.

"Theology. The study of God. But I'm not going to repeat that foolishness to anyone else. I don't believe in it and I sure am not going to spread any of that worthless nonsense to anyone else. If there is a God, I sure don't believe in Him and I'll be damned if I am in any way responsible for further spreading that deceit."

"But…you priest…of the Church?" continued Manu.

"No!" shouted Jonah, loud enough to stun the young kanaka. He instantly brought his finger to his lips again, reminding Jonah of the need for quiet. Jonah regretted his outburst and continued in a hushed tone. "I told you. I am not a priest. Never have been. Never will be. Yes, I was in the monastery. But that was by default, not by choice."

"So you no believe in the white Father God? The one my father teach about?"

"Your father?" questioned Jonah Pessoa, more perplexed as the unplanned conversation continued.

"Yes. My mother, she native…my island. My father…not. Some say, my father, one white man. I never see him. I never know him. Old people tell me…say he wash up on shore one day, in little canoe, but not really canoe. Him look like dead man. Many say he dead but after some days, his spirit come back to him again."

Jonah subconsciously reached his hand up to massage the familiar scar that lay just under his hairline. It reminded him of the time he had spent in the rock-hewn cellar of the monastery, considered to be dead as well. The story Manu was telling him began to feel eerily familiar and a cold chill ran up and down his spine.

"My people take him in. He teach them many strange things. He have great power. He have magic tools with him. Teach my people about the one God, the great white Father God. Him teach that all the gods my people worship…they no be gods. Only one God. In the heavens. My people tear down all the heiaus, destroy all temple, destroy all idols. All people believe in the one God. All my people happy. Learn some words he teach us…English words."

"What happened to your father?" quizzed Jonah, his curiosity piqued by the story.

"One day, white sail appear on the water. My father swim out to it. Him never come back. My mother, she say him tell one last story before him go. Him tell…one day, other white man come to my people, the same way him came. Him say…that man…him also speak English. Also teach my people more about the one God. Him help fight against our enemies, those ones who still believe in the ancient gods. Those who try to make my people forsake their belief in the Father God and force all people to worship the gods that are not gods. Him become great leader to my people."

Jonah Pessoa was not satisfied; he wanted to learn more. "How did you come to be on an English ship?"

Manu paused for a moment before continuing. "My people always treat me…different. Say I am half-white. Say I belong with…other world. Never treat me like all other boys my age. Always…no with the others. Keep me away. Me have only one sister…many year older than me…only one treat me good. Father of her not white. Him one man from the island…die long time ago. I never know him. People treat my mother, sister, and me…bad. Because long time pass and my father, him never return. My people stop to worship the Father God. People from other side of our island come…say we make trouble. Must worship the ancient gods…Pele of the volcano and Hi'iaka, sister of her. My people turn against the white Father God. Only my mother stay…worship him. She die. My sister taken away. My people no touch me after that. No more speak sacred words, the words of English.

One day, sail on the water seen again. My people no want ship to come in. Put me in canoe. Make me go out to ship alone. I go. People take me on board. Take me to big place…many white people…named *London*. I learn speak some English. I learn read and write some. I learn to be sailor. When father of Captain Metcalf go sail…he say I sail with his son…this ship…he ask me come. Say we go…my home, my island. Like see my people. I like return. So I here. Now, meet you. My English still…not so good. You English…very good. You teach me better English."

Jonah smiled at the thought and embraced the idea. He abhorred the thought of teaching any theology related to the Church. However, learning about the ancient gods Manu spoke of interested him; and he loved studying and learning languages. He was impressed by anyone who shared this passion with him. He also would learn from his new found friend.

"I will teach you English. But you must also teach me. Teach me your language. And you must tell me of the gods of your people."

Manu frowned. He did not believe in the ancient gods but his desire to learn English was strong, overwhelming even – he reluctantly agreed.

"I will tell you of the stories of those gods, who are no gods. And I will teach you the language of my people. And you will teach me…best English."

"We have a deal, my friend," said Jonah Pessoa, extending his hand to Manu. The kanaka grasped his forearm instead, squeezing it vigorously. The ever present grin on his face widened even further. His eyes shone bright; even in the darkness of the night, Jonah could see that.

"What is the tongue of your people? What is your language?" asked Jonah innocently enough. Another voice boomed from out of the darkness, breaking the unique spell over the two confidants and shattering the secrecy each of them believed they had enjoyed up to this moment.

"Hawaiian. His people call themselves, and their isles…Hawaii."

Chapter Ten

The voice from out of the darkness was instantly recognizable. Both Manu and Jonah froze.

"Manu is from the Sandwich Islands; the natives there refer to themselves as Hawaiian. No doubt of Tahitian extraction, but no one knows for sure. Not even the islanders themselves are knowledgeable about their ancestry. They have no written records or language. But their knowledge of sea navigation is incomparable. And they make good sailors," stated Isaac Davis, matter-of-factly.

The first mate strode up next to the two; the tension in the cool night air intensified.

"Relax, men. You'll find no trouble with me. Listened to your conversations, though, and I'd like to make both of you an offer. None of us can be found by the Captain engaging in wanton speech and undisciplined activity. Too much work aboard a ship to allow for that. My job is to see that the men aboard are kept busy and engage in productive seaman's work. And that I'll do and do well. But we each seem to have a stake here, in this matter."

Manu and Jonah looked at one another, unsure of what the first mate was leading to.

"Didn't get the chance to get school learning, beyond the primaries. Picked up the rest of everything I know on my own. Learned the craft of a sailor by sailing; by doing. Still…always wanted to go on…for more schooling. Never forgot what is was like to learn.

I can read a chart well enough to steer a ship, and I have enough writing and spelling to keep the ship's log but…nothing like the knowledge one learns when one is in the Monastery…when one is a…*Jesuit*."

The emphasis upon the last word was deliberate and Jonah knew it. He was backed into a corner. To refuse the first mate would put himself and Manu in an untenable position. On the other hand, he had no desire to teach Christian theology, a theology he despised. The thought revolted him. His mind raced, quickly searching for an option, a way out.

"What *exactly* do you believe I have learned that I can share with you. What is it you wish to know… from the Jesuits," offered Jonah.

"I have heard tell the Jesuits learn many things. So many things…things I do not know. Geometry. Astronomy. Sciences of all kinds. Things I wish I knew. Things I would have liked to learn. But I was not chosen as one for the monastery. Many times, I wish I had been. I have heard one learns so many different things, things I always wanted to learn, but was never given the opportunity to…until now."

A silent sigh of relief welled up within Jonah's soul. At least he would not have to be teaching Christian dogma. He no longer even knew what he believed in but he was sure it wasn't the Christian God.

"I can teach you what I know. My time was not long there but what I know, I can share."

Isaac Davis smiled, a tight-lipped grin. Manu's face instantly returned to the wide grin he wore perpetually. But Jonah was not finished yet.

"And, in return, what will you teach me?" he asked of the first mate.

"What would you like to know about, that I can possibly teach you, other than the sailor's lot?" replied Isaac Davis.

Jonah pondered for a moment before answering. It was something which had always held his fascination, even before his mother and he ended up on Faial. Something which even his father had neglected to teach him. "Teach me to use the gun – and the sword," he replied.

Isaac Davis was relieved. If there was one thing he was expert in, it was the sword. And he could load and shoot a musket as well as any man in the Royal Navy.

"By God, so shall it be. You'll learn the sword, and gun, well enough. Hell, you'll even know how to load and fire the cannon before I'm through with you. And you'll teach me geometry, and astronomy…and the Chinese boxing?"

Jonah froze. It was the one thing the Captain had expressly warned him about, the one thing he had said was not to be allowed on board. If he was caught, there would be punishment. And the last thing Jonah wanted to do on board was to alienate himself from the crew and create hardship for himself. But this was the first mate. His hesitancy in responding was ameliorated by Manu, who abruptly chimed in, "And I learn better English; more better English. And more about – the…olo…gy."

Jonah frowned. He wasn't sure whether Manu had understood him or not, or whether his Hawaiian companion was just being obstinate.

He replied to his ship-mate, "…and you'll teach me to speak Hawaiian. And about the gods of your people."

Now it was Manu's turn to frown. Each man looked at the other in turn before all three broke out in simultaneous laughter. A deal had been struck – the ramifications of which would reverberate throughout the lives of hundreds of islanders; although that could not have been known by the three men standing on the deck of the *Fair American* that cold, calm night, out in the Atlantic Ocean. Each man silently retreated to their respective posts.

A regular routine quickly set in. After dinner was served and the crew had settled for the evening, just an hour or so before their morning watch began, Jonah Pessoa and Manu would meet, exchanging knowledge for knowledge, joined as often as possible by the first mate, Isaac Davis, whose interests ran the gamut from the various hand strikes of the Boddhidharma to the astronomy of the night sky.

"Alo…ha," repeated Manu.

"Alo…ha," repeated Jonah once again. "Amazing that one word alone can have so many meanings."

"Yes," replied Manu. "Have many meaning, this one word."

"Kâne," continued Manu.

"Kâne," repeated Jonah.

"It mean…man."

"Man. Kâne. Man," smiled Jonah.

"Wahine," said Manu.

"Wa…hine," repeated Jonah.

"It mean…woman."

"Woman. Wahine," smiled Jonah, wider this time. "I like this word…Wahine".

"Me like wahine, too," responded Manu, chuckling. "Kâua aloha wahine."

Jonah appeared puzzled, unsure of the sentence his Hawaiian mentor had just strung together.

"Say it," he ordered, grinning. "Kâua aloha wahine."

"Kâua aloha wahine," repeated Jonah faithfully, the look on his face one of uncertainty.

"It mean…we love women," explained Manu.

"Yes! We love women. Kâua aloha wahine!" repeated Jonah again, both men laughing with the thought.

Manu paused for a moment, as if he were making up his mind on a delicate matter. Without explanation, he suddenly left Jonah setting on the box crate they shared, returning after a few moments with a leather wrapped object in his hand.

"You teach Manu, now. You teach Manu read English; read best English."

"Very well," replied Jonah.

Manu extended the leather wrapped object to his friend, carefully cradling it as if it held the most precious object in the world. Slowly, Jonah untied the stout leather thong which bound the object and unfolded the soft leather flaps which covered it. Jonah slowly recognized what he was holding; a rare object, indeed, and of considerable value, given the fact that it had been laboriously hand copied. It was a true work of art; maybe even a labor of love, if its transcription were voluntary and not forced by another. Forced in the way he had been forced so many long hours, to copy laboriously the words of the Holy Book.

"Manu. I really…"

His words were cut off by the insistent demand of his Hawaiian partner. "You teach Manu! Manu teach you; he no complain. Now, you teach Manu. Teach Manu read English. Best English."

Jonah stared into the sorrowful eyes of his cohort in learning. The oblique darkness they always held was covered over by a mist, a pitiful gaze that conveyed loneliness and abandonment. Jonah knew those emotions all too well. Only one who was an orphan could ever detect them, lying buried deep under a mask of blithe indifference.

"It…my father's. Belong him. My mother…she give me before she sick then die. Her say it hold… all words… of Great White Father God. The one true God my father teach my people about before him go away. My mother, her say…it hold words of best English. Only thing Manu have left of mother and father. Now, you teach Manu read best English. You teach Manu all about…great Father God in the heaven."

Manu's voice was trembling. Every nerve in his muscled body was on edge; Jonah could see the young Hawaiian was shaking on the insides. It was not until that very moment that Jonah fully realized he was face to face with yet another orphan, one like himself, way too young to be without father or mother. His heart softened. In spite of his abhorrence for the Christian faith, a faith, as far as he could tell, had made yet another orphan of an innocent young man, he agreed to teach his Hawaiian companion…in the English language, nonetheless.

Slowly, methodically, Jonah unfolded the heavy leather cover, settling his index finger on the very first line of text, a beautifully and meticulously adorned work of art. It was grandiose, more exquisite than any script he had ever copied, its scrollwork and bright colors leaping off the page. It was evident to him that the author of this work believed in every word he had recorded.

Jonah's finger traced the words, one by one, as he spoke them aloud. Manu, crowding in beside him on the box crate, devoured every word of the text with his eyes, repeating each syllable aloud as Jonah articulated them, verbally treasuring each consonant, each vowel, as if their sounds alone were sacred, holy, in some way.

"In the beginning…" began Jonah.

"In the beginning…" repeated Manu.

"God created the heavens and the earth…"

"God create…createded…the heaven…and the eart…What this word mean, eart?" questioned Manu.

"Earth. Terra, in Portuguese. It means…the dirt, the land. Well, no, it means more than that, actually. In this passage here, the original Hebrew word means…the whole world. The sea, and the land, our world…"

Manu smiled broadly. So broadly, it led Jonah to stop in mid-speech.

"It like my father teach my mother, my sister, my people. The one God create everything. Him create the sea and the islands I come from. No Kane, no Ku, no Pele, no Hia'ka. Only the one God in the heaven. Just like my father say," proclaimed Manu with great pride.

Jonah seized the moment. "What do your people believe about how the earth was created?"

Manu's face dropped. "Manu no believe in that. But them say, it was a time of deep darkness, before any people. Then come Kane, the god of creation. Him pick up giant calabash, and throw high into the air. It break…two piece. The top piece, shape like a bowl, and it is the sky. The seeds throw all places and become the stars. The other side of calabash fall downward, and became…Eart, Earth…like one word you just teach me."

"The sky then belong to god Rangi. The Earth belong to god Papa. The sea belong to god Kanaloa. Kane say him make a great chief to rule over the Earth. To help great chief, him fill the earth with all things like birds, salamanders, and turtle. Him make Ku god over all forests to grow great trees of koa wood and candlenut, hau and wiliwili. Him make Lono god over all food plants for chief to eat like coconut, breadfruit, and taro."

"Kane tell other gods they find things to make this great chief. Can be wood, clay, stone or bark. He send them far. They search and search. One day, they find big mound of rich, red dirt…or *earth* – like the word I just learn about. They take some to Kane. Him shape figure of a man then breathe life into it. The man walk and speak to the gods. And the gods happy. Them call him Red Earth Man, and say him the first son of Rangi Sky and Papa Earth. From this, come all who are priests, our word for them *kahuna*. And all our chiefs, we call *alii*."

Jonah paused, taking in all of the details of the story he had just been told.

"Well, Manu. That's fascinating. And not that different, truth be told, from other creation myths, including the one in this here book. Actually, there are a lot of parallels between the two. But you mentioned Pele and Hi'iaka earlier. Who are they? I didn't hear them mentioned in the creation story you just shared."

"Them…two gods specific to just my island, my people. Pele, they say, follow a star from the northeast, which shine more bright than any other, and she keep following it."

Sounds like the wise men following the star of Bethlehem, to me, thought Jonah to himself.

"One day, she wake up. She smell a thing in the air, a thing she like smell. She see a high mountain with smoke; the smoke hide the top of the mountain. Pele like it. She make it her new home. She named our island…Hawai'i."

"Pele carry her magic stick up to the mountain where a part of the…*earth*…fall into the ground. She place the stick in the ground. She called this place Kilauea. Inside is big pit. She name it Halema'uma'u. She say this her new home. There was a fire god already living on Kilauea named 'Ailaau. He and Pele fight over Kilauea. They throw fire balls at each other, make big damage to the land."

Jonah shuddered at the picture in his mind. He knew all too well the damage that was done when a volcano erupted. He had felt the white hot sting of those projectiles, more than one of which had struck him, almost taking his life. He subconsciously reached up to feel the familiar scar under his scalp but caught himself in the act and forced his hand back down. Maybe there really was some malevolent force inside volcanoes, occasionally striking out at those who disrespected the land, exacting a heavy toll in human life. It made just as much sense, if not more, than a benevolent all-seeing God, who capriciously injured and killed his loyal servants.

" 'Ailaau run away. Pele alone now rule the Island of Hawai'i. My people fear and respect her. Pele have an egg her mother gave her. It hatch into a beautiful girl. Pele name her new sister, Hi'iaka. She learn to surf the waters between the islands. The shark god, Kamohoali'i, teach Hi'iaka all this."

"Pele fall in love with a man she see in a dream. Him called Lohi'au; him a chief of the island Kaua'i. Pele send her sister Hi'iaka to bring Lohi'au back to Hawai'i, to live with Pele. Hi'iaka have forty days to bring Lohi'au back. If not, Pele punish her by hurting Hi'iaka's girlfriend, Hopoe. When land on Kaua'i, Hi'iaka find Lohi'au dead. She rub his body with herbs and chant to the creation gods for help. They answer her, bring young chief of Kaua'i back to life again. Lohi'au agree to return with her to Hawai'i because he grateful."

"More than forty days pass. Pele think Hi'iaka and Lohi'au fall in love and not come back. Her get angry. Her make big eruption, turned Hopoe into stone. When Hi'iaka return to Hawai'i with Lohi'au, she find her girlfriend, Hopoe, a statue of stone. Hi'iaka very sad. Then she angry and want to hurt Pele. She lead Lohi'au to edge of the Halema'uma'u crater. She know Pele can see them. She put her arms around Lohi'au and kiss him. Pele become very angry; she cover Lohi'au with all lava and flames."

After, the two sisters are sorry for what they do to each other and to Lohi'au. One them, lose a friend, the other one them lose a lover. Pele decide to bring

Lohi'au back to life so let him choose which sister he will love. Pele sure Lohi'au will choose her. When he come back to life again, Lohi'au chose Hi'iaka. Pele hurt but let them sail back to Kaua'i together. Now, Pele still live on Hawai'i but she alone and still hurt. She rule as the fire Goddess of the volcanoes on my island. If people displease her, sometime because they no let one who love someone have him, or her, and make them be with someone else, she cause big trouble; hurt lots of people."

Jonah Pessoa contemplated again how many parallels were there: the forty days at sea, much like the forty days Noah spent adrift during the great Deluge; the resurrection from the dead, similar to Lazarus and Jesus Christ himself. It seemed odd, in some ways. How all these stories could be interconnected, somehow, as if they all came from a single, original source, at one time. What was it Israel de Silva had said? "It is God. All knowledge comes from God and He is the source of it all…see this ultimate connection. Everything that we learn, all that we know, eventually points back to Him." Nonsense! Jonah was offended by the thought and quickly dismissed it from his mind.

"Now you teach me more best English?" queried Manu, eager to continue. Before Jonah could answer, their study was interrupted.

"Learning from the sacred Scriptures, I see," shouted Isaac Davis in a voice louder than what was needed. It was a cramped space at the rear of the ship's hold and even a whisper could have sufficed.

"Well, not one to dissuade any time spent in the Good Book, but I'll be needing you both topside." He paused there, before adding for Jonah's benefit, "that is, if you wish to learn to shoot a British musket."

At just that moment, the hatch to the lower deck slid violently open. A voice cried out in panic-stricken English, a message both Manu and Jonah Pessoa understood.

"All hands ahoy! Pirates! Pirates!"

Chapter Eleven

Captain Cook's vessel, the *Resolution*, lay peacefully anchored in the translucent bay of Kealakekua, on the western side of the Big Island of Hawaii. But all was not well with the famed captain and his tired ship. The stately craft was hampered by rotting ropes, tattered sails and, more notably, a broken foremast. Adding to the worry was the absence of the *Fair American,* a rendezvous with young Captain Thomas Metcalf's ship; one which was weeks overdue.

The seasoned explorer stared through his brass looking glass, surveying the wooded hills of the island, marveling at the mysterious sight. White glimmering towers dotted the landscape, many of them well over fifty feet tall.

"What do ye make of it, Captain," asked his sailing master, William Bligh.

"It be a strange sight, true," replied the venerable Captain.

"Sir – we need to go ashore; the natives must help us. We can trade in fair," stated Bligh, matter-of-factly.

"Something's changed, Mr. Bligh. Cannot put my finger on it but I've got a bad feeling about it. Can sense it in the air. Have never seen the likes of this… before."

"Captain, with all due respect sir, these natives are no strangers to us – and they respect you. I struggle to comprehend your hesitance," answered Bligh. "I've never known ye to be a superstitious man…"

"It's not superstition, Mr. Bligh. It's real; it's palpable. Can ye not sense it, man?" answered Captain Cook, collapsing his looking glass. He squinted nervously across the bow of his ship, the fluttering white towers visible even to the naked eye.

"Truthfully, sir – no; I cannot," responded Bligh. "But the fact remains, we'll not replace these ropes, patch these sails, nor fix that broken foremast without the help of the natives. We need their tapa cloth and the wood for the mast. Not ten days past, ye were like a god amongst them, sir. They could not serve ye well enough, giving ye all that was asked for and waiting upon your every whim, like a king. And the men were thrilled with the favors of the native women, sir, and shall not hesitate to return again. How soon shall I order a group ashore, sir?"

The seasoned Captain paused to study the face of his veteran sailing master. William Bligh was a steady enough seaman and would, no doubt, make Captain of a ship someday. His technical and nautical skills were never in question. It was something more subtle, deeper, which troubled Cook about the man. He appeared to possess no intuitive skills whatsoever. And a ship's captain needed a leader's intuition, above all else, in order to hold mastery of his crew. A man who could not read and understand the mood of his men was doomed to lose their respect…and, in time, their obedience.

The stark cold reality of his predicament, however, dictated actions which his intuition told him were not in his favor. But he had no other choice. And he could not, in good conscience, put his men in harm's way without taking the lead role himself. And the natives had, in fact, stolen one of his dinghies, just last night. Theft of that nature could not go unrecompensed. He would take one of them hostage and hold him until they were willing to barter for what his sea-weary ship needed so desperately. The tactic was a common one among the Tahitians he had so recently dealt with and he was convinced it would work. Still…something down deep inside nagged at him; an uneasy sense of impending dread. The veteran Captain shrugged it off.

"Order six men each into two of the dinghies, Mr. Bligh. I shall accompany them myself," he commanded.

"Aye, Captain," replied William Bligh, a slight grin forming at the corner of his mouth.

The landing party came ashore without a hint of native presence. This time, there were no canoes filled with streaming banners, no Hawaiian royalty clamoring to meet the Captain, no gifts of food or tapa spilling from their arms, no Hawaiian women freely offering their bodies to whomever wished.

The rocky beach front was uninhabited. *Strange; very strange,* mused the Captain to himself as the two tiny craft lurched onto the gravelly black sand. The landing party found nothing of substance on neither the beach nor the sharpened cliffs which surrounded the small alcove where they hoved ashore. Leaving two men with the dinghies, a party of eleven, led by the Captain, slowly made their way deeper into the forest, towards the white masted towers which Cook had made such careful note of.

Within half a mile, the small group arrived at a rocky heiau. The magnificent structure consisted of a raised stone platform, thick walls of sloping boulders rising to more than fifty feet. Atop the stone monument stood multiple wooden constructs, each one crowned by fresh tapa cloth. These splendid edifices were the white towers which had shone so brightly from the bay. But there was not a living soul to be found.

Trekking deeper into the ohia forest, the troop came upon a long wooden hut, thatched across the sides and the top with palm leaves. Peering inside, Captain Cook noted multiple wood and stone carved tiki idols spaced across the earthen floor.

"Look, Captain," whispered one of the crew. "Freshly dug up soil; be it graves?" he asked, trembling at the possibility.

Without answering, the Captain proceeded inside the darkened hall, carefully placing every footfall. Coming upon another gravesite, the Captain's eyes widened in fear. Four skulls, freshly cleaned and gleaming white, lay upon the freshly turned-over earth. The skulls were set in a cross fashion, one each facing the four directions of the globe. It was clear evidence of that which had been rumored among the crew, regarding the natives. It was proof of human sacrifice.

Immediately, the experienced captain knew they were in trouble. Slowly back-tracking, he stumbled out of the sacred hut, ordering his men back to the ship. He knew, from his travels and his time spent among the Tahitians, what had now transpired. Their earlier welcome and effuse appreciation was tied, in some strange way he could not decipher, to the season of the fertility god, Lono. Now it made sense! The sexual generosity of the Hawaiian women, just ten days past; the music, the dancing, and the feasting…all of it a religious exercise of some kind, not in honor of Cook nor his men, but only in honor of their god, Lono.

But now – that was all past. As readily as the natives embraced the season of their fertility god, they would embrace its closure; and its replacement with the rituals and expectations of their war god, Ku.

A cold sweat broke over his body; the great explorer, cartographer, and voyager of the high seas found himself in an absolute panic and screamed at his men.

"Run, you fools. To the ship; run, damn you, run!"

The troop broke out into a mad dash for shore, even as the drums began to beat their slow methodic rhythm from somewhere deep in the forest. Conch shells were blown, their low, haunting tone filling the jungle all around them.

The British sailors raced for the dinghies; rounding a large boulder, they came face to face with a monster.

What stood before them, blocking the path, was a sight unseen by white man, until that moment. Standing upright, clothed like a man, yet more lizard-looking than human. The old creature's eyes were red, the pupils no longer visible. A rough, thick scaly skin covered his entire body.

"Is it man or beast, Captain?" asked one of the armed Marines who had come with the party.

"It be a man, alright. An old kahuna, by the dress of him," whispered the Captain.

"Does he mean us harm?" followed the young Marine.

"I don't know; hold your fire and……"

But it was too late. The young Marine had already leveled his .69 caliber musket, the best firearm manufactured in the world, outfitted to the best fighting force in the world, including the Royal British Navy… and promptly fired.

A deafening explosion erupted from the smoothbore as fire belched from its barrel and a cloud of white smoke filled the air. Eerie silence filled the seconds immediately afterwards, as the shocked crew waited for the blinding smoke to dissipate. The drums instantly ceased as well as the low mourn of the conch shell. All was quiet in a surreal moment of suspense.

Captain Cook slowly made his way up to the fallen native. One large hole penetrated his chest and rich dark blood already pooled at his back, where he lay fallen. The old man was yet alive; but death was certain. As the sailors gathered cautiously around the slain kahuna, his lips moved slowly, deliberately. James Cook, although not familiar with the Hawaiian tongue, easily discerned their intent.

"He has cursed us, men," he whispered ominously. The Captain's teeth clenched violently. He turned upon the young sailor, who had killed without clear provocation. "Damn you, man. I told you to hold your fire!"

The wild-eyed Marine, trembling in fear, stood silent. He made no effort to explain his actions. And then the forest around them erupted.

Chapter Twelve

Isaac Davis, followed immediately by Jonah and Manu, scrambled up onto the gun deck. Jonah was astonished to see the flurry of activity, sailors rushing to and fro in a frenzied burst of action, the most movement he had ever observed the crew about.

Not a hammock was occupied; every man was working his post. Some were busy with opening and securing the hatches while others were filling cloth bags with gunpowder from the many barrels. The cabin boy, youngest among the sailors aboard the *Fair American*, was rapidly carrying cannonballs from the stack and distributing them, one at a time, to each of the cannon stations on both sides of the hull. Wooden slat pails were dipped into the open barrels of fresh water and set beside each gun.

"Not yet lad," ordered Isaac Davis to his wide eyed follower, obviously enamored with the preparations afoot to load and shoot cannon. "I'll teach you that another day. These are all veterans and need no coaching. You and Manu, I need up top; you'll get a gun yet, sure enough."

The three burst onto the upper deck. The ship's purser, Mr.Winscott, was anxiously distributing flintlock muskets to each and every man that would take one, complete with powder horns, charging flasks, and round musket balls by the handful. Those not armed were rapidly throwing water upon the sails and constantly looking astern.

Jonah followed their eyes and spied a small clipper-built brig with a black hull heading directly toward the *Fair American*. Manu went to work immediately, helping the unarmed sailors to put all the canvas out they possibly could. Others continued wetting down the sails, hauling buckets of water all the way up to the mast-head.

The despised Captain Metcalf watched the pursuing ship through his spyglass, a golden retractable three-sectioned marvel which Jonah had observed the captain on the whaling ship also use. The tool fascinated him and, although he himself had never been allowed to use one, he had been told that it magnified the view in the distance, allowing a level of detail no human eye could ever detect. Not even the Jesuit monastery had a spyglass among its expansive repertoire of scientific instruments.

He never lowered his head to face his men and his eye remained pressed to the glass. "She shows no colors. She is full of men. And she is armed," reported the Captain, as if he were the subordinate to Isaac Davis and not the other way around.

"We are rigged out full mast, Captain," replied the first mate. "If we cannot outrun her, by God, we will turn and fight her. Sixteen cannon, loaded for war, sir, and the small swivel cannon on the quarter deck. And every able bodied man atop is armed," he continued. Isaac Davis accepted another .69 caliber British musket from Mr. Winscott and placed it into the hands of Jonah Pessoa.

Despite spreading the fullest compliment of canvas possible, the *Fair American* slowly began to give to the speedy pirate ship. It was evident to every man on deck that they would not be able to outrun their pursuer; they would have to fight.

"Alright then, men," cried the first mate. "She'll be on us in no time now. Load but hold your fire until I give the command."

Isaac Davis turned to his young mentor in the Chinese arts. "My turn to teach you a little bit of fighting now, lad. There be no fighting style in the world that can withstand a full charge of hot lead. Load your musket. Take the powder horn and uncork her. Now pour some powder directly down her barrel. That's fine, not too much or she'll blow up in your face. That's plenty. Re-cork your horn, now."

Jonah methodically followed the instructions, re-slinging the powder horn back over his shoulder.

"Now take one of your musket balls and drop her down the barrel."

Jonah grabbed one of the smooth round balls from out of his shirt pocket and dropped it into the end of the barrel. It slid down the gleaming silver tube before making a slight sucking sound.

"She's as far down as she'll slide without ramming her home. Take her ramrod out, right below the barrel there, and swap ends. Now ram that musket ball home, right down into the barrel. Go ahead, push it down harder. Tamp it a couple of times to make sure that ball is seated directly on the powder charge. Can't have a pocket of air between the ball and the powder. That's good. Put your ramrod back."

Jonah carefully threaded the stout ramrod back into the two silver bands directly below the barrel.

"Now, prime the charging pan. Cock that hammer back until you hear the first click, then fill that little silver bowl with powder from the charging flask."

Jonah did as he was ordered, filling the pan with the fine grained black powder until it spilled over the sides and sprinkled onto the deck.

"Whoa there! That's more than enough. Swipe a little bit out or you'll have a blast in your face big enough to blind you. That's good. Now wait for my order. When I yell fire, cock that hammer all the way back, till you hear the second click. Then aim that barrel right at a man's head and pull on that trigger. She'll do the rest all by herself."

Jonah stood on deck, armed with a British musket for the very first time. Other sailors surrounded him, creating a flank of muskets on the starboard side while the first mate scurried to the helm, taking a position aside the Captain.

Young Captain Metcalf appeared visibly shaken. Even Jonah could read the terror in his eyes; the young novice captain's lips trembled as he tried in vain to demonstrate command.

"Mr. Davis! Mr. Davis!"

"Aye, Captain," replied the first mate.

There was a pause in the conversation as Thomas Metcalf struggled to find the next words. "What are we to do?" he cried out, fright dripping from his words, the inflection in his voice cracking in tenor.

"We'll give them a fight, alright. They'll not take the ship, Captain. I promise you that."

The petrified Captain spun on his heels and promptly retreated to his quarters. His private chef and purser, Mr. Winscott, was fast on his heels. Both men managed to secure themselves within the luxurious captains quarters before an audible click was heard, the ominous sound of both men locking themselves inside the safety of their fortified lodging – and locking out the world of life-and-death combat that was about to ensue on deck.

"Bloody coward," whispered one of the men.

"Hold your tongue!" shouted back the first mate, anger filling his voice. "We've our hands full of it now, men. Take heart and keep your barrels up. Again I say…hold your fire until I give the order."

The first mate scurried to the open hold, cupping his hands as he shouted into the gun deck below. "Starboard. Load cannon! Single ball."

A chorus of throaty "ayes" rang out from the men below. Then, Jonah heard the unmistakable sound of the wooden ports being locked in the open position. Within moments, eight fat cannon barrels poked their flared ends from out of the hull. Jonah watched as another man ran to the small swivel cannon, mounted on the railing of the quarter deck, and immediately rammed a curious cloth shrouded cylinder down her narrow muzzle.

"Now we'll show them what the Royal Navy is made of, lad," whispered Isaac Davis as he passed by, checking the lock of each and every musket. One by one, he took the guns from their hands, pulling the hammer back to check the frizzen. Carefully returning it to the half-cock position, he restored it to each sailor with a slap on the back and a smile which exuded confidence.

The small black brig closed in quickly. The crew aboard the *Fair American* ceased wetting the sails and every man took up his position. Those without muskets quickly drew their short knives. Others grabbed whatever they could find, from the ship's pikes to the deck axe.

As they drew near, the crew of the black ship could clearly be seen. Each man was armed with cutlass or knife, but there were no muskets among them. They appeared to be a motley crew of various origins, not a single coat or vestige of insignia among them. Many appeared dark-skinned, of Moorish descent by their costume. The ship's six portholes were opened and a rotund cannon protruded from each square orifice, an obvious sign of her intent. There would be no bargaining. The small pirate brig wheeled sharply, turning her port side to the *Fair American.* At once, her forward most cannon belched smoke and fire.

Jonah Pessoa instinctively ducked along with the other men aboard as fragments of hot lead tore through the deck, ripping holes into the sails and splintering the wood of the masts and the booms.

"Cannister shot!" hollered one of the men. Jonah knew immediately what that meant, despite no formal training in the cannon. They had loaded their large guns with hundreds of smaller projectiles instead of the single cast iron ball. They wanted no large holes in her hull, had no intention of sinking the *Fair American.* They wanted only to disarm her and kill her crew so that they could take the ship as their trophy.

Despite the enemy blast, first mate Isaac Davis stood, unflinching, at the helm. Jonah thought he detected a slight trickle of blood coming from under his arm, a dark crimson circle staining his white cotton shirt. He turned the ship slightly so that she paralleled the black brig.

"Fire musket!" he shouted. Without hesitation, the men surrounding Jonah stood upright, cocking their hammers back and sending forth a fuselage of musket fire. Jonah stood as well, a split second behind his companions. The instant he pulled the trigger, the exploding flash of a dozen or more muskets surrounding him, and the ensuing cloud of whitish smoke, completely enveloped him. Jonah fired in total white blindness, unable to see even the dark hull of their adversary. He had wasted his first shot and he knew it. He had no time to be embarrassed – the smoke cleared, revealing an unscathed black hull, growing closer and closer to the *Fair American* every second.

Another one of the pirate ship's cannon bellowed fire; scorching projectiles again screamed across the bow. Jonah watched as the young sailor standing beside him yelped out in pain then collapsed onto the deck. His scalp was torn off and blood flowed profusely from the top of his head. Jonah laid his musket down and knelt to assist him even as the hole in his young companion's forehead pumped out green and red bile.

"Fire cannon!" screamed out Isaac Davis. Jonah could feel the thunderous movement under his feet as all eight guns in the deck below roared in unison. A thunderous clap temporarily deafened him and a bank of white smoke clouded his vision once again. Although his ears rang out in pain, he was sure he heard the sound of wood cracking, the heavy thud of a cannon ball burying itself deep into her hull. The first mate would sink her yet! He had waited until there was no opportunity to miss, bringing her in close, close enough to guarantee a broadside hit. Every one of those cannonball had found their mark, thanks to Isaac Davis.

Jonah dragged his bleeding companion to the hold and lowered him into the gun deck. He scrambled behind, climbing down into a smoke-filled well of confusion. The confidence and calm that permeated the upper deck was replaced by fear and agitation as men screamed out orders at one another. Unlike the upper deck, which was open to the sky, the gun deck had no opportunity for smoke to dissipate; the sulfurous by-product of exploding gunpowder lingered in the air, choking, suffocating. The stench of it filled Jonah's nostrils. The men were all coated in black soot. The pails of freshwater, used to swab out the cannon in-between shots, were tipped over and pools of the soot-blackened liquid stained the floor, making its deck a slippery black ooze.

"Get above, boy!" hollered out one of the sailors; it was Elihu Smith. Jonah recognized him only because of the scar which ran the length of his face; it remained white against the dark soot which otherwise covered his entire countenance. "Don't need a sod down here getting' in the way!"

The old African appeared, taking the bleeding young man from under Jonah's arms and dragging him to the hold and then below without saying a word. The sailors slipped across the deck as they scurried to re-swab the starboard cannons and stuff powder charges down the barrels. A cry was heard from above…"All hands on deck!"

It was the voice of Isaac Davis. The command to abandon the cannons could only mean one thing …the pirates were boarding the ship!

Chapter Thirteen

Jonah slipped on the black soot covered steps as he climbed up; he stumbled onto the deck just in time to avoid the blade which sliced in an arc, directly at his head. Jonah rolled over in the Shaolin style and was up on his feet quicker than his attacker could have guessed. The young Portuguese lad delivered a swift kick to the brigand, who missed again as he swiped his curved scimitar at Jonah's head. Grabbing the startled pirate by the arm, Jonah twisted his wrist and turned the blade back into the man's side. One forceful shove and the curved scimitar plunged deeply into the man's own ribs, spraying blood from his torn abdomen across the deck.

The ship's upper deck was a scene of carnage. Men shouted, growled, and died as blood and bile from their sliced open bodies puddled in grotesque swells. Slain pirates and sailors lay in haphazard fashion, splayed across the deck. The dead rested in unnatural poses, heads, arms, legs, and torsos twisted in perverted angles, twisted into awkward positions as they collapsed at the moment of death. Jonah choked back tears as well as vomit; the scene of blood and carnage before him, the smell of it, all of it bringing back visions of the bloody visage of his father's face on that fateful day Jonah had found him dead. He suddenly felt sick.

Jonah spied Isaac Davis fighting for his life, parrying and thrusting with his sword against the scimitar of a turban-clad Moor. Quickly swallowing his emotions, Jonah ran to the fray, jumping and kicking the Moorish attacker from behind. The strike of his bare foot against the nape of the man's neck made a sickening, cracking sound and the man fell forward, directly into the polished steel of the first mate. Jonah landed on both feet, in the traditional horse stance of the Shaolin.

"Fancy fighting, that. Thanks, lad. Almost had my fill of 'em, I did," shouted Isaac Davis, smiling despite the numerous wounds which colored his white shirt, turning it a crimson red in many spots.

"Grab that there musket and give 'em hell," the first mate shouted as he spun around, slicing his sword through the torso of yet another brigand whose back was turned to the young Welshman.

Jonah crouched down and grabbed the blood-stained stock, hoisting it to his shoulder. He flipped the flint-jawed hammer back and whirled around, pointing the barrel at the nearest pirate. Jonah pulled the trigger, anticipating the flash and smoke that would obliterate his vision.

Click.

The hammer fell forward on a musket which had already been fired but not re-loaded. The unexpected silence punctuated the moment with an eerie stillness, surprising the inexperienced shooter.

As Shaolin artists are trained to do with the kendo stick, Jonah rotated the impotent weapon, swapping the butt end for the muzzle. The buccaneer for whom Jonah's shot was intended rushed towards him, sword drawn high above his head. The wild-eyed pirate yelled, his visage a grimace of terror, his eyes wide with fright and madness. The downward slice of the blade clanged against gun metal, sending out a shower of sparks. Jonah held the musket lengthwise, blocking a slice that would have cleaved his skull in two. The young Jesuit refugee quickly swung the butt end around, crashing it into the face of his attacker as the crazed-eyed pirate yelled out in pain. The gun stock broke flesh and bone. Tobacco-browned teeth scattered across the desk, his mouth filled with warm crimson.

In the midst of the melee, Jonah paused for a breath, his latest victim lying prone at his feet. And, then, suddenly, it was over…was that all there was to it? An eerie calm fell over the ship, as raider and defender alike seemed to have reached their limit. A shrieking call from the pirate ship and, instantly, each of the Moorish invaders dropped their assault and jumped back aboard their wicked bark, cutting off all the tie-lines. Slowly, with each swell of a wave, the two ships separated, the pirate captain (if he could be called that), standing at the mast of his blackened and wounded vessel, clenched fists resting on either sides of his waist. The body count had risen to an untenable level and even the denizens of the buccaneer class had to keep enough hands aboard to man their craft. The ill-timed raid on the *Fair American* was a mistake; one that yielded stiffer resistance than the Moorish brigand would have imagined, leaving him no other option than to withdraw and lick his wounds.

"Hoorah! Hoorah!" screamed the English victors, bloodied fists raised high in triumph!

"To hell with the lot of you, bastards," yelled another crewman, exultant and prideful.

"We did it, Mr. Davis! We did it!" bellowed another one of the crew. But the first mate's face was somber. Already he had begun taking inventory of the dead and wounded aboard the *Fair American* and the count was staggering.

"Aye, men. We did it," he responded, his tone muted. The spilled blood and bile was already beginning to bake solid in the unrelenting sun. And his own wounds were beginning to show, the adrenalin of the fight for one's life fading now, leaving behind the sharp pains of wounded and torn flesh.

Captain Metcalf emerged from his quarters, shaking. Mr. Winscott trembled behind him, holding the Captain's waist as he shadowed him out onto the carnage of the deck.

"Well done, men," stated the Captain, uncertainty clouding his voice. Silence reigned supreme as each man looked at the youthful coward before them…presumptuous enough to congratulate the crew when he himself had done no more than run and hide. Disgust and hatred filled the visage of every man left standing, many of them still bleeding from their wounds. The moment was thick with righteous rebellion and would have most certainly erupted into mutiny had not the first mate responded.

"Aye, Captain. Looks like we've four men dead, and twelve wounded." Isaac Davis waited for the natural response from Captain Metcalf but there was nothing forthcoming. Only a stupid silence accompanied by a mortified look of fear…and a look of total absence of awareness, as if the scene before him were not even real. Their eyes met - a long fixed stare. The first mate could clearly read in those terror-filled eyes, the void of knowledge and experience which existed – and the absolute plea to be told what to do next.

"Aye, Captain. We'll take the wounded below to Mr. Carlisle. Manu – you look unscathed enough for it; form a funeral detail and wrap these bodies up. Jonah – help Manu; he'll tell you want you need do."

Then, leaning closer for only Jonah to hear, the first mate whispered, "Well done, lad. You're a fighting man in the King's Navy, alright. And a damn good one at that. Bet ye never fire a musket again without checkin' to see if she's loaded, though, eh? I'll teach you, fair enough…and the cannon, too, in time."

Chapter Fourteen

The first grey streaks of dawn began to creep along the eastern horizon. The faint glow of illumination cast an indistinct light upon the face of the deep. Combined with the boundlessness of the sea surrounding him, Jonah Pessoa could not help but feel a familiar tinge of loneliness. The vastness of the sea was so immense…and he was so small, in comparison; and all alone. But…this was immediately supplanted by a growing sense of victory, of accomplishment. He had survived his first watch at sea; survived it in grand fashion, storm and darkest night now behind him.

Along with the crew, he had fought off a pirate attack, lending his own combat skills to the fray and learning to use a rifle in the process. And he had gained the trust of two new friends, one of them the ship's first mate. As the dawn grew increasingly brighter, his confidence and self-assurance grew. Although he still had much to learn, he felt himself a true sailor now. He could hold his own on a ship. And he was not without friends aboard the *Fair American* – and enemies.

Jonah promptly fell into the sailor's routine, a regimen of work that was not foreign to him. A vintner's work was never done and life in the monastery had reinforced the constant work-ethic that all monks had to keep. He found a life at sea actually more restful than the perpetual prayers, religious ceremonies, academic studies, and script writing the Monsignor had required of his monks, in between the daily grind of milking cows, tending the garden, and harvesting the grains.

All at once the ship gave three unaccountable rolls. The first was not violent, and nothing moved on deck, but the second was stronger, and pitched Jonah down against the rail on the port side. The third roll sent him tumbling. The ship, rolling with increasing violence back to starboard, threw the youngster across the deck in the opposite direction. Every moveable thing on deck was in motion. A striking crash resounded as a number of empty barrels dashed about between decks. The iron hooks of the blocks grated in the eyebolts and the blocks themselves thumped heavily on the yards. The iron trusses of the lower yards snapped and squeaked and chain topsail sheets clanked against the yards and masts, the square sails spilled, and the jibs threshed against the stays.

"Enough!" shouted the first mate. "The sea's a bitch enough on her own. No need you to be adding to it," he roared, glaring at the helmsman who had deliberately shuttered the *Fair American* back and forth across the calm waters, all in an effort to show the greenhorn sailor aboard he was still a long ways from gaining any place among the lot of seaman.

After that, Jonah settled in among the crew, working the sail gear, replacing the rigging, swabbing the deck, tarring the masts, scraping the chain cables, pounding the anchor, patching the canvas, varnishing the hull, painting the gunwale, and working the wheel and spindle, as oft as needed, to sew or repair worn clothing. When not on night-watch or otherwise occupied with his assigned tasks, he reposed in the stern of the hold, away from the prying eyes of the crew.

Jonah found himself the morning watchman on deck, an assignment which guaranteed he stood through the blackest part of night and turned in just after the dawn broke each day. Although his status as the greenhorn aboard guaranteed his watch would come in the darkest hours of the morn, occasional offers to spell him of his turn were met with rebuff. Jonah came to value this portion of the night, in a manner he had never come to know or appreciate while tied to the land. He insisted on keeping the 4:00 am-to-dawn shift and would not yield it to others. There was something special about the aloneness of those hours – standing guard on her deck as the proud ship bobbed rhythmically throughout the night, cleaving the dark waters, silently slipping through the mysterious depths of the great Atlantic Ocean, the canopy of stars overhead a brilliant exhibition, shining forth their majesty each evening in a show worthy of adulation.

The night constellations captured Jonah's imagination as never before and the young wanderer found himself applying the astronomy Monsignor had drilled into him, marking the Pleiades, Orion, and Ursa Major – the Great Bear. Each of them so clearly visible now, so splendidly outlined against a night sky which reflected upon the face of the deep with a power above and beyond anything ever witnessed, standing upon the earth's dull refraction.

Dawn often revealed clouds of flying fish, like swarms of locusts, rising up before the ever-advancing ship and tropical birds floating upon the blue heavens, occasionally lighting upon the mast. Day followed night and night followed day as the routine of a long sea voyage settled into Jonah's bones, not unlike the doldrums of monastic life. The daily routine of a monk and of a sailor shared some things in common: there was always work to be done; repetitive, mundane, but necessary work – but aboard the *Fair American*, after the work day was done, Jonah was the teacher and Manu…and Isaac Davis…were the students.

The monotony of the voyage broke up, from time to time. Black clouds arose from differing parts of the endless sapphire dome that enveloped the ship, and squalls attacked the ship, beating her with rains and wind. The entire crew rallied to trim sails, hustling to complete their tasks. Jonah fell right in, comfortable now with the rigging, the tackle, and that which needed to be done, without instruction. More often than not, the crew would scarce have their jobs completed before a blazing sun would peek out again, drying the seaman within minutes and sucking all the moisture from out of the wood, the canvas, and the pitch in the seams. In no time at all, the unrelenting sun would beat down upon the crew and ship alike with an intensity that led the sailors to wish for another squall, despite the danger.

Enormous whales, larger than any animal ever seen on land, often swam leisurely by during the hours of darkness, keeping the awestruck Jonah Pessoa company throughout his watch. The night-silence was sporadically broken by the hissing jettison of their columns of water into the air, frequently splashing the deck. Occasionally, the gentle giants displayed their vast black bulk, lolling over to one side before silently slipping back below into the shadowy ocean depths. The awesomeness of the site never failed to impress Jonah.

Chapter Fifteen

The *Fair American* crossed the equator in the night, silently, quietly gliding through that imaginary line which divides the sphere of the earth into two equal halves. Jonah first noted the peculiarity of the difference in the night sky; the starry vault above him, his constant companion throughout the early morning watch, held no Southern Cross, no Constellation of the Ship, no Magellanic Clouds.

The unknown firmament set above him now was cast with new and splendid Constellations and starry luminescence. The setting and the rising of the sun occurred with a suddenness of transition. It leapt abruptly above the horizon, and the change from darkness to light came instantaneously. The change from day to night came equally as swift. Sunset at sea in the southern latitude painted a dissimilar canvas from that which the young Portuguese sailor had ever experienced before. Clouds, absent all day, gathered quickly in the western sky, catching the final rays of the sun and presenting them to the eye in striking colors, the tints and hues deeper and richer than any artist's oils ever could.

Two days after crossing the equatorial line, Jonah laid eyes upon the first spit of land seen since leaving the shores of Faial. It stood defiant against the crashing surf of foamy waters as a rocky pyramid, jutting out of the ocean, two hundred miles off the coast of Brazil. Its most prominent feature was a single pointed spire, like the finial of a church. A bizarre horizontal aperture cut across the rocky crags of the coastal edifice through which the ocean waves crashed again and again.

"Hole-in-the-Wall," commented Manu, grasping tightly to the rigging as the ship veered in the rough waters.

"The isle of Fernando Noronha, as she is more properly known," added the first mate, "Although most sailors know her by that more descriptive euphemism of Manu's. They say the Brazilians have made her a place of exile. Place all of their criminals there. Even if true, safe enough for armed sailors of a British war brig, eh, Manu?"

"Them say have no woman on this isle; man only," grunted Manu in response. "Sounds like Hell, to me," refrained Manu, bringing a grin to the faces of all three men privy to Jonah's land-sighting.

A small object appeared shore-ward, rising and falling on the waves. As it drew closer to the ship, Jonah discerned a small sail jutting up from a curious looking craft. Her hull consisted entirely of logs, roughly cut and lashed together. A single mast rose from her bow and was crossed at the top by a yard from which the dinghy's sail hung, similar to a ship's foresail. At the rear was a raised platform upon which sat two figures, holding ropes by which they shifted the sole canvas to catch wind and steer her.

"A Brazilian jangada," offered Isaac Davis, holding the Captain's brass looking glass to his eye. "Call the Captain out from his cozy quarters," instructed the first mate to the group of sailors who had begun gathering around the trio. "It appears she is aiming straight for us."

The sun was just beginning her quick departure from the horizon as the flimsy-looking craft hailed alongside the *Fair American,* the two occupants tying her to the side of the ship with ropes thrown over by the wary crew, suspicious of her intent but willing to accommodate the two – after all, there were only two of them; how much harm could two do against a fully armed crew of the British Royal Navy? And it appeared one of the two was…a woman?

"Permissão vir a bordo?" shouted out the shirtless, dark-skinned man from the jangada, cupping his hands around his mouth as he called upwards. A couple of wooden casks sat atop the rough-hewn logs of the craft, their weight shifting from side to side as the tiny catamaran bobbed in the rough waters. The woman seated at the rear of the raft did not look up, her head downcast.

All of the crew turned immediately to Jonah, known, among other things, for his fluency in multiple languages. If nothing else, it was a silent acquiescence of his unique role aboard the ship, a role that was increasingly polarizing the crew. Most of them had, by now, come to either appreciate the strange young phenom or to despise him, based on their own insecurities, fears…or allegiance to Eusebio.

"It's the Portuguese tongue. He is asking permission to come aboard," replied Jonah to young Captain Metcalf's blank-eyed stare.

"What does he want aboard?" responded the fearful youth, his eyes wide with fright.

"Porque você quer vir a bordo?" shouted out Jonah to the two in their own language, mimicking the Captain's question.

"Tenha as coisas a vender. Água fresca, laranjas, e…" responded the Brazilian, casting a disdainful sideways glance at the woman passenger beside him.

"He says he has things to sell," translated Jonah. "He claims he has fresh water, oranges, and…Jonah paused for a moment, double-checking the inference he had drawn from the Brazilian man's fleeting look at his passenger before continuing…I believe – the woman?"

A shout erupted from the crew as the men simultaneously reacted to the possibility of sex, something which sailors are routinely deprived of during long sea voyages. As Jonah peered down from the deck more closely, he could make out more details of her features. Even with her head downcast, it was evident that this was no young woman; she was well over 40 years of age and possibly quite older than that, although it was hard to tell with certainty. Her head was covered by a wrap of blue cloth which draped down her thick neck. Her rotund shape, poorly hidden by a plain tunic of thin, dirty-white cloth, revealed a fleshy, sun-wrinkled and deeply tanned body that had seen its prime long come and go. Saggy breasts splayed wide across a barreled chest and large, heavy thighs rounded out her form. *And where had a woman come from, off an island that was supposed to be a prison for the miscreants of Brazilian society? Had she actually been banished there herself for some crime? And would she have been sent there, one lone woman among all those men, to suffer the craved deprivations of convicted criminals? Or was Manu wrong? Was there more to the thickly forested isle of Fernando Noronha than just the man-populated prison his Hawaiian colleague had shared,* wondered Jonah silently.

The woman's aged form made no difference to the sex-starved sailors, each one shouting out in English, "Bring 'er aboard; bring 'er aboard!"

Captain Metcalf appeared slightly confused; the internal debate showed on his face. "I need that fresh water. And those oranges would make a welcome addition to the men's diet. But……", he pondered aloud, "I don't know about…"

"It is poor form, Captain," offered the first-mate. "And not proper discipline. Every man here knows what it means to serve at sea. Shore leave is different; whenever we pull into port, the men granted shore-leave are free to do as their consciences, desires, and pockets allow. But bringing a whore on deck? It's unheard of, Captain."

"Bring 'er aboard Captain," shouted out the men, their cries overriding the first mate's. It was the first example Jonah had ever witnessed where the men did not align themselves with their respected first mate; it would not be the last.

"Uma guiné para um barril da água, e duas guinés para a caixa de laranjas," shouted out the Brazilian.

"He says a guinea for one cask of water, and two guineas for the crate of oranges," translated Jonah.

"And the woman? How much for the woman?" cried out more than one sailor in a frenzy of lust.

"A mulher - não vai na plataforma. Permanece aqui. Cada homem que paga pode vir abaixo da corda e retornar terminado uma vez. Cada homem paga vinte guinés," replied the Brazilian, almost as if he understood the conversation up top, spoken in English.

Jonah recognized the look on the Brazilian's face as one who is fluent in more than a single language; it was evident, in that moment, that the Brazilian spoke English, well enough to understand everything that was being said, despite his insistence on using Jonah Pessoa as a translator.

"He says that the woman – she does not go on deck. She stays on the jangada. Each man who pays can come down the rope and return to deck once finished. Each man pays twenty guineas."

"Twenty guineas! Twenty guineas for a poke! That's me whole pay for the voyage!" cried out one of the men. "Ack! – tell 'em he gets three guineas a poke and no more," offered yet another one of the crew. "Aye, aye!" shouted out the men in unison. Jonah glanced over at Captain Metcalf, who nodded in agreement before turning to the first mate. Isaac Davis gave no indication of what Jonah should do before young Captain Metcalf screamed out.

"Don't be looking to Mr. Davis! He is not Captain aboard this ship, I am! I give the orders here, damn you! And I told you to tell that man that he'll get three guineas a poke, for the old woman. Go on, now, tell him!"

The disdain was obvious on Jonah's face, not for the content of the message but for the way in which his friend and mentor, Isaac Davis, had been countermanded by the inexperienced Captain, one who, despite the title he bore, held no rightful authority over a proven and tested seaman like the first mate, a man who could command authority on any ship at sea. He chafed under the inequality of it and it rankled him to a depth he would not have imagined to have to follow the orders of this foolhardy excuse for a leader. He slowly turned to the Brazilian below and repeated the command.

"Nao, Nao," replied the Brazilian. "Vinte guinés para cada homem."

When Jonah repeated the Brazilian's response, indicating that the price per man would not be changed, the young Captain instantly ordered guns to the deck. Lust crazed sailors quickly retreated from view and returned in a manner of moments with muskets loaded, more than twenty guns pointed down directly at the Brazilian trader.

"Tell him, priest. Tell him he receives his price of one guinea for each cask of water, his price of two guineas for each crate of oranges, and our price of three guineas for each poke of the woman. Tell him if he does not agree, the men will shoot him full of holes and take his wares…including the woman."

Reluctantly, Jonah communicated in Portuguese to the Brazilian, confident that the flesh merchant from the prison isle understood every word spoken by the Captain. The phalanx of British muskets pointed at him underscored the point.

"Tree quineas por man ees good. I sell you two casks water and two crates orange," spoke the Brazilian in broken English. "Throw money down and I send up the water and orange. When man come down for ees woman, I stay here. Put sail down. Only one man at a time. Each man bring his tree quineas with him."

Captain Metcalf called for Mr. Winscott to ledger each participating sailor's account against his wages and bring forth the purse. When the coins were presented, the appropriate quantity for the casks of water and crates of oranges was tossed overboard, into the waiting hands of the Brazilian. One at a time, the shirt-less vendor tied his wares to ropes and the prized commodities were brought aboard. It was already dark before the business of lust commenced. Whale oil lanterns were lit and hung from the port deck as the men took turns climbing down the rope to the catamaran, each with his three guineas counted out from the purser. The rafts single canvas was taken down and thrown onto the logs as a cushion against their rough hewn surface. No pretense came before the grunting and pushing commenced; just an exchange of money for access to the woman's thick-set body, a task the beleaguered prostitute appeared to bear in a cold, detached silence. She made no sounds as one man after another relieved himself into her cavernous pelvis.

"Be takin' your turn wit the 'hore this evenin', Mr. Pessoa?" asked the pitted-faced boy.

"I don't reckon' I'll be a-partakin' in this, Petey," replied Jonah, practicing the most slang filled English he had the courage to experiment with. Whether he successfully pulled it off or not, he was safe trying it out on Petey.

"Reckon I otter git me some," answered Petey, a solemn look on his face. It was a look of anticipation…and of fear. "Mr. Winscott says I gotter go lasts, on account of my rank on ship."

Jonah looked incredulously at the youth, his innocent face flickering in the lamplight.

"Don't be rushed into a-doin' somethin' you ain't ready to do yet," offered Jonah in a polished Cockney slang that would have passed for an east-end Londoner.

"I ain't a-skeered, Mr. Pessoa," lied the youth. "I jist not sure exactly what I's suppos to do," replied Petey.

Manu appeared beside them both, smiling, ready to climb down to the jangada for his turn with the sea-borne whore.

"Watch Manu. Him show you what do," he said as he grasped the mooring hitch and lowered himself to the waiting duo below. Both Petey and Jonah gazed from the lantern-lit deck as the Hawaiian paid the Brazilian his three guineas, then approached the naked woman, who lay exhausted, spread-eagled on the canvas.

Then a strange thing happened, a thing that had yet to occur that evening between any of the sailors and the prostitute. The worn out woman, her dark bushy hair revealed, the blue head covering long ago stripped from her, rose up on one elbow, staring at the young Kanaka before her. Gently, she touched the tattoos adorning Manu's body…and she wept. Words were exchanged, a language Jonah recognized only a smattering of…it was the Hawaiian tongue!

Slowly, the woman and the younger kanaka embraced…but it was not an embrace of lust. She wailed earnestly now as she held Manu in her arms. He, too, wept openly, unafraid of how his emotions might be ridiculed by the crew.

After a time, they broke off their embrace and stared into one another's eyes. Manu slowly rose, still clothed, and drew the woman's dirty tunic over her naked form. Circumspectly, the forlorn but apparently happy woman unhooked the only other adornment that remained on her flesh, a tiny necklace of koa beads; she carefully laid them over the head of Manu. Then, without hurry, Manu paced the five steps over to where the Brazilian stood fore, holding onto the coarse hewn single mast – and promptly stabbed him to death, driving his knife three times into the man's lower ribcage with lightning speed. A single low-pitched groan escaped the Brazilian's throat as he doubled over; Manu retrieved the guineas from the man's pockets before he silently slipped the body into the sea. Tying the sail once again to the boom, he hoisted the canvas and deposited all the coins with the woman. One more embrace and Manu was off the catamaran, climbing the rope back up to the deck. As he scrambled aboard, he quickly tugged at the mooring hitch, releasing the jangada from her attachment to the *Fair American*.

Manu, Petey, and Jonah stood silently as the small craft, piloted by the lone woman, disappeared into the dark night.

What seemed like an eternity passed before Petey finally broke the silence.

"Why did you let her go, like that?"

Manu's gaze remained fixed on the last point in the darkness where he had beheld the tiny catamaran, bobbing upon the dark waters. His expression never faltered as he spoke. "Her Hawaiian. Her from my island; of my people; of my family." Manu paused, the silence in that moment ominous. He walked away, uttering a final missive. "Her sister me."

Chapter Sixteen

An equatorial burst of dying magenta set over the calm waters, cloaking the magnificent bay of Rio de Janeiro in dusk. Despite the encroaching darkness, the bay remained alive with the commerce of hundreds of ships, one after another, hoving ashore, steering passage out to the Atlantic, or lying placidly idle, her contents of men and wares in a constant state of exchange.

The crew of the *Fair American* bustled with the expectation of shore leave, the longest period off ship they were to have. Cheerful and animated tones carried the tenor of the conversations as sailors eagerly blackened their boots and brushed their woolen coats in-between their watches. Isaac Davis had warned against it but, yet again, the impetuous orders of Captain Metcalf had overridden the wisdom of the first mate. Mr. Davis had seen it too many times before; lonely, impetuous men, let loose for temporary shore leave in a strange and exotic land where novel and extraordinary delights were easily made available to any who had a coin or sovereign to offer up – they had a tendency to miss the call to port and often the crews sailed away from land with many less hands than they had put to port with only a day or two ago.

More often than not, the locals had to be scavenged in order to fill the requisite number of deck hands, a task that would come easily in a place like Rio de Janeiro but one which always altered the composition of the crew in ways which Isaac Davis found challenging. And it was unnecessary – but the young Captain had yet again placed currying the favor of his crew above sound ship practice.

The fore crew busied themselves with hooking up chain cables from their lockers, overhauling ranges, and casting loose the anchors. In the aft of the magnificent vessel, the sailors scoured up the brass ornaments which adorned the sacred quarter-deck and rubbed the tarnish from off the paint. As the ship drew closer along the west side of the entrance to the bay, Jonah and the crew were struck by the sight – held in awe by the unmistakable landmark which punctuates the glistening waters, its perfectly conical sides, steep and smooth, rising from out of an inferior range of palm covered granite hills – the Sugar Loaf Mountain.

A vast, massive stone structure rose sharply up from the edge of the sea, jutting out from the dark waters on the east, as the passageway continued to narrow in width.

"The Castle of Santa Cruz," whispered Manu reverently, as if the imposing fortification itself could hear them speaking.

Large brass cannons stared down at the ship from over the front wall. A single tall staff rose above the uppermost rampart, proudly bearing the Brazilian flag. One lone sentinel paced the battlement, making his rounds then wheeling sharply when he reached the terminus of his march, never once averting his gaze to the hull of the ship that glided so effortlessly beside him in the deepening twilight. The *Fair American* passed so close, Jonah and Manu stretched forth their hands over deck, attempting to touch the rough-hewn stones which stood like a bulwark against the constant crashing of foamy waves; another hand-breadth closer and their fingers would have scraped against the coral-covered lower edifice.

The *Fair American* was immediately put upon by a bevy of rival ship-chandlers, small oar-driven craft, offering to furnish for the vessel whatever was required. People of every color filled the little barks, shouting out goods and prices, in direct competition against their neighbor, each one unabashedly vying for a sale while simultaneously disparaging their rival's prices and quality of goods.

Jonah licked his lips; the salt-air actually tasted different here. There was a sweetness to it, as if the sea breeze itself was laden with the fruit of the sugar-cane fields which populated the upper mountainous regions.

The starry host shone their finest display, spreading a canvas of starlight so thick it filled the night sky. The surface of the water became calmer, smooth as glass — and it reflected all the overhanging stars in a mirror like fashion; so much so that above and beneath became one another. Jonah could not discern where the heavens ended and the waters began.

The lights of the city, just now beginning to flare up here and there, in thousands of candle wicks and smaller fires, started high up among the dark hills then swept down to the water's edge and blended with the lights of hundreds of ships anchored in the bay – an indiscernible swath of artificial illumination against the blackness that gradually shrouded the hills and the meandering valleys of the city proper, set at the foot of the mountains.

"Permission to go ashore, sir," chorused the men, their fresh-shaven faces gleaming in the starlight.

"Aye, men. Which two of you shall volunteer to stay aboard – keep watch o'er the ship till the dawn?"

Not a sound was heard as the anxious sailors dropped their heads, each one avoiding eye contact with the first mate, lest they be the ones chosen. Silent moments passed; the lapping of the waves against the hull was the only timbre to the night – that and the faintest sounds of drumbeats, just now wafting off the beaches, across the water, and out to the ships; dim but discernable.

"All right, then. I'll have to appoint two men, of my own choosing. Is that how it is, you land-lubbing scallywags?" The affront was not serious and everyman knew it to be nothing more than a ploy to illicit volunteers from the group. The first mate was a man above reproach and every sailor aboard the *Fair American* knew it.

"I'll take the watch, sir," replied Jonah softly, his voice lingering in the cool night air. Isaac Davis replied, "Will no man stand with the young novice? Has he put all of you to shame?"

"I'll take the watch…alone," added the Azorean refugee. Jonah himself was not fully sure why he had volunteered so, taking upon himself the entire burden for the care and custody of the ship…alone. He had long since passed the point where he believed he had to prove himself an able seaman. Yet the idea of being responsible for the ship, of being wholly and completely responsible for the *Fair American*, excited him – more so than the bright lights and the constant drumbeat of music that began to build, louder and louder…from just off shore.

"He can do it,' offered Eusebio, his voice dripping with sarcasm.

"Aye, Aye," rang in a chorus of others, each one eager to get off ship and explore the sinful delights of an evening in Rio de Janeiro.

"Are you up to it, lad?" asked the first mate, serious concern in his tone. Isaac Davis had no intent of putting the *Fair American* in jeopardy or otherwise disadvantaging the young protégé who had so much to offer – including that which he himself coveted to know and learn.

"Outside of a hostile takeover by a dozen men, I know I can do the job. She'll be in good hands, sir. And it would take a dozen or more to put me down, sir," answered Jonah.

It was not an idle boast. Jonah Pessoa had continued to faithfully practice that which Brother Chin had taught him so diligently; practiced every morning, during the darkest hours of the watch, when no one else was awake or up top. He knew he was stronger and quicker now than he ever was with the arts of the Boddhidharma. He was confident he could take on more than his share of fighting men, a confidence which the first mate sensed as well.

"Let the lad take the watch," shouted out Captain Metcalf.

The first mate scorned the rashness of his naïve commander, so casually handing over the care of the *Fair American* to the young ex-monk, a command that he would never have given so flippantly, if the beautiful bark beneath their leather-clad soles were his to control. Yet he knew he had no say in the matter, once the ship's Captain had spoken aloud, in full view of the crew.

"Aye, Captain. So shall it be," shouted out Isaac Davis. "Keep her safe, my lad. We'll be back aboard before the sun rises."

"No worries, sir," replied the confident Jonah, speaking in virtually flawless English.

Jonah watched in silence as the nearly two dozen crew of the *Fair American*, including the Captain; his personal attendant and ship's purser Mr. Winscott; the boy Petey; Jonah's best friend on ship, Manu the Hawaiian; Eusebio, his nemesis; even the ship's cook Stewart, took their leave. The spirited bunch trotted happily off the lowered gangplank which was hastily laid across the bow by the first sailor in line. In no time, the riotous crew disappeared into the warm Brazilian night, dispersing in different directions, each according to their wishes.

In an instant, the *Fair American* went from a clatter of activity to a citadel of silence. Even the creaking of the wood, an ever present meter of sound, a companion to every sailor who has ever kept the dog-watch, was gone. An eerie stillness hung in the air. Jonah found himself surveying the deck, studying the minute detail of every rope coil, wooden plank, and furled canvas but there was nothing out of place but for the unusual hush.

A sense of new found freedom surrounded him. Jonah found himself walking upon the quarter deck, that hallowed ground reserved only for the Captain and his entourage.

Nothing different here than anywhere else on deck, mused Jonah. *Wooden planks the same as every other plank on deck; rope coiled here just as every other rope; railings cut the same as every other railing. What's so special about this section of ship?*

The thought bemused him for a moment before a wicked grin spread across his face. Despite the childishness of it, he could not help himself. Jonah instantly jumped up and down, forcing the weight of his feet to slam into the deck harder than ever.

"Hah! Nothing, just as I thought," he said aloud, to no one in particular – actually, to no one at all. *Just another way of separating people one from another; making one feel inferior to the other, all in an attempt to enforce some system of control,* he thought silently*, like Anton Soto had tried to control me.*

Vicious thoughts raced through his head; thoughts of retribution against the Captain and all those like him. Mental images flooded his mind; images of Anton Soto being beaten to death by his own hands. Vivid pictures of the brightly colored blood and the torn flesh; the sound of it, the smell of it, and the fading glimmer in the gaze of the dying, as Jonah watched him, eye to eye, the life force draining out of him.

Suddenly, inexplicably, a deep-rooted fear gripped his heart. Jonah became silent, listening for noises in the dark. A wild desire for flight and escape came upon him. He was suddenly possessed of a feeling that he must go far away from the ship and move fast, keeping ahead of anything that might be pursuing him. He actually loosened his grip on the mast and found himself running manically for the gangplank, running as he had those first few moments he awakened in the monastery cellars, confused, alone, in total utter abandonment of reason.

Jonah raced across the gangplank …then stopped suddenly, at some invisible barrier between the last footfall that would tie him to the ship and the dark mud of the bay of Rio de Janeiro. He remained frozen for a moment before steeling himself on the inside, as Brother Chin had so faithfully taught him to do. Slowly, methodically, Jonah backtracked across the wooden gangplank, placing both feet firmly on the deck of the *Fair American*. He rationalized the thought of panic-stricken running away against his duty to protect the ship; after all, he was the lone human being on board. This thought served as a cold reminder that he was alone, truly alone, in this universe. Jonah felt that aloneness surrounding him, enveloping him in a wash of sadness and abandonment. He had no one: no father, no mother, no family, no confidant he could turn to. Even on board ship, surrounded by crew, he was the outcast, a mystery to the men, someone whom they could not avoid but treated with an uneasy caution. The feeling was palpable.

No one truly understood him, where he had come from or where he was going in life. Not even Jonah could answer these questions of himself – and this fact further alienated him from even his own soul.

Who am I, really? he questioned silently. *What am I doing on this ship? And where am I going with my life? What am I supposed to do and where should I be going?* he answered aloud, the responses coming on the heels of the question. *Am I destined to roam life alone, constantly lost in a sea of human detachment? Isn't there supposed to be something more, something that I'm destined to do, or become? What is the purpose of my life?* he queried. *If it was not to grow the family vineyards with his father, then what? If it was not to care for his widowed mother, then what?* It was certainly not to serve as a monk in the Faial monastery – that much he was certain of. *But what other choice did I have, but to jump aboard the Fair American when she showed in the lava strewn remnants of the harbor?* But he was no sailor, either. What, then, was to become of Jonah Pessoa?

Jonah made a mental list of the qualifications he believed he possessed, trying desperately to justify his existence, if to no one else, then to himself. Without hesitation, he came up with the first item – *an indomitable will to live*. Despite the sorrow of a childhood marred by a murdered father, a slain mother, and the horror of a volcanic explosion that nearly killed him, scarring him for life, both physically and otherwise, and had obliterated his home and his false start at his own vineyard on Faial, he was alive! He could not escape the sense of destiny which surrounded this fact, emboldening him with a forcefulness that begged description…a will to live. If nothing else, he was a survivor and a future of some nature surely awaited him, somewhere, someplace.

After pausing for a moment, Jonah added to his list. *Am comfortable with being alone.* Despite the fact that Jonah missed the presence of his parents in an unfathomable way, he had learned to deal with it. He had not allowed the monastery to become a surrogate parent, as Israel deSilva had offered, because he was quite at ease with being alone in this world. This was the hand that fate, the volcano, or God, had dealt him and he was prepared to live with that, the rest of his life, if he had to.

Thirdly, Jonah mused, *know how to fight.* Though no expert in Chinese boxing, Jonah had learned enough to defend himself and was willing to kill, if he had to. Anton Soto was evidence of this fact.

Can speak multiple tongues. Know Portuguese, Latin, thanks to his studies under the Monsignor*; have recently learned some English – and appear to have a natural affinity for languages,* which struck Jonah as slightly odd, the instant his mind framed the thought. *Why this is so is beyond me!*

Know how to cope with extreme shock, added Jonah. *And am highly adaptable,* he finished, considering how quickly he had grasped the whirlwind that was his life, from apprentice vintner, to life in a monastery, to a sailor's lot aboard an English war-ship.

Surely life has a role for a man who has demonstrated he can survive the worst travails of life, can live alone, is an accomplished fighter, can speak multiple languages, and knows how to adapt to rapidly changing environments, though Jonah inwardly, smiling as a new found confidence wrapped itself around his soul. *I may not know what it is yet, but surely there is something more to this life, out there for me, someplace?*

Chapter Seventeen

The appearance of dawn surprised him, springing instantly over the depth's horizon. *Have I been on watch all night already?* he pondered. Time had come and gone so quickly Jonah could scarcely believe it but the blazing sun could not be ignored. He had passed the entire night watch lost in self-reflection and did not sense the passing of the hours before it was time for his turn at some shut eye.

The drunken shouts and hoots from the bedraggled and exhausted crew brought him back to rapt attention. One by one, the sailors crossed the gangplank, taking their places amid ship.

"You missed one hell of a night, my boy!" shouted out one, followed by another's taunting response. "Best whores a man could ask for," bragged another. "Eyes of black; liquid intense fountains which capture and hold a man's soul in their mesmerizing grip."

"Aye," chimed in another, "and skin the color of dusk, with rich full lips bursting with the tint of the rose…"

"All right, lads. That be enough," countered the first mate. "No sense in reminding the young man of everything he missed out on so all of you could have your fun. About your chores, now! Keep her up, men!" barked out Isaac Davis. Then, softly, quietly, in a tone only heard by Jonah and the first mate, "Take your leave or take your sleep, lad. It's up to you. I'll see to that. But be gone for no more than the morn, lad. That's all I can cover for with the Captain. We'll be re-stocked by mid-day and intend to catch the afternoon winds out of the harbor and be on our way."

Despite the hours he had spent on watch, Jonah felt no weariness and found himself excited about a chance to see Rio de Janerio in the light of day. Without giving it a second thought, Jonah nodded in silent gesture to the first mate and sauntered down to the end of the gangplank – the same slab of wood that had most recently been a tangible barrier to his understanding of his life's role; and he splashed down into the dark rich mud. Gaining a foothold, he sprung onto the cobblestone path which marked the line between a sailor and a land-lubber and promptly struck off in the first direction which struck his fancy...alone.

The city spread out rapidly before him. A compendium of white stone walls and red tiled roofs greeted him, constructed in a new and strange style of architecture. Spectacular fountains with circular reservoirs were scattered throughout the winding streets – many appearing more like sculptured monuments to their makers rather than utilitarian sources of water, although each one was attended to by numerous souls, each one either dipping and drinking, or carrying bucketfuls away on their heads. Multitudes of folk, both women and men, of every color, shade, and costume were joyously taking their fill, amid occasional outbursts of laughter and strident discourse. Jonah could not help but smile at the scene, emboldened by the fact that he understood every word being spoken. *Portuguese! They're speaking Portuguese!*

At length, he reached a market, stopping in amazement at the host of treasures displayed. Bouquets of fresh and beautiful flowers filled the air with fragrance. Green vegetables, in a size he had never seen, were laid out beside vivid yellow fruits. Pyramids of oranges and stacks of bananas were juxtaposed against row upon row of cocoa nuts, plantains, pineapples, and mangoes, all heaped in profuse amounts. Squawking parrots sat on perches throughout the market, preening their plumage of vibrant yellow, red, and green. Smallish monkeys spun perpetually around their tethers, ranting aloud as they tugged in a futile effort to be free of the ropes which bound them to their masters. Finely turbaned and decorous vendors waited upon the throng of customers, the verbal barter over prices rising in crescendo until the reluctant sellers let their wares go for yet still handsome profits. Robust African women, sacks of coffee piled high on their heads, trotted in single file along the streets, singing and shaking rattles as they went.

Jonah made his way up the public promenade in the bright daylight, his path shrouded on both sides by striking trees, shrubs, and flowers he could not name, despite his Jesuit's training in horticulture. Tall thin palm trees dotted the sides and the summits of the hills. The morning air burst forth with fragrance of roses and myrtles as diminutive humming birds dashed back and forth, chasing one another, their gold and green feathers shining in the intense sun.

The terrace he walked upon gave way to polished marble, dotted with elegantly crafted shrines here and there. Across the bay, the towering Sugar Loaf mountain stood out, like a citadel carved by the gods, or God. Jonah froze for just a moment, admiring its architecture, the giant granite conical sheath rising from up out of the water, statuesque in its phallic-like state.

Jonah paused to look back at the ship and was surprised to see how far he had walked. The *Fair American* was nothing more than a white blip amidst a sea of sails crowding the bay of Rio. He had no idea there were so many other ships choking the waters of the bay and he gained a new found respect for the helmsman who had steered her into the port so artfully, in the dark of night. He exhaled, a tired breath coming from his lungs. He had traversed a very long way, much of it uphill, and suddenly tiredness overtook him. Wiping the sweat from his brow, he plopped down in the shadow of an enormous cliff, which afforded him a view of the entire Bay of Rio, the city proper, and the rapidly steaming hills and verdant landscape.

Suddenly, without warning, he was desperately sick at heart. The lush rolling hills which sloped to quiet bay waters, so reminiscent of the bay of Horta, before the volcano exploded, melted his heart. He had often stood gazing out over her gently rolling slopes which terminated into the sea, during his solo vine-planting efforts. He would be stilled, drinking in her azure beauty, the quiet blue waters lapping again and again at the smooth base of the earth which seemed to slip seamlessly into the deep. How much alike these two vistas were!

Then he remembered the solemn resolution he had come to hours ago, in the darkest watch of the night, in the deepest recesses of his soul…there would be no more fear, no longing, no attachment. How could one miss what one has no attachment to? Quieting, once and for all, the gnawing hunger of loneliness and isolation which strived to be his constant companion required that he come to love nothing, or no one, or no place! That is how he would live his life, then. Love nothing – miss nothing! Become attached to no one or no thing – total freedom to pick up and move on at a moment's notice, which seemed to be a pattern that was firmly entrenched in his young life already. Not that Jonah had wanted it this way, oh no! It was the cruel fate that destiny (or God?) seemed to take delight in measuring out to the young orphan and if that was what Fate, or God, wanted for him, who was he to struggle against it? Better to take the hand that was dealt to him and learn to live with it, the best that he could do; it was, in the end, all that he could do. Sleep suddenly and inexplicably overtook him and Jonah slipped into a deep slumber, leaning down onto one arm before falling into a near-comatose state. Nightmarish scenes crowded his unconscious mind – scenes of retching lava and scorched soil, spitting out from the midst of smoke-filled fountains, raining death and destruction down upon the earth. Terrified screams filled his ears; shattering voices of men, women, and children, shrieking out in unmitigated terror. Then the screams of his mother, wailing his name again and again, "Jonah! Jonah!"

Awakening with a start, Jonah was shocked to discover that all was dark around him. An inky black had overtaken the day; the stars of evening hidden by an ominous firmament, a moon which curiously appeared to be missing from the night sky. Angry at himself, Jonah cursed silently…how long had he been asleep? How could he have been so dilatory? The first mate had granted leave only for the morning. Would the *Fair American* still be in the harbor, waiting on him?

Scrambling in the night, Jonah righted himself and carefully retraced his steps, faltering in the murky darkness, tripping over obstacles which he did not recall in the path on his climb up the hill earlier that day. Without warning, a sharp blow suddenly struck Jonah across the back of his head. Still conscious, he tumbled in the dark, body flailing against the hard packed earth and the thick vegetation which coated the steep sides of the sheer ridgeback. Jonah stumbled off the sharp bank, tumbling over and over again.

Desperately trying to gain a foothold, he grasped wildly in the dark at every branch or plant stem that might stop the perpetual churning of his body, but to no avail. Each revolution brought another bruise, scrape, and bloody rasp as he helplessly careened down the darkened ravine. With one final thud, Jonah's violent descent down the vine-choked hillside came to an end; an end that left the young Portuguese wayfarer unconscious and alone.

"That'll be the death of 'im," seethed his silent attacker.

"Don't ya' think they'll know?" whispered the larger man, accomplice to the murderous deed.

"Won't anybody be knowing what you don't tell," spit out the angry culprit. "You's keep your mouth shut. You got that?"

The accomplice nodded his head in unspoken agreement to the evil pact as both men hurried off in the darkness.

Chapter Eighteen

A sullen overcast sky greeted Jonah's eyes, murky at first but growing in clarity with each passing second. Slowly, one shade of color after another, his eyesight came into focus, emerging groggily from the unconscious stupor. Rain dappled irritatingly upon his face and Jonah shook his head from side to side, to avoid it – but, despite his efforts, the rain seemed to have a mind of its own, following him! No matter how much he twisted his face away from the heavens, the rain continued to splash him. No, not rain – water. Salty water – sea water! Jonah sat up with a start, flexing at the waist…but unable to right himself. Both hands had been tied behind his back and his feet were tethered together as well. A growing realization of his whereabouts led Jonah to recognize the familiar feel of the wet decking beneath his back – the decking of the *Fair American*!

Another splash of sea water struck him in the face, a violent wash directed right at him.

"Awake now, are ye, lad?" whispered a voice, vaguely familiar.

"Hit 'em with the wash again. He ain't woke yet," replied another, his gravelly tone void of any emotion; cold, still, and lifeless. This voice, too, was known to Jonah although he could not immediately place it, groggy as he still was.

"Well, lad, ye be in big trouble now," said the first voice, one he now recognized as belonging to old

Elihu Smith. "Captain Metcalf and the first mate nearly had it out over 'ya. Missed the noon wind a'waiting on the likes of ya. Now we be a-sailing under still skies. The Captain is in a real fit. Liked to leave ye behind but Mr. Davis a be havin' none of it."

The hoarse tenor of the ship's cook, Stewart, chimed in. "Went out after ye hisself, he did. He and Manu, a-tracking you's up and down the streets of Rio…afta, of course, Eusebio and that dolt brother of his returned from lookin' fer ya last night. Them says ye weren't no where to be found in all of Rio. Captain kept a-sayin' you t'wernt worth it and wantin' to set sail. Jist one less headache aboard ship, he says. But Mr. Davis was fixed firm 'bout it. Say's you be needed on ship. Never seen 'em so steadfast about any other sailor. Him and Manu found ya, plum drunk at the bottom of a canyon. Some mean lookin' lumps ya took, too. Big one a-back ye head."

Jonah instinctively flexed his arms to reach back to the wound but roped restraints held him fast to the capstan. He squirmed like a fish out of water, writhing about on deck.

"Now jist hold fast there, lad. Captain's been awaiting fer ya to come 'bout. First mate, too!"

A cry went out, calling for the first mate and Captain Metcalf. Isaac Davis arrived first, a look of suppressed trouble on his face. "Jonah - whatever the Captain says, you go along with it, hear me? Now isn't the time for impudence. You cannot miss roll call on deck and then be found passed out ashore. It was all I could do to keep us from leaving port without you."

Before Jonah could even raise a protest, the pretentious Captain Metcalf arrived, his hands clasped behind his back, looking down upon the hog-tied Portuguese sailor with contempt.

"Well, well. This is what I was convinced to wait in port for? Cost me a full day of headwind, did you? And for what? I don't know exactly what Mr. Davis sees in you, nor do I understand the nuances of the strange relationship between the two of you. But that means nothing to me, you hear? Nothing! You'll be punished, alright, for missing roll call. No sailor aboard my ship misses roll call when we're ready to leave port – and costs me a full day!"

"Mr. Davis – produce the lash." An audible gasp escaped from the slacked mouths of the crew, each one gathered around the capstan to see what was to become of the young phenom in their midst.

"Mr. Davis! Did you hear me, man? Produce the lash. You there – tie this impudent drunk to the mast, face first."

"I was not drunk, sir," protested Jonah loudly, using the best English tongue he could muster. "I was hit on the head, sir. Someone attacked me! Meant to kill me!"

"There'll be no excuses from the likes of you. Very well, then, you'll take your licks. Mr. Davis, damn you! Where is that lash?"

"Captain," stammered the first mate, mortified by the ruthless intent of the ship's commander. "Don't you think it a bit harsh, sir? I mean, the lash for missing roll call? We did find him, sir, after all. And he has indicated no intent to jump ship. There is a large wound on the back of his head, sir, and..."

"Enough! No more excuses from you, Mr. Davis. This here reprobate has cost us all a good day's sailing. I intend to make an example, here and now, of those who violate discipline on *my* ship! You there, loose his shirt from off his back. Do it now!" screamed the petulant pretender.

No one moved. An eerie silent rebellion hung in the salt air as the ship rollicked back and forth in the swelling waves. Eusebio alone moved swiftly, breaking the peculiar gridlock that enveloped the deck and crew. He ripped the shirt from off of Jonah, exposing his bare skin. He then moved to loosen the ropes which tied the young Portuguese to the capstan, intending to drag him, feet still hobbled together, to the mast. He was met by multiple hands, each one clasping onto his, halting any attempt to position Jonah Pessoa for a lashing.

"All of you bastards! Remove your hands from off of him, damn you," shouted the Captain. The crew froze, momentarily. Eusebio drug a struggling Jonah to the mast, then re-tied him, back exposed.

"All right, then. At least there's one sailor aboard this ship that knows how to carry out orders. Very well. Mr. Davis? Fifteen lashes. You may begin when ready."

A stunned and frozen crew refused to act, or even breathe. The Captain turned his head, ever so slowly, towards the direction of his first mate. Glaring with contempt, the Captain moved swiftly, grasping the lash from out of the hands of the boy Petey, who had earlier retrieved the cruel instrument, instructed to do so by Eusebio's older brother.

"Mr. Davis. You will do as your Captain orders you to do! Do you see these men, watching you? They're watching a court-martial in the making, they are. They're watching a career in the King's Navy come to end, if you don't set the proper example and carry out the orders of your commanding officer with haste!"

Young Metcalf placed the coiled up lash into the hands of his first mate, then lowered his voice. His gritted teeth emitted a pitch only the two of them could hear.

"So help me God, Mr. Davis, if you don't carry out my orders immediately, I guarantee you my Father will hear of this. And he and I both will have you before the maritime court on a count of mutiny. Commence my orders immediately and this temporary insubordination will be forgotten. Defy me one moment longer and I'll have your neck stretched before the royal maritime council. Begin."

Isaac Davis swallowed hard as the choice loomed before him. Mutiny against the captain of a Royal ship, especially one as impudent and insignificant as young Thomas Metcalf, was a thought he did actually entertain. One quick blow to the ruddy face standing at his ear and this nightmare would end. The crew would follow him – of this, he had no doubt. But could he void the promise he had made to the elder Captain Metcalf? And what of his career – could it survive this incident? Or would it cost him more than a career…could it cost him his life?

"Stand proud, Jonah, like a man," Isaac Davis cried as he clenched the leather whip in his hand. His lips trembled and his voice cracked as he spoke. "It'll be over soon. Many a mariner has the marks of the lash across his back. There is no shame in it, lad. Take it like a man."

Captain Metcalf grinned impishly as his first mate stepped up to the mast and uncoiled the instrument of flogging. The crew remained fixed in trepidation as the scene unfolded before them. Isaac

Davis reached back slowly and flung the whip forward weakly, striping the back of Jonah Pessoa so lightly even the boy Petey could tell it brought no pain. Two more such strikes and the Captain bellowed out.

"Harder, man! Stop this nonsense at once! Harder!"

Isaac Davis increased the force in his forward arm movement, but only slightly so. The whip continued to fall on Jonah's back, but left no visible mark of its presence. Jonah remained silent, bearing the painless stripes with uncertainty and confusion. Was his friend and mentor doing this deliberately? Or did being lashed at sea mean only this level of mild discomfort, which was miniscule.

"Harder!" screamed out the Captain.

Isaac Davis increased the severity, but only in the tiniest of increments, gauging each stripe only slightly harder than its predecessor. Jonah finally flinched, the last stripe actually stinging his flesh.

"Harder! Harder!" railed young Metcalf, blood lust boiling over in his face and his eyes.

Isaac Davis minimized the application of force, although raised welts became evident on Jonah's back. Still, not a sound came from the young Portuguese wayfarer.

"Damn you, man, damn you!" howled Captain Metcalf as he rushed to the scene of the injustice. He grasped the lash out of his first mate's hand and began whipping Jonah with all of his might, leaning back and throwing his full weight into each forward strike.

Instantly, Jonah lurched at the white hot touch of the leather upon already sore flesh. An involuntary scream exploded from his lungs, something he believed his training in the arts of the Boddhidharma would have never allowed for. He felt ashamed and embarrassed, despite the searing pain which wracked his body.

Again and again, Captain Metcalf struck, horrifying the crew as they stood in shocked silence. The ship's commander bereft of all composure, struck out as a wild animal in an orgy of blood lust. Jonah Pessoa continued to scream at each strike, blood flowing freely from his wounds now.

Without warning, Isaac Davis reached out his weathered hand, clasping the wrist of the Captain as he prepared for yet another strike.

"How dare you! How dare you touch me, you insolent bastard, you…"

"Captain! That's fifteen, sir. Fifteen lashes."

The craze-eyed Captain Metcalf stared up into the becalmed face of his first mate…and saw something there. Something which challenged him deep down, a thing which confronted his innermost being in a glimpse of truth that they two shared…and shared alone. It was a reckoning of souls, so to speak. A timeless moment in which the secret soul of the young Captain was measured against that of his first mate…and was found lacking, woefully lacking. In that single solitary instant, Metcalf came to know and accept, unerringly and forever, that he was the lesser man between the two of them – much lesser; and would always be so. Nothing would ever change that; not in this life, nor the next. And that cognition both shamed and frightened him.

Captain Metcalf ran from the deck, slamming the door to his quarters behind him. A stunned and silent crew looked on as their first mate slowly and carefully un-tied the ropes which bound Jonah Pessoa to the mast. He gingerly propped up the young Portuguese sailor between his arms and led him across the deck, laying him face down on one of the canvas sails.

"Doctor!" he commanded, in a voice no sailor on ship hesitated to obey. "Bring the salve and treat those wounds. And bring him double the rations. Don't dawdle, now, get to it. The rest of you – be about your duties. Manu – help the doctor tend these wounds, please? Thank you. Stop staring, now! Go on with your duties or you'll be the next one striped."

The men knew it an idle threat but responded promptly, evacuating the bloodied scene of the only lashing most of them had ever seen. And hoped to never witness another.

Chapter Nineteen

The *Fair American* rounded the freezing cold of Cape Horn on Christmas morning and made her way into the warmer waters of the Pacific Ocean without incident…but the mood on deck remained foul and foreboding. There was neither mention nor celebration of the sacredness of the 25th of December, despite the presence of a Jesuit seminarian on board. Extra rations, common among sailors at sea during a Holiday, did not materialize. Nor was there the customary religious service provided, typical among the British Navy. The silent absence of both were ominously noted among the men.

For his part, Jonah remained somber, going about his duties on deck with nary a whisper to another. Even Manu, his closest companion aboard ship, was excluded from any conversation – the much anticipated meetings down in the orlop deck, where languages and theology, as well as academics, were discoursed, exchanged, with mutual satisfaction between Manu, Isaac Davis, and Jonah, were abandoned without notice.

Manu and the first mate showed up, on time, on the pre-arranged schedule but Jonah never appeared, that first night after the beating…and he never appeared at their rendezvous location again. Neither Isaac Davis nor Manu felt compelled to discuss this with him. The futility of doing so was plain for all to see. The inquisitive, intelligent, multi-lingual sailor, who had slowly begun to gain the trust and confidence of some of the crew for the past five months, had retreated into a sullen loner, with rarely a word escaping his lips. The unjust horror that had become known aboard the *Fair American* as "the incident" had gripped the entire vessel, transforming its crew into a somber husk of unspoken rivalries, prejudices, vendettas, and hatred – both for, and against, the former monk from the monastery.

The oblivious Captain continued on, as if nothing had happened. But the psychological scar that had been carved into the heart and soul of the *Fair American* ran just as deep as those physical scars upon the youthful back of Jonah Pessoa…and the explosion that was brewing would come to head soon. How soon was a question that would be answered more swiftly than anyone had expected. And the spark that ignited the fire would prove as inconsequential as ever – but, as it always is with men who are sequestered in tight quarters for long periods of time, it is the most trivial of infractions which provides the impetus for pent-up emotions to explode; and when they do, no one is safe from the white-hot angst which spills over everything… and everyone.

As the morning watch ended, Jonah found himself helping the sailors haul in a hapless dolphin which had been speared and brought aboard deck. The crew gathered around, gazing in wonder at the rainbow colors which its slick skin assumed in the throes of death. It was a pitiful sight. Jonah immediately regretted taking part in the capture of such a beautiful creature, only for the purpose of observing it die. It seemed such a waste of life, a living creature, sacrificed, not for consumptive use of some kind or for food, but solely for the purposes of looking upon it as it expired. Jonah felt ashamed. He slowly backed away from the group in disgust, the emotion evident on his face.

"Troubles with killin' this here fish, Father?" mocked Eusebio. The sailors encircling the dead dolphin looked up in unison at the young Portuguese.

"Looks to me like the holy man don't appreciate us taking this here fish. Like, somehow, he don't like the killin' of it. Like, somehow, it bothers him – likin' he's better than the rest of us. Likin' killin' don't suit him none," mocked Euesebio.

Jonah's eyes searched the circle of men standing around, one by one, from the innocent blue gaze of Petey, to the mysterious dark gaze of the Turk, to the hate-filled eyes of Euesebio. Other than Euesebio, he was not convinced that the others would attempt to take him in combat. He decided honesty was the best reply; honesty tempered with diplomacy. He replied in the English tongue to his shipmates, a tongue he was rapidly becoming fluent in.

"It is not for me to instruct my fellows in the ways of the sea. I am among the newest aboard ship." It was here that Jonah could have stopped, should have stopped – but that which was within his nature could not let him stop. That…and the scars which adorned his back, a transgression that slowly built within him. Retribution silently screamed within him for an outlet, an avenue to redress the wrong, once and for all, against not only his attacker but against those who had silently stood by in complicit participation, none rising to his defense.

Hatred had taken a hold in his heart, a familiar companion to the young refugee from Faial - a twin to loneliness, which gripped the soul of the confused orphan, who still could not make sense of the life he had been dealt, questioning endlessly the *why* behind the misfortune that seemed to follow his every path. The bitter scars which covered his back seemed only to match the hidden mark below his scalp, the mark he subconsciously rubbed with the tips of his fingers even now.

"But…does it not seem a shame to take the life of one of these poor creatures purely for the sake of watching it die? Is this not a waste?"

"So, the priest will teach us now, who have been at sea for years? I think it time we teach this priest something," replied Euesebio, moving slowly out from among the group. He advanced upon the young Portuguese with one hand hidden behind his lower leg.

Jonah spied the movement and prepared himself. Stepping back, he assumed the one-legged stance of the crane. His well trained feet would kick whatever Euesebio held in that hidden hand from him the minute he brought it forward. After that, any foot or hand he could put on his opponent's neck would end this struggle swiftly. He did not want to kill the sailor but neither did he feel remorse about the eventuality of taking yet another life. He pondered this absence of innocence for just a second and realized that it bothered him. Why didn't he care more about killing yet another man?

"Enough!" cried out Isaac Davis. Jonah had not spied the first mate among the circle which had brought up the dolphin. But, then again, the first mate rarely missed anything that occurred on deck, regardless of the hour of day or night. It was an eerie, almost spooky, omnipresence which the first mate seemed to have. Nothing happened on board the *Fair*

American that Isaac Davis didn't seem to know about…and know inevitably quick.

"Break it up, men! Now! You have your orders! All of you – disperse and get to work! Turk – cut off the dorsal fin for Stewart and throw the rest of that fish overboard, now! Jonah Pessoa – you're way past your watch; be needin' some shut-eye by now, no doubt? To the orlop deck with you! Euesebio – scrape the anchor chain. Go on now, don't dawdle."

Jonah, quite ready for a few hours of sleep after his morning watch, caught the eye of Isaac Davis as he turned to the hatch. There was just a hint of recognition there, something which both Jonah and Isaac Davis mutually accepted. The one, using his authority, to protect the other, keeping at bay the danger that would have engulfed him. The young Portuguese tried to convey his appreciation but was unsure whether or not the first mate denoted it.

A tumult of shouting erupted. The attention of the crew quickly turned to the waterline off the starboard bow. Both the first mate and Captain Metcalf attended to the cause and appeared to be in full concert with the efforts of the men as they rotated around the deck's perimeter, watching and giving orders. Jonah took his cue from Manu and joined with the sailors as they circled from starboard to bow to port to stern, cautious to stay off of the quarter deck.

"We like kill this one," replied Manu in broken English, a look of consternation on his face. "All sailor like kill this kind."

Instinctively, Jonah accepted his friend's verdict. Jonah would go along, for the time being.

A flash appeared in the water and Jonah caught a glimpse of the curious creature as it swam leisurely and questioningly around the ship, as if it were accustomed to such a ritual.

"She thinks were a slaver, she does. Takes us for the Tecora, no doubt. Figgers she's a-gonna get her a free meal. Must be used to feeding off the offal. No doubt, with a hand or foot too, here and there, maybe a whole one, if'n he's sick and not worth any money".

"Or dead already," opined one of the crew.

Suddenly, Isaac Davis hurled a harpoon into the water. There was a mighty thrashing as the rope attached to the butt of the harpoon danced and swirled about wildly. The first mate's powerful throw buried the dart half way through the unsuspecting creature.

The sailors shouted with one accord, the moment the harpoon struck. A roar of victory ascended from the crowd on deck, as if a long-time enemy of the crew had been destroyed. In no time, a bowline was knotted and thrown over the port side, expertly lassoing the thrashing tail. The struggling being was escorted to the port gangway and all hands came along to help heave the pitiful creature onto the deck.

"Shark!" shouted out multiple men in unison, as if their voices had been queued by an orchestral director. Once upon the deck, the female behemoth began to swing her strong tail back and forth, shaking the deck with the brute force of her strength, even in the throes of death. The enormous shark was greater than twelve feet in length, with an underbelly of pure white. Sharply serrated teeth, in the shape of triangles, lined the upper and lower jaws and ferociously displayed themselves with every yawning gasp of her mouth.

Her diabolical eyes, round orbs of perfectly whole darkness, gazed out at her assailants with an unblinking hatred.

One of the sailors fetched an axe and sprang forward, ready to sever the unruly tail. The able seaman swung the axe high over his head, poised and ready for the downward stroke just as the ship's surgeon, Doc Swisher, shouted out, freezing the young man's arc in mid-stride.

"No! No! On the head," he exclaimed. "Hit her on the head!"

No sooner had the ship's surgeon uttered those words than the great fish rotated over and over again, encircling the harpoon's rope around her scarred, two toned, gray and white skin. The great tail swung in a wide arc and struck Doc Swisher, just as he leaned over the great marine specimen, throwing him backwards into the arms of his fellows. He collapsed onto the deck, breathless and clutching his mid-section in a silent groan.

The crew instantly unleashed a torrent of blows, striking with wooden capstan bars, fishing clubs, and every other instrument at hand, each wallop accompanied by a stream of curses.

"God-damned killer!"

"Murderous bitch," spat another as he clubbed the dying shark.

"Man-eating monster!" yelled yet another, striking with his wooden club again and again, each downward stroke punctuated by a single syllable of obscenity.

A burst of common, universal hatred consumed the crew. They struck in a frenzied orgy of violence, singularly directed upon the great white shark, a stand-in for the simmering cauldron of violence which had engulfed the men ever since the “incident”. In no time, she succumbed to the beating; the thrashing and twisting of her body ceased. The black orbs of her eyes glassed over.

Assault with the axe was sanctioned by a silent nod from Captain Metcalf. The tail was immediately severed from the body in numerous places, each stroke invoking a quiver of the great fish’s muscular membrane. The shark’s throat was gashed across with a knife and the stomach opened up, its contents examined.

“Ayie!” screamed a sailor, recoiling from his close inspection of the entrails. Doc Swisher, recovered from his assault by the shark, ran to the stinking viscera and promptly lifted an object out from the gut pile.

“Yep. She’s been feeding upon human flesh alright, boys,” he remarked, lifting the object high above his head for all the crew to see. The grotesque token dangling from his fingers glistened with a coating of mucus from the fish’s digestive tract but could be clearly discerned in the morning light – the complete, articulated bones of a single human foot, up to and including the ankle.

“By God and the King, throw the damned beast over!” screamed the young Captain, visibly mortified by the sight which Doc Swisher held in his hands. The looks on the faces of the crew, seeing their ship’s Captain’s self-indulgent horror, reflected their disdain of the lad, too young and immature to be holding the reins of authority over the likes of them, sea-hardened veterans of the mast, old hands who had beheld much worse than the sight in front of them. Smirking faces, trying hard to maintain discipline, turned in unison to the true leader aboard.

"You heard the Captain, lads. Throw that sea-bitch overboard," roared first mate Isaac Davis, trying desperately to keep some semblance of order on the *Fair American* whilst maintaining the established hierarchy of the British Navy.

The pitiable shark, beaten about the head, throat slashed, disemboweled, with tail chopped off, was cast disdainfully into the sea. As the water closed over her, the pectoral fins stirred the water feebly, lethargically driving the certainly dead fish deeper into the depths of the dark waters. It was an ignoble end. Silently, Jonah Pessoa wished something more for himself, when his time came. He had no clue how rapidly that moment would approach.

Chapter Twenty

Amid the chaos and confusion of killing the shark, no one noticed how close Eusebio had moved into Jonah…until it was too late. Gleaming silver flashed in the morning sun as a marlin pike sliced through the air, meant to plunge into the neck of Jonah Pessoa. But the uncanny second sense which the young ex-monk had learned through many painful hours of training with Brother Chin saved him yet again.

Jonah ducked just as the barb grazed the back of his neck, splitting the surface of the skin but going no deeper than that. In a whirl, Jonah spun underneath the plunging form of his opponent, crouching at the waist and leveling himself against the deck with a single hand. In that selfsame movement, one leg swung about, tripping his would-be assassin over backwards. Before the crew realized what was happening, Jonah had wrested the spike from Eusebio's hand and plunged the sharpened shaft of iron into his throat, fatally pinning the sailor onto the deck.

A death rattle gurgled through Eusebio's lips as he frantically grasped at the spike with hands that seemed not to obey his commands. His feet kicked wildly for a brief moment before collapsing…and then an eerie silence enveloped the astonished crew, suspended in time. Even the waves of the ocean appeared to be stilled.

"By God, he's killed 'em. Killed 'em, he did. Jist like the old man. Murder! Murder," raged Eusebio's brother. Before another word could be spoken, the elder sibling rushed Jonah. In a single stride, the young lad from Faial managed to spin his attacker about, grasping his head between arm and shoulder. One quick, but firm, twist and Eusebio's brother fell to the deck, his neck snapped like a dry twig. There was no sound whatsoever from the elder sibling of Eusebio as he lay sprawled out, the second corpse to fall beneath Jonah's feet within moments. A look of horrified shock fell over the first mate's face.

"Lad, what have you done?" he queried.

"They both tried to kill me," replied Jonah, in perfect English. He remained crouched in the defense posture taught to him so many months ago by Brother Chin.

"Nay, Nay, but he killed 'em both. A murderer he is. Knew it afore we let 'em aboard," answered one of the bunkmates of the dead brothers. Despite five months at sea, Jonah had yet to move his sleeping quarters up to the gun deck, where the crew all slept. Only he and the boy Petey remained below.

"Take him," shouted out Captain Metcalf, his visage gripped with fear. "Take him and hold him fast!"

"Lad – you best surrender and let me work this one out," answered the first mate, his voice conciliatory…but cautious.

"I've done nothing wrong other than defend my life," protested Jonah. "They both have wanted me dead since the day I came aboard. You know this."

Jonah slowly wheeled round, surveying the crew which had gradually surrounded him…while they maintained a safe distance away. "You all know this. Every one of you," shouted Jonah. "For no cause, the two of them have always sought to take my life. What sin have I committed that any among you can lay to my charge."

"Tell him, Mr. Davis," answered Captain Metcalf with a smug look on his face. "Well…go on – tell him."

"The brothers, Jonah," answered Isaac Davis, slowly, perceptibly, "were kin to the old man. The one which Elihu tells he watched you kill…at the Azores, where we first picked you up. Those two are, were, Eusebio and Eduardo Soto. His two sons."

A wash of paleness flooded Jonah's face as the irrevocability of what he had just done sunk in. Not only had he killed Anton Soto…but he had killed the man's two sons, his only offspring in this life. An entire lineage, a familial line, had been stamped out, gone forever, because of him. The blood of a generation of Sotos was on his hands.

Jonah dropped his guard, his hands retreating to his sides. With or without cause, and there could be no argument there was cause…three men from the same line, the only men from that line of proud Portuguese ancestry…were gone forever. The finality struck him in an instant…and he bowed his head, resigned to the fate that awaited him.

"Well, now. Cost me three sailors, he has. Good salts, men of the sea each one…can't replace that. Mr. Davis – bind this violent young brigand and take him below. His fate will be decided on the morrow," said Captain Metcalf.

"Aye, aye," shouted the crew, a crazed lust burning in their eyes. Only Manu and Isaac Davis appeared forlorn at the thought of what awaited Jonah Pessoa.

"Lad, give me some time," whispered the first mate as he tied the hands of the young Portuguese refugee. Jonah offered no resistance and went willingly, somberly, to the gun deck with Manu standing beside him. The shouts and jeers of the crew rose immediately …and fell silent just as quickly with one turn of the head of the first mate.

"I've no cause to discount the lad, Captain. If he says he was attacked, he was attacked. It's no secret that the sons of Anton Soto wanted to avenge their father's death," pleaded Isaac Davis.

The ever-present Mr. Winscott stood silently against the rich oak-paneled cabinets, his arms folded across his chest, a look of stupidity upon his face. He rarely, if ever, spoke in the presence of young Captain Metcalf. The strange nature of the relationship between these two remained a mystery to Isaac Davis, as well as the rest of the crew, although it was whispered among the men, at night, that they were lovers.

It was a rare occurrence for the first mate to be summoned into the opulent quarters of the Captain's chambers. The stark difference between the squalor which the men lived in and the luxurious trappings of the ship's principal, never ceased to amaze and bewilder the first mate. The cause for which he had been summoned was never in doubt. Captain Metcalf knew he was in a quandary and needed a scapegoat. He himself could never command the ultimate actions of his crew without Isaac Davis supporting him…this he knew to be true.

"He's a strange one, this rogue priest. But the King's discipline, and his authority, is mine aboard this vessel. Do not challenge me on this one, Mr. Davis."

"Can we not hold the lad until we return to England, sir? The Admiralty can hold a proper court at that time."

"This reprobate has cost me three good sailors, already!" shouted the impetuous Captain.

"All the more reason to hold him aboard, sir. We're short of deck hands now. And the lad has shown he is a capable seaman. We can use his help on deck, sir. Don't worry about the men…I can handle them, all right."

"Like you handled them this morning?" remarked Alan Winscott.

The wry retort stung the first mate. Despite the foolhardiness of the Captain, in bringing aboard Jonah Pessoa in the first place, Isaac Davis had always prided himself in his ability to command the men who worked under him. In more than twenty years at sea, he had never had an act of violent murder amongst a crew which called him first mate. It was, in fact, a professional and personal failure; and Isaac Davis knew this to be true. Captain Metcalf sensed this inward agony in his first mate, the first hint of weakness he had ever detected in the man whom he had come to distrust, fear…and to hate.

"He'll pay for this with his life, Mr. Davis. And you'll carry out my orders. On the morrow, he shall be hanged from the mast."

"You can't do that, Captain!" shouted Isaac Davis. The emotional outburst caught the inexperienced Captain and his sole entourage off guard…and he responded in kind.

"I can! I can! I can! I am Captain of this vessel, sir, and you follow my orders!" screamed the petulant young Englishman, his face pinched red with anger, eyes shut, both fists clenched at his sides, pumping wildly.

Alan Winscott arched his back against the panels, his eyes growing wider in fear. He obviously had seen, or known, this type of behavior before, from Thomas Metcalf. And it frightened him.

"The men won't stand for it, Captain," remarked the first mate.

"The men will stand for that which their Captain orders, as carried out by his first mate. And you *are* my first mate, are you not, Mr. Davis?"

The first mate's silence was all the answer Thomas Metcalf was going to get.

"First thing on the morrow, you will see to the execution of this murderer aboard my vessel. That is all, Mr. Davis."

"Yes, Captain," replied the first mate, whisking himself away as quickly as possible from the ghastly stares of both Thomas Metcalf and Alan Winscott.

There appeared to be no way out for Isaac Davis. Yet he was bound and determined to save the life of the young monastic protégé, who had meant so much to him during the few months they had shared upon the deck of the *Fair American*. Somehow. Someway.

Chapter Twenty One

Rollicking waves ferociously tipped the *Fair American* as she struggled to keep an even keel. The roaring of distant thunder rumbled across the purplish-hued skies, punctuated by occasional bursts of brilliant streaks of lightning. It was a terrible morning to die.

The crew was assembled, in silence, as Jonah Pessoa was brought out of the darkness of the ships' bowels and onto the deck. He was adorned with nothing more than his borrowed clothing from the sailors slop chest – and the koa bead necklace Manu had slipped over his head, in the night, whispering only, "she bring you good luck." There were no others words exchanged between them, nor any other sailor in the gun deck.

Strange, that the only night he would ever spend sleeping among the men on the gun deck was to be the last night of his young life. He thought he heard the mournful sobs of young Petey, one deck below, throughout the evening…but he could not be sure. The ship's chef, Stewart, had brought the young convict a plate of food that evening, complete with cheese, butter, a double ration of salted beef, double salted pork, biscuits, and a cup of wine from the Captain's store. It was the best meal he ever had aboard the *Fair American*…because it was to be his last.

His hands remained tied, although the martial arts trained monk could have easily slipped his bonds during the night. A gloomy dawn greeted his troubled visage. The morning was eerily reminiscent of the very first day he had spent aboard the ship, those many months ago…and he found he could not escape the irony of that fact. He looked upon the faces of the crew, unable to discern their intent. None dared return his gaze, their eyes averted ever so slightly.

"Am I going to die?" he asked of Isaac Davis. The first mate refused to answer. Couried to mid-ship, the condemned young man made no petition for mercy or judgment.

"Mr. Davis – where is the hangman's noose?" shouted out Captain Metcalf.

"There'll be no hanging today, sir," replied the first mate, mustering his voice with as much authority as he had ever used.

An audible gasp escaped from the lips of the crew, amazed at the events developing before their eyes.

Before the Captain could retort, the first mate continued, "The condemned shall have the sailor's execution. He shall be cast overboard and left to the mercy of the sea, to do as she deems just."

Isaac Davis leaned into the young man, cutting away the ropes from his hands. He whispered ever so softly, "It is the best I can do for you, lad. Swim under her belly and to starboard as soon as you hit water. Manu and I shall try our best."

He paused, the words struggling to escape his throat, before continuing, "I'm sorry Jonah. It truly is the best I can do for you. Pray God your fate be as generous as your namesake in the Good Book."

Jonah nodded, knowing better than most the details of his Biblical moniker. Yet, he could not shake the sense of betrayal he felt.

"Please don't hold it to my account, Jonah. I've done everything possible, under English law," whimpered the first mate. It was uncharacteristic of Isaac Davis and Jonah noted the extreme emotion in his voice…but he would not absolve the first mate of his pending action, one that would most certainly be fatal. Their eyes met briefly and in that moment Isaac Davis knew the transgression he was about to partake in would be unforgivable…that he was dooming an innocent man, one who had done no more than defend himself, as he also would have done. There would be no forgiveness.

Jonah stood, hands now free, as a pre-ordained group of six men hoisted him up, without tumult on Jonah's part…and promptly threw him overboard.

"Very well, then, Mr. Davis. You may resume your duties," snorted Captain Metcalf, parading back to the private retreat of his quarters, Alan Winscott skulking behind him.

The shocking slap of cold sea water roused Jonah from his fatalistic melancholy. Instantly, he began diving deeper, scrabbling to submerge himself under the belly of the ship. Feeling her transom, Jonah swam deeper until he rounded her underbelly and clawed upward, as Isaac Davis had instructed him to do, his lungs bursting for a gulp of air. Desperately breaking the surface of the waters, Jonah was surprised to see both Manu and the first mate, standing alone. As the drowning young man bobbed up and down with the waves, the two men starboard pitched an empty powder barrel overboard.

As the *Fair American* faded from view, Jonah draped both arms over the barrel, its buoyancy providing the only respite from the pull of the dark waters which would have otherwise drowned him. The two solitary figures, still standing starboard, remained fixed. They did not move as the outline of the ship crested over turbulent waves and became nothing more than a dot on the shifting horizon of the Pacific Ocean.

Unsure if it was the sounds of the ocean or the howling of the morning wind, Jonah Pessoa strained to hear a refrain coming from the first mate yet again and again, as the ship faded from view…"it was all I could do; it was all I could do."

A quick survey of his surroundings brought utter despair. Jonah knew, instinctively, that he could not survive in the open ocean…and there was no land mass anywhere in sight. His instincts screamed at him to begin swimming, but in which direction? No one bearing appeared more favorable than another. Panic stricken thoughts raced through his head – should he follow the *Fair American*? By now, she was already lost to view and the crescendo of rising and falling of angry waves completely disoriented him. He had no clue as to which direction he should go, if any.

So this is how it ends? he thought to himself. *What a waste of a life! Survived a volcano…only to die at sea! I'm too young to die,* he screamed inwardly, as one gulp after another of sea water splashed across his face. For the first time in a long time, he found himself praying – to a God he had insisted, until now, he did not believe in.

Please…let me live! Oh, God, please let me live! I'm sorry…I'm so sorry.

The sound of his own heart rate pounded in his ears. Desperate to pull his body out of the paralyzing waters, he tried to heave himself onto the barrel, but it would not cooperate. With each desperate push of his muscles downward, the oak barrel resisted, its buoyancy working against him. It slipped and rotated in the slick waters, tiring the young castaway in short order. Jonah's muscles soon became stiff. His legs, which had kicked tirelessly since he was thrown overboard, turned numb. Without realizing it, his whole body began shivering. It was an involuntary reaction and he was shocked at how quickly his strength was fading.

Brother Chin would be disappointed, he thought. *How little control one has over one's own body. I should be stronger than this. I am stronger than this,* he remarked, silently at first, to no one other than himself. Then, out loud, as if the speaking of the words themselves gave him resolve.

"I am stronger than this! I shall not die out here," he shouted.

"God, give me the strength, but I will not die out here!"

Marshalling the last ounce of reserve energy he had, Jonah determined to make one final push. Sucking in a deep breath, he steeled his legs together and bore down on the floating round of oak with as much force as he could muster. The barrel sank under water, bobbing beneath his weight for just a moment. It was all that he would need.

Jonah thrust his body upward, throwing himself long-ways across the slippery curve of the barrel. In an instant, the air filled drum resurfaced. But Jonah was now spread-eagled across its form, his legs dangling on either side, his hands stretched across to grasp the iron-banded edge. He straddled the barrel, pushing himself upright, more like a rider astride a horse than anything else. His aching muscles worked perpetually to keep him balanced aboard the shifting vessel and it was all he could do to keep from sliding off. And yet, despite his dire predicament, a slight grin of accomplishment crept across his face. He was out of the water!

Thank you, God, he whispered silently to himself. For the first time since splashing into the salty abyss…he had hope.

Chapter Twenty Two

Day turned to night, without the appearance of salvation. The overcast skies were the one consolation Jonah had, as he was spared the blistering heat of the tropical sun. But as the dull grey skies transformed into the inky blackness of a star-less night, a new terror seeped into his soul. He thought he had seen the telltale sign, a time or two, but was unsure of his thoughts. A full day adrift, without fresh water to drink, had already begun to dehydrate him, playing tricks with his mind; disorienting him. He doubted the occasional glimpse of a shape in the water was a true form.

Am I losing my mind? he thought, as the bulky shapes appeared and then vanished as quickly as they had come.

Jonah shivered against the absolute darkness as it blanketed the waters. The temperature dropped suddenly, making it that much colder. In the blackness of night, Jonah was totally and completely blind.

Suddenly, they were there again, revealing their presence in unmistakable fashion, their dorsal fins slicing the waters surrounding his insignificant little float.

Instinctively, Jonah drew his legs up and out of the water, bending at the knees until the heels of his feet lay against his thighs. Were it not for the months he spent training his body under Brother Chin's tutelage, he simply could have not held his legs there for more than a moment or two. As it was, his weary muscles were already cramping and he was unsure how long he could hold that position.

One by one, the sharks appeared, occasionally bumping the floating barrel with their nose tips. Each time, Jonah struggled to maintain his balance, knowing the absolute outcome of his fate, if he dared slip into the waters. As the attacks became more brazen, Jonah resorted to the only thing he knew in defense on oneself; the arts of Boddhidharma.

Tensing his hand into the finger-slice position, Jonah waited until the next shark's head appeared at the surface. In one quick strike, he sliced across the beast's large black eye, blinding it and drawing blood.

Instantly, the great fish thrashed about, twisting wildly in the waters; the movement almost upended Jonah but the desired effect was complete. In seconds, the water was filled with blood and the other sharks quickly began cannibalizing their injured sister, tearing into her flesh and striking violently at her wound.

Jonah watched, captivated, as the blood lust feast filled the water surrounding his pitiful float. He wondered…how different were these sea beasts from man, when his blood lust is full and blinding rage fills his heart? How different from he, himself, who had taken the lives of three men already. The lack of differentiation stung him.

Dawn broke instantly, the brilliant sun exploding over the horizon of the now calm waters. Jonah was both relieved and troubled. Being able to see one's surroundings was always better than being blind but the heat of the tropical sun was something he knew could be brutal. Even sailors aboard the *Fair American* took their turns below deck, out of the unrelenting rays of the sun…but there would be no such respite for Jonah, endlessly straddling the oak barrel which had become his only haven from drowning.

A quick glance around brought no new hope for the young castaway; water in every direction and not a spit of land in sight. There would be no use in attempting to paddle anywhere. He was at the mercy of the tide and it would take him wherever it willed – or take his life, if meant to be. It was a solemn conclusion but one he had arrived at, during his first terror filled night at sea. Hope, which had sprung within him so readily, when he managed to fight off the shark attacks in the middle of the darkness, receded just as quickly. Despair was now his only companion.

Utterly exhausted, Jonah collapsed onto the barrel, lying prone across her as sleep overtook him.

He awoke, having no concept of how long he had slept, although he could not shake the nagging feeling that much more than a single day and night had come and gone while he was unconscious. The sun was down and nightfall was just beginning to darken the world around him yet again. His throat was parched and his tongue swollen in his mouth, making it hard to swallow. A bright red burn covered the side of his face that had lain exposed to the sun. But the stars were just beginning their faintest glimmer in the heavens and the moon had already begun her slow rise.

From somewhere deep inside him, he felt a slight tremor of hope. He was familiar with the outline of the night sky; had studied astronomy at the monastery and had not forgotten what he learned. Perhaps he could actually begin to navigate?

The moment the thought entered his mind, an enormous shape emerged from out of the waters. The wave it created rocked the tiny flotilla Jonah was perched upon, almost upending him. He struggled to maintain his grasp and keep the barrel, and himself, upright. Suddenly, it was there beside him, its enormous eye staring directly at him, surrounded by a bulk of crevices and barnacles, her slick skin shining in the moonlight. She was the largest whale Jonah had ever seen.

Both man and beast froze, each one staring at the other. Oddly, Jonah did not fear, although the enormous creature could have easily destroyed the odd being astride a piece of oak with one small shift of its massive bulk. After what seemed like an eternity, the giant animal slowly submerged, but not without a gentle swipe of its gigantic tail. The wash from the dismissive movement sent Jonah reeling across the waves, in a direction opposite what he would have determined, given the alignment of the stars in the night sky.

Is she, too, trying to condemn me to the sea! My God, what else can I do, cried Jonah from the deepest depths of his soul, convinced that the sea Goliath had just pushed him out in the direction of the boundless ocean, away from the path he would have navigated. Desperation, coupled with exhaustion, overtook him; he passed out.

Chapter Twenty Three

The water-logged oak barrel jarred to a complete halt. It shook Jonah from unconsciousness and he briefly lifted his eyes but saw nothing.

God, this is it, thought Jonah. *I can't hold on any longer. Let the waves take me; I'm ready to die,* he muttered to himself. His body, utterly unable to grasp hold another moment, slipped into the waters. His exhausted muscles, no longer his to command, involuntarily relaxed and Jonah welcomed the cool respite washing over his sun-baked flesh. He opened his swollen mouth, prepared to take in the sea water that would drown him. At this point, all will to live was gone and he actually welcomed the calm of death; at least, his endless ordeal at sea was finally over.

Splashing overboard, Jonah was shocked to feel solid ground beneath his body. His face still lay in the ocean, slurping in sea-water; but that was not all of it. Air filled his lungs as well. Confused, he drifted in and out of consciousness. Fleeting images came in and out of focus and Jonah was unsure of whether he was alive or dead. Suddenly, a pair of lithe arms struggled to pull him forward, his form scraping against the black sand; then a wet face, hovering above him.

It was the most beautiful face Jonah had ever beheld. Moonlight danced upon her shiny black hair, glistening with the dew of the ocean. Jonah rasped out a single question in a barely audible whisper, defaulting to his native Portuguese tongue – "Are you an angel?"

There was no response but as her delicate fingers made their way across the koa-bead necklace which still draped the half-dead castaway, a broad smile, revealing the most brilliant, white-perfect teeth Jonah had ever laid eyes upon, shined upon him. Darkness closed in around his vision and Jonah lapsed again into the peaceful abyss of nothingness.

Chapter Twenty Four

Angry screams cascaded from every direction of the thick ohia as Captain Cook and his men rushed for the shore. Stones rained down upon them, dashing wounds in their flesh. The furious swoosh of wooden spears crisscrossed their path constantly.

The British sailors' desecration of a Hawaiian heiau, and their killing of the lizard-like shaman, or kahuna, had sealed their fate. Cook, for his part, should have prepared his men better; but nothing he could have shared would have settled the minds of his men as they stumbled upon what they had.

Charred human bones, laid out in the shape of a cross; the blackened skull with its grotesque grin, staged like a trophy atop the carefully constructed cairn, all of it inside the small stone enclosure, not unlike a tomb of sorts. Only this was no place of homage for a respected dead elder. The five gilded brass buttons, each one bearing the emblem of the Royal Navy, arranged in a circle around the cross-shaped bones, revealed the tell-tale story. This victim had been a British seaman, and an Officer at that…but how could that be? Was it possible that Cook was *not* the first Englishman to have reached these Polynesian isles, out in the middle of the great expanse of the Pacific Ocean? And, if not, who then had come before him? And what had happened to him…or them, if it were a full ship's crew?

The Hawaiian shaman had screamed at first, shocked and horrified by what he saw standing inside the small heiau as he entered – men, white men, dressed just like those dead bodies which had washed ashore…were these their spirits, their ghosts, come back to honor their bones? Would they be satisfied at the reverence which the old shaman had shown their remains, honoring the dead strangers' bodies with the purification fire and the totem he had put together so respectfully?

For their part, Cook's party was just as horrified at what their eyes saw standing before them. The bald-headed old man, obviously native, was covered from head to toe in yellow scab-like lesions, his skin a rough scaly texture, not unlike that of a lizard. His pupils were wildly dilated and pale yellow surrounded the remainder of his eyes. His unexpected and sudden appearance, along with his scream and his form, startled the men. Before Cook could give any orders, the Marine with him leveled his musket and fired, firmly convinced he was shooting at a demon, and not a man. The tumult that followed brought total chaos, as the British troop ran from the heiau while the shouts and shrieks of the natives, unseen but heard from every direction, surrounded them.

Two sailors fell to the ground simultaneously, moaning aloud as long wooden spikes buried themselves deep through the midsection of both. There was no hope for them and the others knew this; leaving their brethren to writhe in death, the remaining group ran on, desperate for their very lives.

Clamoring onto the black sand beach, Cook was horrified to discover the bloody remains of the two sentries he had left behind. Seaman Gore and King lay sprawled out, disemboweled, their heads cut from their bodies. The two small dinghies remained beached, apparently untouched.

"To the ship! Quickly…there's nothing we can do for them now," shouted the Captain. "Row, damn you, row!"

The first dinghy filled with five men was already in the water, easing away. But the look of sheer horror on their faces, as they tugged desperately at the oars, surprised even the seasoned Captain, whose back was turned, helping to launch the final boat. Captain Cook instinctively spun around…and met his death.

More than eighty Hawaiian warriors, decorated in full battle costume, their brilliant plumages fluttering in the slight breeze, descended upon the remaining sailors. They had yet to wade into the still blue waters when the frenzied natives fell upon them, slashing and cutting. Shark toothed war clubs sliced as cleanly as the finest British steel, and the azure waters of the tiny bay quickly turned crimson with blood.

Captain James Cook was struck on the head and promptly fell on his face into the surf. Pouncing upon his body, the Hawaiians repeatedly stabbed him, driving their koa wood knives into the regally costumed Captain until his clothing was torn to shreds.

The young Marine, still standing ashore, had managed to reload his flintlock with shot while on the run. He turned, firing into the crowd of screaming natives. Instantly, four Hawaiian fighters toppled, their bodies riddled with hot lead, blood streaming obscenely from abdomens, chests, and heads. The devastating barrage gave no pause to the onrushing army, and the carnage continued unabated. The young Marine was pierced through the chest with a long spear and impaled onto the blood-spattered sand, another grotesque totem to the slaughter. The last two seamen ashore fought valiantly, wading backwards into the surf…but to no avail. Each was overwhelmed by the sheer number of his attackers. They fell into the shallows, their blood blending into the turquoise waters with each gentle wave of the tide.

The first dinghy rowed on, relatively safe from the spears still being hurled in their direction. The Hawaiian army massed at the beach, taunting the sailors and raising their weapons above their heads in triumph. The five seamen reached the *Resolution*, unscathed but terrified; and without their beloved Captain.

"Load the cannons with canister shot," murmured William Bligh, watching the devastation ashore through the Captain's telescoped looking glass. He strained to assure himself there were no survivors among the landing party; if one Englishman were yet alive, he would forebear with his plans. But the magnified view confirmed his worst fears. All were dead, including the Captain, whose limp and lifeless body was dragged out of the waters and onto the beach for more desecration by the natives.

What a fool, thought William Bligh. *A Captain is never the one to put himself at risk; that's what the damned sailors are for, the scurvy wretches! And now, Cook has gotten himself killed, trying to ensure his men made it safe? What a waste of a British officer! That's one mistake I'll never make,* promised Bligh to himself. *When I get command of me own ship some day, there'll be no question who is the absolute authority amongst the men.* He lowered the brass looking-glass slowly with somber deliberation.

The Hawaiians remained tightly assembled on the beach, eyeing the *Resolution,* unaware of the terror that was to befall them within seconds.

"Loaded, Mr. Bligh," replied the men aboard ship.

"Very well, then. They've given us the perfect target, have they not? Killed a Captain of the King's Royal Navy, have they? We shall see to that." He paused for the briefest of moments; a glint of vicious loathing flashed in his eyes - and then he issued the command.

"Fire when ready!"

An awkward silence lingered for only an instant before all three of the *Resolutions'* starboard cannons fired into the naïve congregants, still bunched together on the beach, shouting and relishing in their victory. The boom from the ship's weaponry thundered across Kealakekua bay, shattering the skies and silencing the Hawaiians on shore. Choking white smoke enveloped the deck, temporarily obscuring the horror that was unfolding on shore. Dozens upon dozens of native warriors collapsed, right where they stood. Faces, arms, legs, and bodies were instantly shredded in an explosion of bone and flesh. The profuse bloodshed coated the survivors and drenched the sandy soil in a layer of scarlet horror.

A confused Hawaiian army immediately retreated to the safety of the thick ohia forest. But the slaughter which had occurred that day left behind a stain on the land in a way that would forever haunt the island. In a single day, the blood of a royal kahuna, British seamen, and Hawaiian soldiers had all been spilt, in an orgy of conquest, fear, hatred, and spiritual violence; *it* seared itself into the rocks, the sand, and the waters, all of which had opened up to receive the life blood. And there *it* would remain – forever.

Chapter Twenty Five

Jonah awoke to the caress of hands, deftly working the muscles of his back as a body sat astride him. Slowly, cognizance of this world came to him and he realized he was laying face-down in the black sand, puking water with every shove of her palms. Stronger than he first realized, her two hands pushed hard, shoving up into his shoulder blades, her body weight shifting forward with each thrust. He retched sea water with each of those thrusts, a small pool of the fetid upchuck forming around his face; but he was too exhausted to move and could do nothing but lie there, grateful for life but wondering where he could possibly be. Everything around him remained dark, and he lapsed into unconsciousness yet again.

He awoke this time, stronger than before. His eyelids fluttered briefly and he was vaguely aware of a moan escaping his lips; was that sound coming from him? Instantly, the angelic face that had appeared, pulling him from the waters and, he had no doubt in his mind about this, was the same body and hands that had sat astride him, pumping the seawater from out of his lungs, saving his life…was before him again. He had not dreamed it; she was real.

“Quem são você?” he whispered…but only a look of confusion came over her dark eyes. Jonah’s thoughts raced for a moment; realizing he had spoken in his native tongue, he asked the question again, this time in English.

"Who are you?" Still no response from the dark-skinned, raven haired girl with the bright smile and the perfectly white teeth. He closed his eyes, his mind filtering through the linguistic possibilities, a smattering of languages which he possessed, rooted in the Latin he had studied so laboriously in the monastery at Faial, in a greater number than most men ever would know.

"Qui sont vous?" he tried, in the French tongue…nothing.

"¿Quiénes son usted?" he asked, in Spanish, rapidly reaching the end of the languages he could, at a minimum, converse in, if not fluently.

"*Mai e `ai*?" replied the young girl, a quizzical look on her face. Jonah's eyes instantly brightened as he recognized something within her words, if not their exact meaning…he did recognize one of those words, a word that Manu had taught him.

Eat…in Hawaiian, the word was *ai*…she was definitely asking him something about eating…and she was speaking Hawaiian! And he was famished.

"Mahalo Nui Loa," replied Jonah, thanking her very much…in the Hawaiian tongue.

The young girl's face lit up, eyes shining brightly as a wide smile crested across her lips. She ran from the small thatched hut but returned shortly with sustenance.

Baskets of known, and some unknown, food were set before him, in quantities beyond his ability to consume. Jonah recognized the distinctive taste of the cooked ahi and steamed pork, both of which he swallowed voraciously.

Coconut, banana, breadfruit, yam, and sweet potato were before him and he ate more than his fill, accompanied by the ever present bowl of thick paste, a culinary indulgence he had never know before.

Shoveling two fingers into the purple goo, Jonah was disinterested by its bland taste, at first…but a starving man who has teetered on the edge of life for, how long? How many days had he been at sea? Feeling ashamed for his apathy, he quickly resumed eager consumption of the *poi,* as she had called it. The taste grew on him with every bite.

Her name was Lilena, and she had found his unconscious form adrift in the surf three nights before.

According to her, the great whale she had been watching, for three evenings in a row, came unusually close into shore that night. Lilena was drawn closer to the strangeness of this event, curious as to the whale's odd behavior, perilously close to beaching itself upon the sands. As she entered the surf, the massive sea mammal descended into the deep, making one final demonstrative flip of its tail, sending a crashing wave into shore. The rush of the water completely upended her and when she righted herself, Jonah's form was floating directly towards her, face down.

The evening was too dark for her to make out all the details but she recognized an unconscious human form floating directly at her…and that she needed to help that one to shore, assuming he was not already drowned. The rest of the story fell into place for Jonah, as he remembered her pulling him onto the beach, her pumping the water out in order to resuscitate him, but no more.

And there was the necklace, always that necklace. Except for the moment Manu had first put it around his neck, he had all but forgotten its presence there…until Lilena. It was an obvious source of fascination for her and Jonah began to wonder if the longing look in her eyes, every time she stared into his face, had more to do with that necklace than it did with any romantic notions he had imprudently allowed to foster in his head. What kind of fool was he, to think that he had seen something more in her eyes that just empathy for a drowning man…she was only interested in saving a fool's life…and, obviously, in the damned necklace.

Kamehameha rubbed the pockmark which was forever embedded in his right cheek, his keen mind turning over the events of the last few days. The missing slice of flesh, already covered with scar tissue, served as a perpetual reminder of his victory over the strangest enemy he had ever faced; and added yet one more to the list of leaders who had fallen before him, as had been prophesied – he was destined to be a *Killer of Kings*.

The drowned bodies of the white strangers who had washed ashore just days prior to his great battle against the British and their leader, the one they called *Captain*, were a mystery to him; where had they come from? Were they of the same tribe as those who had come ashore, to spy out his plans? Had they come ashore to retrieve their own dead? His instincts told him no; these two events were not related. But the sameness between them, their common clothing, their magic tools, the tongue they, or at least the one who survived, kept speaking, convinced him they were of the same stock. It was no accident only the one had survived among the floating bodies which had pre-dated the war with the British Captain; it was destined by the gods.

The one white man he now had in his captivity, the one his wives were carefully nursing back to health, the one who called himself *Isaac Davis* – this one was sent to him. He would learn everything he could from this one, would make him like unto one of his own sons and, in return, this one would show him the power of his magic - the strange wood and metal instrument which Isaac Davis had clung to; the heavy metal log which had been attached to the floating wreckage that also washed ashore; the barrel of foul-smelling black sand which Isaac Davis guarded so carefully…these were the things which the gods had put into his hands, and his hands alone. The prophecy continued to unfold, piece by mysterious piece, and his destiny was slowly being realized. And now that he had defeated the British landing party, and killed their King, or *Captain*, there would be no stopping him.

Eight years ago he had wrested control over the districts of Kona, Kohala, and Hamakua, killing outright his cousin, King Kilwalao, after days of bloody battle. The entire western half of the island was now his and his alone. Only the Hilo, Kau, and Puna districts to the east remained beyond his control, governed by Kilwalao's brother, King Keoua. Diplomatic attempts to consolidate his power through a marriage compact with King Keoua's youngest daughter, Lilena, had been rebuffed. Now, there would be no mercy.

All of the island, not half, was going to be his. The lonely childhood years of scorn, ridicule, and estrangement he had suffered at the hands of his cousins Kilwalao and Keoua, banishing him to the forlorn coast of Kohala, were to be avenged and there would be no forgiveness. Lilena would become his wife and all of Hawaii would become his domain.

His grand stone temple, the largest structure ever built, dedicated to the war god Ku, was almost complete. Day and night his laborers worked, piling stone upon stone. The slain bodies of the British Captain and his dead sailors were even now being prepared for sacrifice and would be the first to be burned there; others would follow – many, many others. Yes, even the white Captain from the ship was a *King* over the men who had come ashore, was he not? The *Lonely One,* he had been told by others his name meant, was indeed a *Killer of Kings*. Keoua would be next.

Chapter Twenty Six

Lilena and Jonah spent most days together. The young Portuguese castaway made the most of his language skills, reciting and repeating with her all the Hawaiian words which Manu had taught him. In turn, he shared the English and Portuguese translations with her – although she appeared to favor the English tongue – as well as the inevitable crowd which gathered around every time Jonah sat with Lilena for a translation session. Jonah was amazed at how quickly Lilena grasped languages, a skill set the two of them seemed to share in some mysterious way. The admiration the rest seemed to have whenever he spoke in the English tongue was a peculiarity which he also made note of.

Lilena's father, King Keoua, seemed especially pleased with the appearance of the young white-skinned lad within his domain. The deference he was shown amazed him and Jonah could not help but wonder why this was so. The looks of surprise and awe followed him wherever he went; regardless of age, both old and young often trailed him, observing, watching, and waiting upon him. In fact, he and Lilena were never truly alone.

"Why," he asked, one balmy summer evening, just as the two of them set down together at the water's edge, the gentle waves of the bay of Hilo lapping at their feet. She hesitated, a look of consternation clouding her otherwise joyful face.

"Why," he prodded, driving deeper. It was obvious she was holding something back. Jonah was grateful to her, for saving his life, for all that she and her father and village had done for him. But he sensed something below the surface of their affections, an expectancy that had yet to be spoken aloud, given breath to, but there, nonetheless, waiting…waiting…

"Do you know of the book?" she responded to his question with one of her own.

"What book?" he replied.

"The book – the book of the white Father God," she replied.

Without saying another word, Lilena rose to her feet and walked away, leaving Jonah confused and disappointed. His heart ached for the beautiful dark-skinned girl, darker than any of the others he had come to know since washing ashore. She was different from them, in some subtle way. He yearned to hold her; to have her. It was a singular, fierce emotion, stronger than he had ever felt for any other. He was no virgin, having known what it was like to take his pleasure from a woman. But it had never gripped him before like this. This was above and beyond all of that – it was both overwhelming and frightening; he felt a gradual loss of control every time she appeared, as if, somehow, for the first time in his life, he could let go and be himself with her, like no other person in the world could, or would, do for him. No pretense, no hiding, no masking the pain and the hurt inside. She would know, somehow – and she would understand, somehow – and she would not reject him, somehow, for the ugliness he kept bottled up inside; not reject him for the damage that marred his soul, the fear, anger, the loss, the confusion and, yes, even the hate. The hate he had nowhere to direct to, other than the amorphous concept that plagued him wherever he went; the concept of God, a single benevolent entity that watched over all and controlled all. A concept he had come to despise. Others had told him to let go, to forgive, and to understand – but he could not do that.

And now, there was her. No, what he felt for her was something new, and deep, and strong – and it scared him. Fear mixed with shame overwhelmed him and he cursed himself for having driven her away.

Relief washed over him when she returned within moments, carrying a woven basket. Seating herself against him, tighter now, her warm skin touching his, she brought forth surprises; things Jonah could not believe had found their way to the people of the Sandwich Isles, as Isaac Davis had referred to them.

A brass tinder box, complete with flint striker; a brass powder flask, its gleaming gold cover long ago glazed over with the green of corrosion but still filled with black powder – was it dry and still usable? A broken sextant, similar to that he had observed Captain Metcalf use aboard the *Fair American,* but much older in design with its glass ocular missing and the markings on its arc long since corroded and…a heavy leather-bound tome, its binding long ago rotted away and the cow-hide covers torn, faded, and curled.

"The book," she stated, matter-of-factly as she handed it over to him with a reverence reserved for sacred objects.

Jonah carefully turned the pages, one by one, its English script barely visible in most places, the ink long ago faded, but discernable to an eye such as his, an eye that had known the labor of hours and hours spent in the scriptorium of a monastery – it was, without a doubt, the earliest English translation of the Bible he had ever seen, a hand-written version he guessed was from the early 1500s.

"Where did you get this?" he answered, excited at the age of the rare document he was holding in his hands…and simultaneously bewildered by the fact that, twice now, the Christian text had unbelievably found its way into his life, presented by those who could not read it. First, Manu, aboard the *Fair American* and now, Lilena.

"Long time past…one white man come to my people…bring many magical things…bring this book, also…"

My God, thought Jonah, *it can't be. It simply cannot be...is this the same story Manu told me? Can it be? Is this tribe, Lilena's people, the same tribe Manu comes from? Are these his people? Is this Manu's tribe?*

Lilena continued, "…this man. Him wash ashore – just like you!" she grinned, telling the story with increasing excitement in her voice. "Him teach words from this book – no other person can read. My village follow him; teach us many things…"

*Oh my God! It is!...these people, this village... this is Manu's people! The story's the same!...*then he recalled the other part of what Manu had said. The part about another white man, returning some day, to restore the faith in the Christian God and lead the islanders against their enemies, overturning the idol worship which had violently erupted when Manu's father had left his island family behind, and…

"First white man tell prophecy before him leave," she continued. "Someday another come, just like him! That one read to us from sacred book again. That one know all magic of these things," she gestured, waving her hand above the sextant and corroded brass accoutrements which were specific to a black powder musket. Was there one of those somewhere in the village?

"Me wait for three nights when see great whale; me have dream of great whale and what she bring to us; me dream of that one, who can read the Book and teach us again, the ways of the one God. My father, him wait, too. Him wait for this man to return; my father, my people, no believe in those gods which others on the island force us to worship. We wait…for ***you***!"

The impact of her words struck Jonah in the heart. This was the last thing he had wanted or expected. He did not even believe in God himself; unrequited anger still simmered in his heart over the untimely death of his father, his mother, and the pathetic justification the priests in the monastery offered as Divine excuses for the unjust travails of his young life. He was blinded with rage – he simply could not come to grips with the Christian God of the Church, an unpredictable and capricious Deity who meted out favor to some while delivering calamity to others, with no apparent reason for either. His inner rage, held in check, still boiled over at the concept of God as had been taught to him by his family, the Church, and the Monastery. Then he remembered the recent solemn oaths he had made, afloat in the vast ocean, alone and forsaken, his life all but vanquished…and how, in fact, salvation had indeed come his way, in the form of this beautiful island maiden.

Before he realized what was happening, she had leaned over him; a warm, full kiss graced his lips, astonishing him…at first. She pulled slowly away from him, holding his wide-open eyes in a gaze of wonderment and hunger.

The rage and confusion he had felt only a second ago dissolved away instantly. Never had Jonah experienced such a range of emotions, so quickly and so deeply. And never before had they been able to be so swiftly and completely quieted by another, with just the slightest caress of those thick full lips…he was gone, hopelessly gone, and he knew it, knew it like he had never known anything before in his short life.

"Yes," he replied. "I know this book…and I can read to you from it."

With no real direction, Jonah decided to let fate decide where he ought to begin although, to tell the truth, he was somewhat averse to beginning with the first verse in the book of Genesis, having started this cycle once already with Manu. He carefully opened the beautifully hand-scripted pages, already torn on their edges and pockmarked with defects of time and moisture. The pages fluttered briefly in the warm breeze and then settled where they lay; he began:

"In the beginning was the Word, and the Word was with God, and the Word was God…"

She had come to him that night, that first night after he had read to her, to all of them really, from the Scripture. King Keoua had called for his finest warriors and his kahunas to gather around and listen as the young white man read from the Secret Book, read the magic words in the unknown tongue, that tongue only the white man understood; until just recently, when his daughter Lilena had also begun to be able to read and speak it, as well…a linguistic phenomenon that caused the whole of the village to take note.

She had brought them both bowls of sacred awa and the two of them sipped it together in the quiet of the dark. She said nothing as she slipped silently beside him that evening, laying her head upon his torso, their naked chests touching one another, the gentle rise and fall of his breathing a rhythm that furtively matched the beating of her heart. He opened his mouth to speak but she silenced him with nothing more than a gentle brush of her fingers upon his lips, a gesture that required no explanation. Her oval shaped face, framed by soulful dark eyes which danced with a strange fire, a perfectly sloped nose, and thick full lips entranced him. Shiny black nipples, really nothing more than small hard buds upon a flat chest, fully formed hips, and rich long dark hair completely enveloped him in her smoldering looks and when she slowly took him into herself, he felt as if time had stopped. There was no time, no world around them; sublime nothingness gripped him in her magical trance…until that strident grunt escaped her lips, a low rasping moan, flexing convulsions through her entire body; and then she collapsed, falling onto his chest, utterly and completely spent.

Jonah knew then, in that single transcendent moment, as had had never known before in his young life, that he wanted desperately to live for something beyond himself – he wanted to live, live forever, if possible…live for *her*. And that meant he needed to be…honest with her.

"I'm not…who you think I am," he whispered, tentatively, the words choking out of his throat, half-spoken in fear, fear of what could, what would happen next. How could he live now if he lost her? He had lost every person whom he had ever loved; how could he risk losing her?

"You are," she replied simply, her head resting sideways upon his chest.

"No. No, I'm not…"

She reached her hand up to his neck, tenderly fingering the koa bead necklace which lay there.

"Yes, you are."

"It is only a last-minute token, given to a dying man, about to drown, by one who was a friend and wracked with guilt; that's all," he replied.

"It is the most sacred and exclusive gift of my people. No one but my people has these. It is not possible that one like you could wash ashore, presented to me by the great whale, yet adorned with this kind. All but dead, yet now you alive; you know our tongue, somehow? You read and understand the words in the magic Book, somehow. None of this could be true…unless…you *are* him," she answered quietly.

He opened his lips to reply but her deft finger blocked his speech yet again.

"Shhhhh," she whispered, gently pushing back the hair from his forehead, her delicate fingers gingerly searching under his hairline, searching for something deliberate, a thing in particular, until she found it. Soft fingertips gently traced the outline of the odd-shaped scar that lay forever imprinted upon Jonah's scalp, hidden, or so he had thought, under a thick layer of sandy hair.

"It's a scar…" he began.

"I know," she whispered in reply, her tone low and secretive. Only the rhythm of the pounding surf against the black sand beach outside accompanied their voices; all was otherwise silent, an eerie stillness that added to this moment of glorious mystery between the two of them, alone together, in the dark.

"It's the shape of *the* symbol," she answered, a slight grin forming from the corner of her mouth. "I knew it would be there."

Jonah reached up to remove her hand, fingering the tiny scar hidden beneath the coarse sandy-colored hair which covered his scalp. He was stunned to discover the too-familiar scar, that which he massaged every so often, reminding him, when he needed or wanted to, of the volcanic catastrophe which had orphaned him for life, tossing him so cruelly into the hands of fate…had transformed, changing its shape. The head wound which Brother Israel de Silva had treated and stitched so carefully…had taken the form of two opposing arches, each one inverted against the other, coming together at their apex, in a crude symbol of….a fish! 

No, No, No…this cannot be! Jonah silently raged, distant fear welling up within him from some unknown source; a panic born of some fear and shame from a distant past, long ago and far away; yet still so ever present, seething slowly just underneath the surface of the conscious mind.

"You don't remember, do you?" she cooed, gently stoking the back of his neck.

"Remember what?" he whispered, half-afraid of the words that would follow, words that he strangely knew were coming, in advance, as if he had known them all along.

"You actually don't remember, do you?" she questioned again, a slight hint of forsaken desperation in her voice, a solitary tear from her eye wetting his chest. Jonah remained silent. A torrent of mixed emotions raced through his soul; the fear of what he was about to hear actually muted him. *It cannot be true; it must not be true!* he sighed.

"It was the time of the Romans," her narrative began, her head still laid across his chest, neither one making eye contact with the other. Jonah felt the movement of her lips against his chest as she spoke the words; words that were increasingly coming forth in near-flawless English.

"The Emperor had declared conversion to the faith of the one God, and our sect…illegal…punishable by death."

She paused, waiting for something from him; that something that did not come.

She continued, "They put us in prison, after we refused to recant…the four of us…the fifth one, the one who did not confess to his belief…was spared." She paused. Still nothing.

"My breasts hurt so; they brought my baby to me so I could nurse and instantly my heart was filled with joy. Nothing in this world could compare with the look on my baby's face, being nourished from my breasts, and in that dark, dank cell, the whole world was once again light and unbounded joy to me...for a while."

She paused. Her silence punctuated the still night air, making the dark palpable. Jonah dared not break that spell, and…he could not bring himself to believe her, not the things she was saying. But why, oh God why, did her story *feel* so familiar? A panicked shiver ran through his body; Jonah tensed every muscle he had, in an effort to hide this involuntary reaction. He did not want her to know.

"After my baby was full, they took it away… and I knew then that the hour had come. They led us before the Roman Governor. He asked one last time for us to recant our faith and make the nominal sacrifice of worship to the Emperor…but we would not. How could we?"

A fleeting glimpse, a scene from some long distant past, flitted through his mind as she spoke. Jonah could actually smell the sweat of the Roman soldiers around him as they stood encircling the morning fire, the wood crackling, the hushed whispers of the men as they watched in amazement, the balance of life and death a simple matter of momentary denial, a denial that could be easily made up for in the future…but the obstinate Christians, as they called themselves, would not yield! Damn them! All they had to do was recant, a simple verbal recital and a tiny pinch of incense thrown briefly on the fire, in honor of the Emperor…and they could go free! It was so perfunctory – they did not even need to believe in it; just do it! They could then be free to practice their own strange religion, free to move on with their lives, free to raise their children…she could raise her child - their child! God, was it so? She claimed it was his, but how could he know for sure?

He observed, above and outside of the scene, as the drama unfolded in his mind's eye.

"Is it true that one of you has converted to this strange new religion?" quizzed Hilarianus, the Roman Procurator over this northern most region of Africa.

Carthage was more than just a Roman outpost on the Gulf of Tunis. It was rapidly becoming a major port for the merchant fleets of multiple nations to find safe harbor…a rising town, with a rising prosperity. And a young Roman officer, a local boy but one who had found favor with the occupying Romans, could rapidly make a name for himself, if he followed all the rules and pleased the Emperor. And that was exactly what Collum intended to do.

He was young, full of life, and the future before him was unbounded. Then he had met her and everything had changed. She was different; unique. Of a noble Tunisian family, but humble and unassuming. Very young, and very beautiful, oh so beautiful…yet also so very strange. Her new-found religion had ostracized her from even her own family – but she would not bend. Her attempts to convert him had been only partially successful. One of her favorite games was to leave a mark in the area where they two had arranged to meet. Always the single arch  awaiting its twin, to be drawn by him. He would faithfully follow suit, completing the other half of the puzzle, forming the secret mark of the fish,  some bizarre homage to a supposed miracle performed by the sect's founder, a young Jew whom she had said fed hundreds of his followers with just a few fishes brought to him. Then, and only then, would she be willing…and if he failed to complete the sign, there would be no consummation of their love that night.

He feigned enough belief in her bizarre faith to get her to fall in love with him, and from that point on, he had her. Or so he thought.

"I asked you a question!" Is the rumor true? Have one of you also fallen under the spell of this foolishness?" barked the Procurator.

Collum and the other soldiers each looked at one another, their glances revealing the dismay they held for the outcast group of believers…and their strange God.

"This young lady tells me that one of you is her fellow convert, a disciple of this one they call the Christ, or Messiah, or the One True God…it's all so confusing to me. Speak up! Who among you claims the faith of these reprobates?"

Suddenly, without warning, Jonah's head began swimming, as if he were blacking out. Everything went dark for just the briefest of moments. And then…he was no longer observing. The eyes he was looking out through were no longer those of one from outside the event; instantly, he found he was living in the moment. He viewed the scene from one of the Roman soldier's eyes. His pulse quickened and his heart raced; sweat beaded upon his forehead and an oppressive dread overcame his entire being. It was as if he were Collum, observing the ancient act of long ago through those eyes! He was actually standing there, in the bright heat of a Tunisian morning, the unnecessary flame from the courtyard fire blazing hot against his legs, legs braced by kneepads of gleaming brass. A red tunic and skirt wrapped his frame; a stamped cuirass adorned his shoulders and arms, completing the outfit. Strapped around his waist lay a leather scabbard, filled with a short sword. Jonah, or Collum, stared in amazement, slowly twisting his arms as they dangled at his side, viewing them as obscene strangers, foreign appendages that were somehow oddly attached to his body – a body that he did not recognize, one much darker in tone, the skin a deep ebony hue.

Jonah's mind whirled as he struggled to escape from the duality of the mental trap he found himself in; but to no avail. At least for this moment, even as his mind screamed that this had never been true, could not ever have been true, he *was* this young Roman soldier, sometime in the first century, witnessing the death sentence of a small group of early religious martyrs …one of whom he had lied to, had made love to, and was now about to betray in the utmost – a betrayal of both love and faith.

She had loved him first because she believed in his conversion to their sect; a conversion that left him deeply conflicted, as far as Collum (or Jonah) was concerned. He was not fully convinced of their beliefs but…he had been impressed with the underground sect's passion for their beliefs, their ultimate commitment, their single-minded devotion to the One God, and their willingness to sacrifice everything, everything, in service to that God. The Romans, whose pantheon numbered in the dozens, would no more put life at risk for one of their gods than would the pagans, theirs. But these Christians…they were so damned different!

Yet he did feel deeply for her; and he had felt something amazing when he confessed his belief and allowed the sect to secretly baptize him. Was her child truly his own? Even of that he was not sure; but who else would she have been with? These Christians were very circumspect. It had taken all of his efforts to get her to agree to consummate their love; she would not have been with another – no, the child had to be his!

The moment of horror faded away; Jonah was back in his own body, his own consciousness, in his own time, listening intently to her story. She continued:

"I longed for the one I loved to speak up, to profess his belief…to own his child, his woman, and our God…but he did not do so. And I would not betray him. We were led out of the courtyard and into the small coliseum. The crowds roared in their lust for blood. There were wild animals and a single gladiator roaming the arena's earthen floor." She paused again, desperately waiting for some semblance of recognition from him; it did not come.

"A wild bull charged our small band and I was thrown into the air by his horns, landing with a cracking thud on my back; the pain of broken bones racked my body but I sat up, adjusting the ripped tunic, with as much dignity as I could muster…and ran to help the others. A leopard was introduced into the arena and rushed us, biting and clawing. Blood rapidly covered our torn flesh and yet, for some strange reason, the she-cat withdrew, pensively pacing backwards away from us, as if she could not bring herself to actually cause our death. The impatient crowd screamed with unrequited passion as we were left yet alive, torn and bleeding, kneeling together in the dust and the heat.

A strange pause filled the moment and then… the gladiator came. He was a young man, not unlike you in some ways. He approached with great deliberation. One by one, he wielded the sword of finality, dispassionately piercing the hearts of my fellow believers first, leaving me for the last. As he stood over me, wielding the bloody sword, the look of fear and trepidation on his face was palpable…and then he made the thrust into my chest – but it was not fatal. As he withdrew his blade, I glanced throughout the screaming crowd to find you, standing there in the shadows, dread and guilt flooding your visage. Our eyes locked and I whispered the only words I could think of, in that moment, the last words I would speak to anyone in that life, void of any blame or condemnation - - - and I told you, *I have given my love to you; you have given your love to me.*

I returned to face the young soldier, his countenance twisted in horror at my continued existence. The others had died so quickly; why was I still alive? I could tell that he had never experienced a thing such as this. His hand trembled, the dripping sword wavering in the bright sunlight. I reached out with trembling arms, guiding his blade to my throat, and with the last portion of strength left within me, thrust his gore-filled edge into me, ending it for him…and me."

Long moments of silence passed; Jonah was sure she had fallen asleep atop him. His mind reeled at the consequences of what she had shared. He struggled to incorporate the bizarre out-of-body occurrence he had just experienced; nothing like that had ever happened before. Perhaps it was the awa. It was only a dream; it had to be! He knew he was in love with this girl, a love beyond anything he had ever known before; and he was equally troubled with the knowledge that this girl was undeniably insane.

"Aloha Aku No. Aloha Mai No," she whispered, eyes closed, half-asleep, her head still pressed against his chest.

Jonah remained silent, unclear of all the words or their meaning. Without lifting her head to discern whether or not he was awake or asleep, she repeated in halting English, softer now, eyes still closed. "I give my love to you. You give your love to me."

More sweet silence passed between them before she whispered a final refrain, a commentary which puzzled Jonah, "but…God, this time…you're *so* white."

Chapter Twenty Seven

"He has one white man also," reported the breathless young courier from the western side of the island, bowing on one knee before his monarch.

"Keoua has torn down all the altars and heiaus. The people do not worship Ku or Pele any longer. This white man reads from a secret book; he reads and teaches in that same language as your white man does. They all worship the one God, now. Keoua has removed all kapus; the women and men eat together, now. This white man also has one stick of thunder."

"It is the prophecy of Kapihe," replied the King's chief kahuna. An audible gasp escaped the small contingent of the King's entourage, followed by silence.

Kamehameha's eyes flashed in anger. Did his rival have at his disposal what he imagined was his, and his alone? Was there somehow another, besides Isaac Davis, who had survived the massacre of the *Fair American* off the Kohala coast? And did this one also have the cannon and black powder, the instrument of great death which Isaac Davis had shown his warriors how to use, mounting it upon his own war canoe? Was it not this instrument alone that had brought the King of Maui to defeat less than one moon past, in a single bloody battle, adding to his kingdom the isle immediately to his north? And yet the whole of his own island remained elusive, the west side claimed by Keoua as King.

“There is more,” continued the young reporter, pensively, his lips trembling in the presence of one such as King Kamehameha. He dared not look up, keeping his head and eyes downward while speaking.

“Continue,” ordered the King, his eyes brooding. The young man swallowed hard, afraid of sharing the knowledge he had acquired, sneaking through the villages of the Hilo and Puna regions, claiming to be a spiritual wanderer when, in truth, he had been dispatched by one of Kamehameha’s chiefs for the express purpose of gathering information on Keoua’s armies and their strength.

“Keoua has given this white man one of his daughters in marriage; she is already with child.”

“Continue,” ordered the King, rising up from his throne.

“It…it…it is…Lilena.”

Kamehameha roared, his face twisted in rage. The guttural war scream echoed throughout the thatched hut. Without hesitating, he made a single motion of his hand; the royal guardsman nearest the young man drove his koa wood spike directly through the back of the unfortunate teller, impaling him to the ground. Bright red blood pooled at the King’s feet as he stood impudent before yet another victim, one whose crime had been nothing other than bearing news his King was displeased with.

“Bring me Isaac Davis,” shouted Kamehameha.

Multiple warriors scurried at his command, rushing to find and bring the white stranger before their monarch. In moments, a harried and perplexed Isaac Davis was ushered into the royal longhouse. His eyes fell first upon the impaled young Hawaiian, still bent over before his King in a posture of supplication…and still alive, apparently, low moans and gasps escaping his lungs. A final puff of breath fluttered through his lips as his body lurched forward, now perfectly still.

Isaac Davis approached gingerly, the puddle of bright red widening around the corpse between himself and the King, a king he had sworn to fight for. What else could he do?

The fierce slaughter aboard the *Fair American* had been complete. It began first with the mood aboard ship; it had turned strange, after the throwing of the young Portuguese refugee from Faial overboard. Some of the men maintained it had brought bad luck and began to secretly conspire against Captain Metcalf. Others maintained it was the right thing to have done but maintained that the heavens would exact their revenge against the brash young Captain for whipping the lad as he had done. Then the foolhardy Captain, despite his first mates repeated misgivings, had anchored her in Kawaihae bay, off the Kohala coast. The men were desperate for fresh water and food, their stores all but depleted.

When canoes filled with natives approached, he had warned the Captain to arm the men and have them ready for defense; but Metcalf would have none of it. The cannons remained impotent, their barrels clean and free of any powder or shot. The Marines aboard kept the armory locked, upon the Captain's orders.

The natives appeared friendly and Captain Metcalf welcomed them aboard, desirous to trade, barter, and gain victuals for his crew.

"Captain, something's not right," he warned. It was not a thing he could demonstrate, just a feeling, a seaman's instinct. An instinct honed by years of life aboard a ship, exploring, trading, and dealing with people of all kinds, from many nations across the seas.

"Good God, man, can't you see they're a friendly lot. Look at all they have in those canoes," Captain Metcalf responded, his eyes widened with greed. The open rebuke shamed his first mate in the eyes of his men; and it continued.

"Getting afraid of a couple of savages, are you, now? Well, well, I'll not let your childish fears ruin our chance to trade here, now, shall I? Order them all aboard and let's see what we can take from these poor barbarians, shall we, for a brass nail or two?"

The heavenly stars were already twinkling in their host by the time the boarding began; one by one, over twenty Hawaiian men were hoisted on deck, each one laden with gifts of food, feathered caps, and tapa cloth. There were chiefs among the boarders and they made a great show, adorned in their full length capes and robes of brilliant plumage, bright red and yellow feathers woven in the most intricate of geometric patterns. They bowed and scraped before the young ship's Captain, presenting him with one reed basket after another. It was all the grinning Thomas Metcalf could do to maintain his composure, the unearned adulation feeding his youthful ego.

Suddenly, without warning, the heavily-cloaked chieftain pulled a koa-wood knife from under his robe. Thomas Metcalf was the first to fall, his hands filled with a basket of breadfruit as the Hawaiian drove the polished wooden shaft deep into the Captain's mid-section. The young Captain never even managed a whisper as he slid down onto the deck, his mouth and eyes open wide in terror.

Horrified screams erupted as the Hawaiians, following the cue of the chieftain, flung back their feathered capes and began butchering the crew with a speed and ferocity that captured the sailors completely off guard. Shark-toothed war clubs slashed and cut crewmen to bloody ribbons while others were strangled by the use of the whalebone handled garrotes. It was a gruesome scene and he made every attempt to rally his men to arms; but there were none to be had. Not even the ceremonial sword afforded British Royal officers was accessible to him.

The impudent Captain Metcalf, in his rush to make trade, had doomed his crew to their fate, slaughtered at the hands of a relatively small Hawaiian contingent.

Fighting for his life, Isaac Davis managed to club more than one of his attackers to the deck with his bare fists as he retreated towards the stern; but any hope for the ship, or the crew, faded before his very eyes. There was not a man left standing on deck; even Manu lay dead, his throat slashed open. The poor cabin-boy Petey lay strangled, not six paces away from where he now stood, bloodied and cut…but yet alive. Glancing over his shoulder, he spotted one of the native canoes bobbing alongside in the dark waters…and he made an instant decision; a decision that would change the course of the remainder of his life.

He leapt off the deck in one fluid motion and landed with a thud into the native crafted bark, rocking it violently in the waves. Unseen in the dark, a Hawaiian warrior yet remained at the canoe's helm. When the white skinned stranger landed at his feet, the Hawaiian warrior promptly beat him senseless with the canoe's paddle, then stabbed and clubbed him to death;

or so he supposed. Although unconscious, he was not dead. His still body remained in the bottom of the canoe while the Hawaiians scavenged the British warship.

The triumphant party set fire to the hulk of the *Fair American*, then returned to the Kohala shore, bringing spoils of their conquest with them; among these, firearms from the ship's armory, one hand-cannon (torn from its deck mount), barrels of black powder, ornate British officers uniforms from the Captain's cabin…and his own body, presumed dead and available for sacrifice.

Kamehameha was not pleased. He had not given orders for the *Fair American* to be attacked. His recent battle with Captain Cook's landing party, and the barrage of cannon fire from the *Resolution* in retaliation for the bloody slaughter, left him wary of these white men. Yet he seized the opportunity, securing the spoils of the *Fair American* for his own and, upon discovering Isaac Davis still breathing, ordered the utmost care and medicine be done, hoping to save the man's life.

Isaac Davis remembered only partial glimpses of time for the first few days. He knew he had lost his sight and feared he would be forever blind. He relied on his hearing to discern what occurred around him but this proved difficult; he did not know the Hawaiian tongue, only a few words he had picked up from Manu.

Yet, day by day, under the utmost care of Kamehameha's physicians and healers, his sight slowly returned. He quickly found himself under the tutelage of Kamehameha's personal family and inner circle. This puzzled him at first until the realization came to him…he was not much more than a trained pet, a novelty that would be expected to perform in the strictest obedience, at the King's behest; perform or die.

Faced with his choices, Isaac Davis made a conscious decision. At least a part of him told him that he owed Kamehameha his life; were it not for his intervention, and a genuine concern and care for his well-being, he would have long ago been sacrificed to the local Hawaiian deities. If, in return for his life and well-being, he owed a debt of service to the King, then he would faithfully do so. One King was no more righteous than another, be it King George III or King Kamehameha.

He dutifully fulfilled the specific wishes of his new monarch; teaching the English language to select subjects, among them the King's many wives; and training his warriors in the use of the musket. *Load powder. Load ball or shot – or use small rocks if no other ammunition is to be found. Charge priming pan. Cock hammer. Plant butt stock firmly against cheek. Close left eye. Sight right eye down the barrel. Pull trigger. Repeat again until the last enemy falls or they surrender.*

He had even gone so far as to mount the rescued hand-cannon from off the deck of the *Fair American* onto the King's personal war canoe, making it the most powerful war-ship among the Sandwich Isles. It, and it alone, had tipped the scales of battle when they sailed against the King of Maui, blasting Kahekili's men off the cliffs as they scrambled to escape.

Kamehameha had honored him for this victory, making him equal to his other war chiefs and giving him in marriage to one of his own kin, a royal Hawaiian wife. And yet the irony of it never failed to trouble him, late at night, when his regal wife and rapidly burgeoning family had long gone to sleep – and he was alone with his thoughts, only thoughts he knew, and no one else, thoughts no one else could possibly ever know. He was using items from off the very ship he was first mate to, in furtherance of one whose warriors had attacked and killed every one of his brethren aboard that ship. And meant to kill him as well, had chance, fate, or some Hawaiian deity he was not even aware of, not intervened, leaving him alone as the sole survivor of the *Fair American.*

Why? Of all the men who kept her deck, and there were many such men, good men, men whose lives had yet to be lived, why was he the only one to survive? Why not Manu, who was actually Hawaiian, although he once claimed his loyalties lay with the clan on the westward side of the largest isle, and no other isle or clans would he ever bow down to. Or how about Petey, just a lad still, no more than 12 or 13 years old…how fair was it that Petey had died but he had lived?

He bowed in the presence of the King, keeping his eyes fixed forward on his regent and the royal guardsmen. He remained acutely aware that nothing separated his fate from the dead young man impaled to the ground in front of him, but the capricious wish of Kamehameha at any given moment of time.

"Who else survived the wreck of your ship," demanded the King, his voice filled with curiosity mixed with rage.

Odd, Davis thought, to hear the King refer to its destruction as a wreck, as if some calamitous force of nature, a violent wind or crashing sea, perhaps, had done her in when, in fact, it was the King and his warriors he now served who had deliberately, and deceitfully, raided her, killing everyone on board. Why was he so conflicted over this? Kamehameha had saved his life!

"No one, my King. I, and I alone, remain to serve you. There were no others."

"Do not seek to deceive me, Isaac Davis. I know there is another; a white man such as yourself…and that he teaches the tongue of the English, as you do. And he, no doubt, teaches the use of the *gun*, as you do. And he does these things on behalf of he who tormented me throughout my youth, my sworn enemy, Keoua."

Isaac Davis was struck dumb; no one else had made it off the ship, had they? He had watched them all die, everyone, as he struggled for his own life. He was the last man standing aboard her deck, when he jumped, was he not? He was sure of it. Perhaps the King's information was…wrong?

"There were no other men left alive, on the ship, when she was…it was…*rescued* by your men, my King. Of this I can assure you," he replied, careful in his use of words, still not fully fluent in the Hawaiian tongue. And still cognizant of the dead body grotesquely propped up in front of him, a fresh testament to those who displeased the mighty Kamehameha.

"There is another!" screamed the King at his white convert. "I feel it in my bones. He will lead the people away from the great Ku, and away from Lono. He will destroy our traditions and overthrow our culture. He reads the English tongue, your tongue, to Keoua's people from a secret book and he teaches them to fight with the gun and he must be destroyed! And you, Isaac Davis, shall destroy him! You are the one I have chosen to destroy this white man. Begin the preparations for war and maintain at the highest vigil. We march on Hilo when Ku ordains the time is right!"

Isaac Davis bowed before the King as he gingerly stepped backwards, "Yes, my King. It shall be done as you please."

"And Isaac Davis," continued the distraught monarch, his point yet not fully made, "make sure this white man, whom you claim not to know? Make sure he is killed in the battle; by your own hand. Not one of my warriors are to touch him; this I have already determined. Your hand, and only your hand, shall be the one to take his life," growled Kamehameha, a crazed gleam filling his eyes.

"It shall be as you wish, my King," answered Isaac Davis, continuing to step backwards out of the great thatched hall, all the time wondering, *Who? Who could this white stranger among Keoua's army be? Who, absent the Officer Corps of the Royal British Navy, could have the intelligence, the training, and the requisite education to be actually fulfilling all those things the King has claimed? And how did one such as this come to be ashore the leeward side of the Island*?

Chapter Twenty Eight

Keoua's army grew in confidence every day. The strange white man among them, although reserving the gun for his exclusive use, often delighted in showing how the massive firearm belched smoke and fire, koa tree limbs his favorite target. In turn, select soldiers taught Jonah Pessoa the sacred art of Hawaiian Lua, carefully denoting the pressure points and demonstrating how easily bones could be broken when just the right spot was selected, using the skeletal carcasses of the wild boars which roamed the wet side of the island in the hundreds.

They were more than a match for any military action Kamehameha would send against them; a conflict that was destined to come; it was only a matter of time.

Lilena's swollen belly signaled the entire village of a unique event, the first time a royal would be giving birth to a child of mixed race. The gleeful anticipation was not universal; rumors circulated among some of the elders that Keoua had damned his people, allowing one promised to Kamehameha to be given to a non-Hawaiian, a white foreigner from afar who knew not nor honored the religion of the ancients. To this charge, King Keoua incessantly repeated the prophecy of Kapihe, a prophecy all knew had been given in the presence of Kamehameha:

"THE ANCIENT KAPU WILL BE OVERTHROWN, THE HEIAU AND LELE ALTARS WILL BE OVERTHROWN, AND THE IMAGES WILL FALL DOWN. GOD WILL BE IN THE HEAVENS; THE ISLANDS WILL UNITE, THE CHIEFS WILL FALL, AND THOSE OF THE EARTH WILL RISE."

King Keoua had often pondered this prophecy, in light of the white-skinned castaway in their midst, now a son through marriage. This one alone among them had knowledge of the musket, a thing which had been left in their care years ago by another foreigner; one who also spoke and read the secret language in the Sacred Book, also left in the care of his own family.

This one had a quick grasp of their own tongue; he led them in their understanding of the one great God; and had helped the tribe tear down the altars and heiaus, forever setting in motion the destruction of the old kapu system. No one need bow down and tremble in fear when royalty, including himself as King, passed through.

How many lives had been taken in vain, simply because the shadow of an innocent had been cast upon one of the ali'i class; or had eaten a banana; or had sat down to feast with the opposite gender? The kapu of the old ways was harsh; too harsh. Life was something sacred, not to be taken away from one because of some simple infraction, meant to do nothing more than reinforce the power of a select few over the many.

Keoua hated the old ways, even though he had been born into that select class. There was simply no desire in his heart to exercise ruthless control over his subjects. Since he was a young boy, he had always had a desire to see his people happy, fulfilled, and free of tyranny – and if that meant his own power was in some way diminished, then so be it! The islands were to be united, yes they were. And it would be the religion of the one God that united the peoples of the islands, not the horrific bloodshed of a warring despot. Yes, this one his daughter called Jonah was the fulfillment of the prophecy of Kapihe – he had to be! How else could these turn of events be explained? The only missing piece was Kamehameha. His negative influence had to be abated and it would take war to do that.

Reluctantly, Keoua had resigned himself to this fact. But he would not attack his troubled cousin; let the Lonely One come to him, if he must. Jonah would lead his army in defense of his villages and then push the unremitting invader back to Kohala. The One God would fight for their side, no doubt. And righteousness would reign over the islands. If Kamehameha himself would only accept the prophecy of Kapihe, he also would see that the end had come for the ancient ways and he, too, could follow the One God. Not Ku, nor Lono, nor Pele, but the god of the sacred book…and peace would be the food of the people. How Keoua yearned for a lasting peace, to live without the constant threat of war!

"Kamehameha's soldiers! Over the ridge!" yelled the watchman from his outpost, high above the sloping cliffs which rounded the bay of Hilo. Jonah marshaled a first line of defense, calling out for the first five hundred pikemen to arm themselves.

"My King," proffered Jonah Pessoa, in the Hawaiian tongue, "let me take the first line. I can hold it against their soldiers, of this I am certain."

King Keoua nodded silently, confident in his young charge.

"Take the gun," the King offered, calling for the prize possession to come forth from his own private store. Although Jonah was the only one who could actually shoot the weapon, its care and custody always reverted back to the King. No one but he held the musket, the Sacred Book, and the other accouterments which had been left so long ago, by another unnamed stranger. One whom Jonah recalled had been responsible for the family line which Manu hailed from.

Strange that, after so long a time, Jonah had just now recalled the story Manu had told him aboard the *Fair American*; the story of a predecessor to this side of the island, a man who had brought a British musket, a copy of the Scriptures, and a possibles bag, complete with ball and black powder. Jonah would need to follow up with Lilena on those details, some day.

"Form a pike phalanx along that ridge, in the shape of the half-moon," ordered Keoua. "Offer peace and let them know we do not wish to fight. But we will defend our territories," instructed the King.

Jonah nodded in silent affirmation. He trusted the black powder musket and its ability to inspire dread among the native Hawaiians. He was confident that one blast, and one alone, would send the vanguard of Kamehameha's invading army scurrying for cover. There need not be massive bloodshed. He loaded the .69 caliber musket with great deliberation, gently tamping down over 120 grains of black powder into the wide barrel, even now beginning to show the tell-tale signs of rust, despite his best efforts to keep it clean. He carefully drew the flint-jawed hammer back to half-cock, an audible click signaling its resting place among the intricate gears and springs of a finely crafted lock, no doubt forged in the delicate hands of a Spanish or British gunsmith many years ago.

"Do not go," pleaded Lilena.

The fear in her soulful eyes sent a shiver down Jonah's spine. Her look carried within it a sense of loss that spanned eons of time. He recalled her desperate story, that first night they had made love…and it shook him to the very core of his being. She had never mentioned it again, and their lives together had since took on the normalcy of any young couple, ignited with the heat of passion and youth. But the conviction with which she had told it remained with him, a gnawing sense of some awful truth which ate at his soul whenever they made love.

"I'm not afraid to fight," replied Jonah, cognizant of his skills, honed long ago under the tutelage of Brother Chin in the bowels of the Faial monastery.

"I cannot afford to lose you, my beloved," she whimpered, her left hand involuntarily drawn to the growing swell that was her belly.

Jonah smiled and put forth his hand, gently rubbing the taut skin which surrounded her unborn child, his child…memories of his own father flooded his consciousness. No doubt this child would be a singer as well and he was determined to teach it to sing the mournful lament of Portuguese fados…when the time was right.

"Nothing will happen to me," replied Jonah, the uncertainty in his voice only serving to reinforce her trepidation. Despite his bravado, Jonah, too, sensed something deep inside, an impending dread that he worked hard to suppress. Mental preparation was just one of the many skills he had learned from the art of Boddhidharma…it would be fatal for him to go forth into battle, not confident that he could win.

He shook the sentiment from his heart and steeled his will against what was to come. He had killed

Anton Soto with nothing more than his hands and feet, he had killed more than one marauding pirate on the deck of the *Fair American* with both steel and gun and he had killed both of Soto's sons. He had survived the volcanic eruption at Horta, and drowning at sea…no, he had not come this far, only to die at the hands of the local Hawaiians in a petty struggle over land and religious beliefs – his destiny contained something greater than that – it had to!

"I won't go without you, *this time*," she stated, matter-of-factly.

Jonah stepped forward and embraced her as their lips met, losing himself in the warmth of her arms, the smell of her hair surrounding his face, the heat of her breath upon him, in him…entwined with a distressing thought, a thought that heralded loudly in his subconscious – the thought that this would be the last time he ever kissed his beloved Lilena.

She broke off their embrace suddenly and walked away, leaving him perplexed and confused. She was strange in that way, as if she lived in two worlds at once, constantly juggling the moment with some surreal other, a bizarre parallel stream of consciousness, or knowledge, or understanding of some kind. Or was it just that she lived in her own world, apart from everyone and everything else around her? Jonah knew then and there that he could not, would not, ever truly understand this striking, otherworldly girl; but God, how he loved her!

He shouldered the musket and walked out to join the hundreds of pikemen, even now milling about, waiting patiently for his presence to lead them as they climbed the gently sloping hills to face the Army of Kohala.

Chapter Twenty Nine

A mournful sea-breeze howled from off the warm waters of Hilo bay, its eerie pitch alternately rising and falling, adding to the surreal landscape. A cloudless sky set the backdrop for the morning sun which shone brightly, illuminating the lush green slopes in an angry amber hue, as if anticipating the bloodshed that was to come. The morning dew had already evaporated by the time Jonah and five hundred warriors had amassed in the low grass of the first rise, grouping themselves in a large semi-circle, successive rows of warriors holding their 12 foot long wooden spears, capped with sharpened stone points, at the vertical. Hundreds more Koa warriors, those equipped with shortened spears, shark toothed clubs, strangulation cords, trip weapons, throwing axes, and koa-wood daggers, remained in reserve.

Jonah surveyed the mass of Kamehameha's warriors opposite them, occupying the high ground of the small ridge opposite. The fearsome front line was outfitted with gourd helmets, each one a terrifying mask. The bright feathers which extruded from the tops of their helmets only added to the chilling effect. Large dual eye holes were carved into the gourds and woven reeds draped from their mouthpieces, providing protection for both chin and neck. It was a practical battle accoutrement as well as a frightening aesthetic.

He could only guess at their numbers but it appeared that thousands upon thousands of koa warriors stood in formation, successive regiments of soldiers in wide flanking positions, at least twice as long as his phalanx. They numbered more than the eye could see and a flash of panic ran through him. How could they possibly defeat an army this large? And from where had all those soldiers come from? It was not possible that this many men had amassed from the west side of the island alone…had Kamehameha convinced the armies of Maui to join him against Keoua?

The only separation between the opposing divisions was a shallow depression between the two hills, cloaked in short grass, the occasional boulder of lava jutting forth from the ground, here and there, pock marking the terrain.

The young Portuguese outcast strode forth alone, as he had been taught was the local custom, to make a solo challenge. Once they saw a demonstration of the force of firepower within his hands, they would certainly retreat, would they not?

All remained still as Jonah paced forward, steeping up onto one of the high boulders between the two factions, elevating himself. What he saw shocked him even further; rows upon rows of armed soldiers remained massed in reserve, thousands and thousands of warriors. The sheer size of Kamehameha's army was more than Jonah could have imagined. There had to be a least five-thousand fighting men, if not more, lined up. A deep-seated resignation fell upon him and Jonah battled to stay focused…numbers alone were never the sole key to armed conflict and Jonah re-assured himself that he could champion Keoua's army to victory; after all, he had the musket, did he not?

Not a word was spoken as Jonah shouldered then leveled the British musket into the open sky, yards above the heads of the opposing vanguard but pointed in their direction. He wanted a show of force, not to actually kill anyone. With a single pull of the trigger, a fiery roar belched forth from the barrel, a large cloud of yellow-sulfurous smoke filling the air. The deafening sound echoed across the hills and Jonah was sure the vanguard opposite his would turn and flee in terror at the sight and sound of the advanced weaponry he alone possessed. Pausing for the smoke to clear, Jonah reloaded the musket, dropping his head as he re-filled the barrel with powder and rammed home another lead ball from the pouch at his side. Lifting his head again, Jonah was surprised to see that no one from among the front line of the army of Kohala had so much as flinched.

Curious, Jonah squinted against the sun as a small commotion erupted - bodies shuffled at the apex of the opposing line. Four, maybe five, soldiers emerged ahead of the troop and knelt to one knee, appearing as if to point their spear tips forward.

Without warning, small puffs of yellow-white smoke collectively erupted from that line; a lead bullet whizzed past Jonah's head, close enough that his right ear actually felt the compression of the air as it passed, followed a split-second later by the sound of the gun's retort, the stiff breeze off the bay carrying the noise away from its point of origin.

Oh God, they've got muskets! whispered Jonah silently, dropping off his stone pedestal, instinctively ducking down. Thirty yards behind him, two of his pikemen tumbled backwards, writhing in blood as the hot lead rounds tore through flesh. *How? And where did they get muskets?*

The air above him filled with the sound of whistling. The bright morning sky actually darkened as Kamehameha's army launched a massive missile attack. Thousands of slingers and javelins rained down upon Keoua's troop with a devastating effect. Stones and spears found their mark, felling dozens; the bodies twisted and contorted as they fell bleeding.

Jonah retreated to his line as war yells erupted on both sides and the two armies, without orders, rushed towards one another. Mass confusion reigned as the melee battle began. Men stabbed, clubbed, and beat one another, face to face. The lines of demarcation became intangible, each man struggling with the opponent nearest him. Jonah managed to pull off a single shot, killing a feather-clad soldier before his musket was rendered of no more use than a club.

"Take it," he ordered a young Hawaiian soldier near him, handing the black powder weapon over. "I don't intend to lose it to them; take it back to the King; and tell him to send out every man he has."

The young warrior grasped the weapon as if it were a holy object and immediately turned, running down the slopes toward Hilo.

Jonah turned just in time to avoid the slash of a shark-toothed club. He bent at the waist, flipping his opponent over his back. He turned and threw his arm around his attacker's neck, twisting hard until he heard the tell-tale snap of breaking bone. He could actually smell the foul breath of the man whose face lay pressed against his own arm and face, the crazed eyes looking up into his own, pupil to pupil. Reaching down, Jonah retrieved the shark-toothed club and re-joined the fray, ducking, turning, and slashing as he went forward.

The groans and shouts of wounded and dying men filled the air. Blood and bile covered Jonah from head to toe. Had he killed ten men, twenty men? Dead bodies piled up and the crimson slickened grass soon became a slippery stage of the macabre. His forces were being slowly outflanked and pressed backwards. Where were those reinforcements he had ordered?

Amid the confusion and horror of death up close and personal, Jonah found himself stilled by something strange. Faint booming sounds wafted up the hill from behind him; periodic rumbles of a kind that his experienced sailor's ear knew all too well. But how could that be?

He turned back towards the bay, frozen in horror at the site. Double-hulled war canoes were plying their way up and onto the beaches of Hilo. Puffs of smoke periodically exploded from the bow of one in particular; the delay between the discharge of the cannon and the sound reaching his ears a common phenomenon of the wind.

Not only were Kamehameha's canoes attacking from shore, one actually had a swivel cannon mounted on the bow, not unlike that which he had seen and used aboard the *Fair American.*

A classic pincers move had put the army of Keoua in a weak position. No wonder the requested reinforcements had not materialized. Half of Keoua's army was locked in a life and death struggle with an invading force from the ocean while the other half was rapidly losing to Kamehameha's ground force on the hills above the bay. The military stratagem of Kamehameha was second to none; and, somehow, he had managed to obtain both muskets and a swivel cannon, adding to his advantage.

Oh God, how could it have gone so wrong, so fast? cried Jonah.

"The King has requested you return to Hilo immediately," panted the breathless courier. Jonah balked. He had no intention of leaving his men fighting while he deserted them. "You must go at once; the King has ordered it so. The men will retreat as well."

Jonah surveyed the scene of bloody carnage. His men were fighting backwards, retreating with every step. His forces had taken their toll on the army of Kohala, in turn. But the body count was in favor of Kamehameha by a ratio of more than two to one; and Hilo was under attack from the sea as well.

"Sound the alarm," ordered Jonah. The designated tone of retreat was blown from a myriad of conch shells at the rear of the phalanx and Keoua's army turned, fleeing down the slopes towards Hilo. Oddly, Kamehameha's men did not give chase.

Chapter Thirty

"You must leave at once."

"My King," replied Jonah, bloodied and exhausted, "I cannot forsake the battle."

"This is something you cannot understand. It is not for you to understand. It is for you to do," answered Keoua.

"But the village! The village must be kept..." said Jonah.

King Keoua interrupted before the young Portuguese fighter could finish.

"Nothing is more important than my daughter and the child; her child - your child. You must take her to the City of Refuge. If you can reach it, before they catch you, you shall all be safe. Even Kamehameha honors the City of Refuge and no harm shall come. A contingent of my soldiers and their families shall accompany you, on this journey. Flee to the south, to the land of Puna and Kau. No matter what happens here this day, a remnant of my kingdom shall remain untouched. I shall stay and fight – this battle is not yet over. My men may yet prevail. But you must lead this contingent away to the City of Refuge. Do not hesitate and do not falter. If your allegiance to me, and to the God whom you have taught us about, whom you call Father, is true, then you shall all make it. May the one true God keep you safe and protect you on this journey. Flee at once."

Reluctantly, Jonah marshaled the women and children into formation, surrounded on all sides by a regiment of 100 warriors. Everything within him shouted out to stay and join the brutal fighting on the shores of the Hilo bay, the screams and cries of which still rang out across the mid-day air. But, Lilena and her father had convinced him, against his wishes, to lead a remnant population out across the barren lava deserts of Puna and Kau towards asylum in this City of Refuge. To what ultimate end, he was still unsure…but it was that which he had promised to her father; it was a promise he would keep.

The beleaguered throng slowly made their way south, away from the village of Hilo and the fighting that remained. Jonah turned his head every so often, looking back at the sounds of the warfare as it ebbed and flowed, sometimes confident Keoua's army had actually gained the upper hand; sometimes despondent they had not, never sure exactly how the fighting would truly end. Could a truce be reached? Was Kamehameha intent on the utter destruction of every man, or could a cessation of hostilities yet be arranged? Did he have to rule everything? Could not the man leave something to others? What strange force propelled him, what unrequited need or rage forced him forward in a never-ending craving to conquer all?

Every look back was greeted by the forlorn smile of his beloved, her bow-legged waddle an accommodation to the child within her, nearer to delivery with each day. She managed a weak grin but Jonah was not fooled. She hated leaving her father behind; only the knowledge that she would be with Jonah convinced her to leave, as well. The girl, or woman, really, was no coward. She, too, would have fought with club or spear, had she been given the chance.

The exhausted multitude of refugees slowly climbed over 3,000 feet above the bay of Hilo before making camp that evening on the rocky lava flats to the south. Jonah gazed down at the far-away twinkling of firelights in the Hilo village, unsure of whether or not this signaled victory or defeat for Keoua and so many of the people he had come to care about so deeply these past months, people he called his own.

He crouched beside their campfire, somberly eating the jerked pork, sipping water from the gourd in between bites.

"I don't understand where we are going," he complained to Lilena.

"The City of Refuge is ancient," she answered. "No one really knows its origin. It has simply always been this way. When one is being pursued, either in war or because of some wrong done against the family of another, if one can reach the City of Refuge, one is safe from all retribution. Outside its gates, if caught, all is punishable but inside, no harm is done. To breach the walls of the City of Refuge is forbidden and one who does so, in pursuit of another or to exact some revenge, is immediately put to death. Not even kings are above this kapu."

"And, when we get there?" replied Jonah.

"Then we are safe. We can plan what happens next after that but first, we must get there," she whispered, slowly bending over with a grimace on her face.

"Is it coming now?" he cried, leaping up from his crouched stance.

"No," she answered, catching her breath. "It is…just the beginning. We have plenty of time, my love."

Her resolute self-assurance calmed him in a mysterious way, as no other ever could. It was an assurance borne either of deep conviction or experience, which one he was not sure…but, then again, she had never given birth before, so how could she know?

He looked up from the flame again to see her grinning at him…and he was filled with confidence once again. She had a way of doing that for him.

The morning dawned, a sulfurous stench filling the air. The odor was one not unfamiliar to those who frequented the lava flats near the Kilauea crater but this morning it was much stronger than ever before.

"Pele is angry today," offered one of the old women. "She does not want us here."

"That is nonsense," answered another. "There is no Pele. Have you learned nothing, all these months the white man has been among us? Have you understood nothing which he has read to us from the secret book? There is only the one true Father God, the maker of the heavens and the earth…and no others," she replied angrily.

The elder woman cast her head down in shame, muttering to herself dejectedly. But her words had scattered throughout the camp nonetheless. And her belief in the old ways was not universally dismissed. There were others who muttered under their breath as well. The absence of King Keoua emboldened some and not everyone shared the King's absolute faith in the strange white man, regardless of his knowledge, his languages, and his abilities.

Jonah, for his part, shared in her fear. He, too, knew that smell, knew it all too well. But it was not a fear of the spiritual that led to his anxiety but a fear of that which was completely natural, a work or force of nature.

"Steer away from the crater," he ordered the soldiers.

"There is no other path to the City of Refuge," cried Lilena. "We need to move quickly…or we shall not make it," she replied, looking back over her shoulder towards the Hilo bay.

Jonah followed her gaze to the north, down the long but gentle slope towards their home village. Far away, almost imperceptible to the naked eye, was a moving chain of humanity.

"What is it?" queried one of the soldiers.

"People," answered Jonah, without further explanation.

"Others from the village? They come to retrieve us? Keoua has secured peace or has triumphed," shouted one of the young boys, exhausted and tired from the forcible march away from all that he had ever known.

"Can you tell?" asked another of the warriors.

Jonah squinted, peeling apart the distant landscape with his eyes, looking for the tiniest hint of confirmation that these were not Kamehameha's warriors, on the trail of the refugee troop from Hilo, headed toward the City of Refuge. Jonah understood what it meant, if they were from the army of Kohala. It meant that Hilo had been conquered, Keoua killed, and that the "Killer of Kings" was fanatically pursuing this last remnant, in order to capture Lilena, the sole remaining royal of Keoua's blood-line.

If Maui had indeed been subjugated, or joined in league with Kamehameha, as Jonah suspected from the size of his fighting force, then Keoua's royal line remained the last barrier to Kamehameha's claim over all the islands…as this possibility dawned upon him, Lilena shook him from his reflection.

She gripped him on both sides of his face, forcing him to look her directly in the eyes.

"It is time to go, Jonah. We must leave now." Absent King Keoua, Lilena was, in fact, the only remaining royal and her words, and her wishes, carried great weight with the people.

"We leave at once," cried Jonah." But veer away from the crater. We shall cut across the flats," he said, pointing to the east. Nothing but jagged lava, broken tables of volcanic rock punctuated by fissures deep enough to swallow a man, lay before them.

"I cannot," cried Lilena in desperation. "I'll never make it across that; and that way is not known by my people. The path to the City of Refuge is due south, along the rim of the crater. They'll catch us if we go east; too slow and too many obstacles. Our only hope is to follow the rim trail and do so quickly," she responded, the calmness in her voice from the night before conspicuously absent.

He had never seen her scared before, since the moment she had rescued him from the sea, he had not so much as seen a glimmer of fear in her eyes; ever. But this was different; she was genuinely afraid…and this alone scared Jonah as well.

"I know you're afraid," she said. Without admitting it, Jonah could see the fear in her eyes as well – but there remained resoluteness in her, a determination to go forward in spite of the fear. This was true courage, a thing he had always prided himself with – but her inner reservoir was deeper than his own, deeper than any man's. She was, in truth, the most courageous person he had ever known.

"We cannot linger and we cannot cross the flats. We follow the crater rim trail," she stated, almost as if she were giving the orders for the group and not Jonah. He hesitated for only a second before the men, women, and children around them gathered their meager rations on their backs and proceeded…to the south.

It was evening before the weary team stopped for a break, dining on dried fish and pork from their victuals. Spread out across the rim of the crater, the ragged expedition was relaxed, men and their families reclined, some taking a much needed rest while others milled about, busying themselves with mending clothing or their woven baskets.

Jonah's fears were allayed by now; her strength had flowed into him, making him stronger, a stronger man than he would ever be without her. His thoughts soared briefly to their future. It was a future he could not imagine, without her in it. His twisted and grief-stricken young life had all been just a prelude; a prelude to this. She was his destiny; her and their child.

Everything, everything he had come through, the loss of father and mother, the abandonment to the monastery, the long nights spent alone with no one to turn to, the skills he had acquired, the fighting, the languages, and, yes, the theology, all of it without recognizing its ultimate usefulness, it had all prepared him for this time. He would use them now, to build a new society - with her. He could, he would, teach them all the ways of that which he knew. Their lives together would be a beacon for others, raising their child with knowledge of the ancient Hawaiian ways and knowledge of the one Christian God. Respect and acknowledgement for both. And yet, he remained conflicted; too much sorrow had been dealt him in this life. He simultaneously blamed God for it all; still so angry – yet he sensed the need to respect that one supreme Deity as well. But he had also come to respect the local Hawaiian deities too, convinced by a number of observations during his brief time among them that prayers and sacrifices offered to Pele, and Lono, among others, appeared to have some effect upon the material world. Were they not also spiritual beings, who could and would respond, when honored? Could not one believe in both? The two were not mutually exclusive.

Suddenly, in an instant of epiphany, it came to him. So much of what the Hawaiians believed, had believed for thousands of years, was already found in the biblical Scriptures. Their creation story was not a radical departure from the story found in Genesis; in fact, it was eerily similar.

Jonah was not convinced he truly believed either one but the likeness was striking, too striking to be coincidence. And there was more; the strange rite of male circumcision, springing from the Hebrew and Christian faiths, was routinely practiced by the Hawaiians – how was this possible? In all his travels, across both oceans and their many ports of call, no culture, not already exposed to these faiths, practiced circumcision. How had it come to be the norm among the Hawaiians?

And a City of Refuge? Where, other than the text found in the Torah, did such a novel idea spring from? Was it really possible these things could have arisen independently, or was there some grander scheme at work, some larger, universal force coalescing time, people, and place, for a distinct purpose? And what was Jonah's role in this master design?

There was no need to fight and die on behalf of one way or the other, nor in defense of one God as opposed to another. Too much blood had been shed under the foolishness of just such a premise. But, if they had to fight to survive, he could do that too. The British musket remained at his side, an ample supply of both powder and shot; he was skilled in hand-to-hand fighting, and his studies in the monastery had prepared him with a substantial body of knowledge…knowledge one needed, in order to lead.

Although much closer to the caldera than he would have wished, the overpowering sulfurous stench from the day before had all but dissipated. Whatever fears he had, recalling the volcanic explosion on Faial, which had taken the life of his mother and almost succeeded in killing him, as well, were gone. Jonah lay down on the hard ground, his eyes heavy with slumber and exhaustion; Lilena curled up into him, both of them falling asleep within moments. The entire troop took their cue from the royal couple and laid down to rest under the darkening of an evening sky, alight with the stars of heaven. It was the most peaceful sleep Jonah had known in years…and it was to be his last.

Chapter Thirty One

It was still dark. The rising sun had yet to crest over the eastern horizon when the earth began to tremble violently beneath them. A single deafening thunderclap split the air, its volume louder than any human ear could bear, instantly awakening over a hundred sleeping voyagers. Children screamed, wide awake now, as blistering sand, ash, and huge stones gorged forth from the Kilauea crater, encircling a solitary column of rising fire which spewed forth violently, straight up into the heavens. A hundred and more asylum seekers roused fitfully from their slumber, shrieks of terror piercing the dawn.

"Pele! Pele! It is the revenge of Pele!" screamed more than one among them. Jonah and Lilena scrambled to their feet…and promptly fell again as the shifting ground beneath them rocked sadistically, as if to thwart their very efforts at escape.

"Run! Run!" shouted Jonah, grasping Lilena around the waist. Mass confusion reigned as men, women, and children scattered in every direction, tripping again and again as the earth beneath their feet waved and rocked, their yells for one another, and cries of mercy from the goddess Pele, piercing the morning sky.

No, shouted Jonah to himself, *this cannot be! Not again. Please, God, not again!*

The emerging glow of daybreak was instantly swallowed up by a dense cloud of darkness; a grey-black mass filled the heavens above. At once, both lightning and thunder roared from the midst of that roiling cloud…followed by a hailstorm of hot cinder and sand, showering the rim of the crater for miles around.

Blistering embers, thicker than the black sands of the beaches, blanketed the fleeing fugitives. Cries of fright, terror, and pain were instantly muffled as the suffocating black death enveloped them, whole bodies swallowed up at once.

"Go! Go, damn you," shouted Jonah. Lilena struggled to right herself, slipping and falling four, five times, before she managed to remain upright for more than a second. Two royal guardsmen made their way to her, their charge from the King being her safety and security, above their own lives.

"Take her, and go," screamed Jonah. The thought that he might lose her, after having come this far, was too great to bear. And he would not lose the only love left in his pitiful life to the capricious circumstances of another volcano. This enemy of nature had tried its best to claim his life once before; but it would not happen again! Not to him, nor to his beloved.

Her fingers tried desperately to grasp his as the guardsmen pulled her away. "No, No!" she cried, but to no avail. Their clutch upon one another was broken and, in an instant, she was gone, hustled away under the choking cloud of gas which surrounded them all.

The scorching heat was intense. Jonah felt the skin on his arms and face beginning to blister. Breathing was impossible; he choked, coughed, and spit in an effort to regain a precious breath.

Quickly scanning the ground, Jonah reached down and picked up the possibles bag and the musket, grabbing it by the barrel. Instantly, he dropped the firearm, its blistering steel barrel too hot to hold. A bright red welt formed immediately in the palm of his hand. He knelt again, hoisting the musket by its wooden butt stock and cradling it over his right shoulder. The intense heat of the wood burned against his flesh; gritting his teeth, Jonah bore the pain and scurried on, bowing low and dodging red-hot projectiles which continued to pelt the ground all around him.

He cleared the outer perimeter of the dark cloud, stumbling forth into clear air just as his lungs were on the verge of collapse. Sucking in a single enormous breath of precious oxygen, he collapsed…righting himself on hands and knees, he glanced back over his shoulder, the ghastly scene too horrific to contemplate. His head swam as he struggled to keep his balance but the darkness of unconsciousness overtook him…and he fell, face forward.

Chapter Thirty Two

Hands slapped at his face, again and again. In that bizarre twilight, between awake and unconscious, Jonah heard vague sounds, repeating itself again and again. Within seconds, the sounds became clearer…

"Jonah, wake up! Please, Jonah, wake up!"

His vision cleared and the sounds slowly became recognizable; his name, again and again, being called. The repetitious smacking on his face aroused him, and he slowly sat up. Lilena, her two royal guardsmen, and a withered old woman, a thick mane of frizzy white hair cascading down her back, appeared crouched in front of him. *Funny*, Jonah thought, *I don't remember that white-haired old woman among our company.*

"Jonah, please…get up! They are coming. Please, get up!" she cried.

Jonah stood, uneasy on his feet. The two royal guardians helped him, each one on either side, hoisting him by the arms.

Still confused, Jonah wheeled about, unclear as to the how and why of his present circumstance. Why was he lying on the ground, unconscious? What had happened?

Glancing back over the macabre scene, the horror of it all came flooding back. The volcano, the eruption, and the death…death everywhere he looked. A thick layer of grey-black soot lay over everything, wispy steam still curling up from pockets here and there.

Rounded mounds protruded from the ashen blanket, softly formed outlines of human forms; just the crowns of blackened skulls, in some cases. Dotted throughout the obscene landscape were whole bodies, frozen in effigy. Some sat upright, statuesque forms of adults and children huddled together, their last act in life an embrace of familial affection. Others actually remained standing, caught in mid-stride, their eyes nothing more than sunken hollows, mouths gaped open in grotesque terror, a trail of final footprints preserved in the steaming rock immediately behind them.

Jonah could not contain himself. He wept openly. Bitter emotions, coupled with horrific memories, overcame him. How could God let something like this happen? Again?

He turned to face Lilena.

"Pele?" he questioned, his voice cracking with fear. She shook her head back and forth, responding in the negative.

"Then…why? Why only us five, and no more? Why did all of them have to die, but not us?"

Lilena did not respond. Her stoic demeanor, in the face of such devastation, confused… then enraged him. For the first time in their brief togetherness, he was…angry at her.

He opened his mouth but was silenced once again by the softness of her fingers against his lips. "We have to leave now, Jonah. They are close, very close. You must come with me," she said. "Do not falter this time."

Jonah turned at the bellow of the conch shells blowing in the distance. He knew that sequence of sounds. It was the rallying cry of an army, an army in hot pursuit of its foe. It had to be Kamehameha's men, coming for them.

Without another word, he collected his musket, his possibles bag, and limped off towards the ohia forest, the five of them headed south to the City of Refuge. Jonah dared not look back – and neither did any of his fellow comrades.

Chapter Thirty Three

The Birthing Cave at Kau

Jonah fired first, his aim lethal. The flame-seared musket operated flawlessly. The feather-caped Hawaiian chieftain was already dead by the time Isaac Davis returned fire a split-second later, placing a round lead ball just to the left of Jonah's heart. The confusion of near-simultaneous shots, belching flame and smoke, clouded his vision. Jonah's body spun violently backwards with the impact, the hot lead ball tearing through his chest. He collapsed, eyes cast sideways - fixed upon Lilena.

A hailstorm of short spears filled the darkened grotto; the two royal guardians dutifully filled their sacred obligation, each taking multiple spikes to the chest as they buckled to the ground in front of her.

Jonah, still barely alive, watched in horror as Kamehameha's soldiers slowly advanced toward her. She stood perfectly still as they came, unflinching, even as the sharpened spear point was tenuously placed at her neck, wavering and trembling in the hand of her assassin. Slowly, with great deliberation, she reached forth both of her hands, placing them around the thick koa-wood shaft – and promptly shoved the spear point into her own throat.

"Aieee!" yelped the battle-seasoned warrior holding the spear. He stumbled backwards in fear, withdrawing the bloody spear point from her. Lilena stood for a second before her legs began to buckle. Collapsing, she deliberately turned her body so that she fell directly upon the slain torso of Jonah Pessoa.

Her trembling fingers struggled to seek out his face, tracing the features of his forehead, his nose, his eyes, and his lips.

"Aloha Aku No. Aloha Mai No," she rasped out, with the last vestige of life within her…then three words more…"my beloved Collum" – and then she was gone.

Chapter Thirty Four

Jonah awoke, blazing pain radiating throughout his body. He breathed laboriously, his lungs working desperately to bring in oxygen − all but impossible. Was he yet alive? He inhaled short, ragged breaths, just enough to keep him conscious – it was all he could manage. He flexed his arms, only to be held back by some unseen force. Slowly turning his head left and right, Jonah noted his hands were tied on either side. All was open sky above him; in fact, that was all that he could see – the open sky.

He arched his back, screaming out in pain. His bones had been broken in multiple places and a crimson oozing puss formed on his chest, just to the left of his heart. He could not move. Nothing worked; neither his arms, nor his legs, nor his mid-section responded to his will. Slowly, piece by piece, cognizance of where he was came to him.

Jonah was tied, flat on his back, completely immobilized…and naked. Looking down, Jonah spied the edges of rough cut brush, the myriad branches piercing into his back, the underside of his legs, and his neck. His fingers frantically scrambled for some tactile response, some feedback, anything. But all he could feel, below the sticks underlying the entirety of his body, was rough-hewn stone.

So this is how it truly ends? he wondered. *Tied to an altar, a sacrificial offering? God, why didn't I just die in the cave, with her?*

Multiple faces surrounded him from above, looking down upon him; the faces of Hawaiian kahunas, soldiers, and others.

"He is yet alive," muttered one, his voice incredulous. "This is good - call for the King…and Isaac Davis," responded another.

Jonah wriggled violently but the excruciating pain of his wounds was too great for any more effort on his part. Resigning himself to his fate, he relaxed, collapsing back upon the bed of fire stock underneath him, staring directly up into the blue sky. Rhythmic chanting began in the distance, a constant beat of drums and low voices.

A broad face appeared above him, completely unadorned. A simple face, really, not unlike the faces of hundreds of Hawaiian men he had come to know, some of which he had loved as brothers; others, he had killed, as enemies.

This face, wide across the forehead, was crested by a thick mane of black curly hair, shiny but cropped short. Wide eyebrows outlined a set of dark eyes which turned ever so slightly downward at their corners. An eloquent nose with broadly flared nostrils framed a smaller mouth, thick-lipped, curved about with a round chin. He was yet a young man, certainly older than himself, but not by that many years. Jonah knew, without a doubt, who this man was.

"I know you understand our language," stated the man. Jonah did not respond but his eyes betrayed him; a brief glimmer of recognition in those eyes was all Kamehameha needed.

"You have caused me a lot of grief. Lilena was to be mine and mine alone. Now, she is dead. And you will soon join her. My god, Ku, has delivered you into my hands."

Even as Kamehameha spoke, Jonah could smell the scent of burning fire, the pilot torches even now being brought up to the altar of stone.

"The prophecy of Kapihe is fulfilled. I have united all the islands. Every chief who opposed me has fallen, including those of your color and language. There are none left to challenge me. I have your foreign weapons in my arsenal, and my own white man to teach their use to my soldiers. My progeny, and mine alone, shall reign over these islands forever."

"You are mistaken, O' King," sighed Jonah, speaking in the Hawaiian tongue. He addressed the native monarch by a royal title, in spite of the fact that Kamehameha was setting Jonah ablaze, as a sacrifice to the war god Ku, even as he spoke.

Kamehameha's eyes burned in amazement.

"The heiaus are not torn down, nor the altars and images overthrown. You cannot be the fulfillment of this. There is yet a time to come, when all these things shall be fulfilled – but that time is not now. You seek to serve one god, while opposing another. But this is not the fullness of that which was spoken by Kapihe," answered Jonah.

The crackling of a bonfire beneath him had begun; Jonah felt the intense heat rising up from underneath him. The scent of his own flesh beginning to burn sickened him. His time was short, very short.

"You have shed too much blood. Your progeny shall not reign for long. Others will surely come and dispossess them of all this land until…that time comes."

Kamehameha remained silent, transfixed by the words of this dying white man. If nothing else, his courage and his conviction, in the face of death mesmerized the King; he could not resist listening.

"There is no war between the gods, O' King," continued Jonah, his throat already parched from the extreme heat enveloping his neck. Jonah felt the flesh of his scalp crinkle up tightly as the flames licked around his head; a nauseating sizzle echoed in his ears. He choked on his own bile as it rose up in his throat; every last ounce of his being was given over to forming the words, the words Jonah knew would be the last words ever uttered by him - at least in this life.

"The gods...do not make war… against each other; that is our doing."

He swallowed hard, the mucus in his throat turning glue-like, clogging his vocal chords. The pitch of Jonah's voice changed, becoming a throaty rasp, punctuated by periodic gasps.

"They do not strive to conquer…or overtake one another… It is we…who do that, on their behalf…falsely claiming their names…and their purposes…in support of our own…selfish conquests. But…this too shall end. All come…from One and to One…all shall return…In that time …all, and each, …shall have their place…and be honored. Then...and only then…shall lasting peace…come to these islands…Another shall reign, on that day…and that other…shall never come from you."

Jonah's head turned weakly to one side, his eyes catching a final view of this life, the sight of Isaac Davis standing in the shadows, dread and guilt flooding his visage.

Jonah Pessoa, Portuguese, Orphan, Jesuit Monk, Shaolin-trained fighter, Linguist, Sailor, Lover, and Father, died…engulfed in the flames of a sacrificial rite.

Kamehameha's anger exploded. Though the incinerated body in front of him was already dead, the King swung his stone-headed war club in a frenzy, again and again, smashing the blackened bones upon the altar into fragments. Ten, twenty, thirty strokes, and more, until the hot remains crumbled, spilling off the sides of the stone platform, surrounding his feet in a pile of heated human rubble.

Breathing heavily from the exhaustion, a gasping King stood back. The entourage surrounding him paced backwards as well, providing a wide swath of open space behind the enraged Monarch. Even the chanters and the drums had ceased.

"Isaac Davis!"

"Yes, my King," answered the frightened first mate, stepping forward from the shadows, timidly.

"It is over. Is it not?"

"Yes, my King. It is over."

"There is not, nor shall there be, any other lineage to rule over my islands?"

"It is as you say, my King."

"For as long as time shall stand?"

"Yes, my King, for as long as time shall stand."

The mighty King Kamehameha stared into Isaac Davis's eyes - and held them there. His fanatical gaze bore a hole through the very core of Isaac Davis's being, probing, somehow, searching for some crack, some glimmer of doubt.

Isaac Davis trembled, sure that the King would see it there, see the fear which Jonah Pessoa's last words, almost prophetic-like, had planted there. A fear that he dare not give voice to, a fear that the near future would, indeed, see the islands lost, lost to strangers from afar - but resurrected again someday, united under the single rule of a Hawaiian sovereign…a sovereign that would *not* be of Kamehameha's lineage. He shuddered, holding his breath, while the King continued to stare into his soul.

Then, suddenly, the King turned and walked away. It was over. Finally.

Thirty miles to the south of Hilo, just off the Kalapana coast, a moonlit night kept watch as a single canoe, slowly, ever so silently, paddled across the tranquil waters towards the island of Niihau. Its only occupants – a grizzled old woman, crowned by a frizzy mane of long white hair…and, laying in the hold, wrapped beneath her feet…a newborn infant.

Chapter Thirty Five

November 2016 – Honolulu, Island of Oahu

Gleeful throngs, numbering in the thousands, packed the courtyard fronting Iolani Palace, creating a buzzing mass of humanity. The Honolulu police had blocked off South King Street for three blocks in an effort to protect the joyful crowds. The celebrants danced, kissed one another, and broke out into sporadic applause, awaiting her appearance.

Conch shells blew and puniu drums thumped incessantly. Every square inch of the courtyard perimeter was packed with people, decked out in leis; even the thirty foot palm trees fringing the paved walk and the steps leading up to the Palace had been layered with gorgeous ovals of plumerias, tuberose, carnations, orchids, and pikake.

Enormous cruise ships lay stolidly docked at the Aloha Tower waterfront, awaiting the signal, their deafening steam horns at the ready. Encircling these behemoths lay a swarming mass of yachts, sailboats, fishing boats, canoes, home-made rafts, jet-skis, and children on inner-tubes, splashing about, each one decorated with flowers, leaves, vines, or fern fronds, the pent-up emotions ready to explode.

Today's announcement was already a global sensation before it happened; news and film crews from across the world had set up days in advance, camping out in tents, decked with video, antennas, cameras, microphones, and recorders in a swarming sea of technology.

As if on cue, the morning clouds dissipated, yielding to a golden sun which blazed over the city as they waited, waited with a patience borne since 1893. They needed wait only a few moments more.

Kaila Kuahuula, or simply *Kay*, as her colleagues in the Senate had referred to her, studied the documents one last time. Her reputation as a stickler for details was well deserved.

An eye for the minutest of cross-references, an insistence on literal linguistic interpretation, and a keen intellect, especially when it came to Law, had served her well in life, from the Kamehameha school at Keaau, to the University of Hawaii and, ultimately, to Harvard Law School. Never anything less than a 4.0 grade point average, regardless of the level of study.

Service as a law clerk for a Supreme Court Justice followed by successive terms in the U.S. House of Representatives and the U.S. Senate had not appeared to slow her, nor age her. She still retained that youthful look, despite her forty plus years, and was often mistaken for a woman ten years younger.

A single strand of silver or two was just now beginning to appear in an otherwise lustrous head of jet-black hair, cut short but stylish. Olive-skin, lighter than many of her fellow native Hawaiians, had often led to mocking chants of mixed-blood, a *haole* hiding somewhere in the deep, dark past, they would claim, as she was relentlessly bullied on the playground. But she knew better; her pedigree was beyond challenge, stronger and prove-able beyond that of her jealous childhood tormentors.

Evidence of her lineage, mother to grandmother, to great-grandmother, and so forth, through a succession of native women, was irrefutable. The male partners in each of those historical pairings had been rapidly lost to antiquity, undecipherable after four or five generations and, in the end, becoming irrelevant. But the women; she could trace them all the way back to Noelani, daughter of Lilena, daughter of Keoua, the rightful King of Hawaii.

The secret sect on Niihau, where her family history had been so meticulously preserved and documented, was more than enough to silence most critics. There would always be some who did not believe, who claimed an equal, or even superior lineage; but that was beyond her control. She had brushed them all aside; had done so her entire life. The sands of Hawaii were littered with the shattered careers of political opponents whom she had vanquished.

Kay the Conqueror, pundits had wistfully nick-named her. Let them – she was not sure that she truly disliked that moniker. Among her many attributes was resoluteness, a dogged determination to fulfill whatever destiny life had in store for her – nothing stopped her, not as a child, nor as a student, nor as a Congresswoman or Senator. But this single-mindedness had extracted a price, as well.

There was no man in her life. Not that she was unattractive; quite the opposite. A svelte body, paid for by hours in the gym each week, kept her in excellent shape. High set cheekbones, an aquiline nose, full lips, and almond-shaped dark eyes set her apart from many women.

Exotic, a reporter from the Washington Times had written, when she first arrived in the House of

Representatives, many years ago. *What sexist drivel!* she had said to herself then…now, well…her thoughts were not quite that harsh.

She had her share of suitors throughout her life and she was attracted to men, in return.

Her term in the Senate had proved peculiarly flattering as young men, some much younger than her, deliberately sought out her affections. Power was an aphrodisiac; that was certain – even for the men. But nothing ever seemed to stick. Perhaps that was the way it was meant to be? Perhaps this, today, was her destiny, a destiny which required her full and undivided devotion?

"Kay," queried Yunis, her most faithful staffer, a former Senate Page from her time spent in that illustrious institution, "or should I call you by something else, something more *regal*?"

"Don't be a shit, Yunis," she replied, her voice low and smooth, its tempo reserved yet playful.

"The crowds are getting really, really restless. The CNN guy has been pestering me since before sunrise and the other network staff have been clamoring for a time-specific. What do you want me to tell them? Are you ready, my ____?" he answered, a charming smirk forming on the corner of his mouth at the empty pause in his words.

Kay looked up from her studies; a well-manicured index finger slowly drew the custom Cartier eyeglasses down off the bridge of her nose. She stared at him over the rims.

"I'll tell them you'll be out *soon*," he said, scampering off, his arms filled with documents.

Kay scoured the mountain of legalese in front of her yet one more time. United States Public Law 103-

150 she knew verbatim, had actually memorized every word of it. Effective in November of 1993, passed by a two-thirds voice vote in the House, the Senate voting 65 for, 34 against (God, how she had worked hard for those 65 ayes!), and signed by the President, as a Joint Resolution…the *Apology Resolution*, as it had come to be known.

Among other language found there, it specifically enumerated and acknowledged that the overthrow of the Kingdom of Hawaii occurred with the active participation of agents and citizens of the United States and further acknowledged that the Native Hawaiian people never directly relinquished to the United States their claims to their inherent sovereignty as a people over their national lands, either through the Kingdom of Hawaii or through a plebiscite or referendum.

She leafed through the U.S. Supreme Court decision of March 31st, 2009. It addressed the Apology Resolution's legal effects…for the most part, neutering it, rendering it, for all intents and purposes, impotent.

Then came November of 2008….a new U.S. President was elected – who hailed from Hawaii, the first time in the history of the United States that a U.S. President was elected whose place of birth was… Hawaii!

Implausible, precedent-setting, incredible in its ramifications…but it happened, nonetheless. And Hawaii's interests, beyond a presidential vacation or two, were promptly relegated to the back-burner.

Re-election to a second term brought little hope that anything but the status quo would remain for her beloved homeland. As he finished out his second term, 2016 marking his final year of tenure as the most powerful person in the world, looking more to posterity and legacy than anything else, intense rounds of secret negotiations were begun.

Senator Kay Kuahuula was surprised to find the President's interests in the matter so aligned with that of her native peoples.

A vote in Congress was out of the question. But…the Office of the U.S. Presidency carried with it some unusual caveats, reserved powers, *inherent powers*, as some pundits had named them. And the Executive Order she held in her hands at this very moment spoke volumes about the President's true viewpoint on the issue of *inherent powers*.

Extremely complicated legal arrangements were already done. God, lawyers would be arguing the nuances of this one for the next 50 years! But Kay, a lawyer by profession and the principal architect of the deal, was satisfied it would stand the test of time. She had drafted most of it herself.

Statehood for Hawaii would remain. The military and intelligence interests alone trumped all other concerns. As long as Hawaii remained a State, those national security interests would, and should, continue unabated.

Yet the mainland itself had set the precedent; it was riddled with instances where a formerly sovereign people, conquered and dispossessed of their lands, were restored and granted full sovereignty over some of those lands and the rights to self-governance, *domestic dependent nations*, was the phrase coined by the courts.

The mainland was pockmarked by over 300 Indian reservations, sovereign tribal lands. Many of those tribal groups had successfully expanded their powers, including extending rights and privileges to their members that other U.S. citizens could not access.

Sovereign tribal governments with their own laws, sovereign tribal security forces, sovereign tribal enterprises, profit-making ventures, and so on.

She had worked diligently to form hundreds of executable joint powers agreements with every private sector, public sector, and governmental entity that would be affected; worked and re-worked until the President was satisfied that it would stand the test of time and its legal status would rest under the fierce scrutiny of attackers; and there would be attackers. Hell, pretenders to the throne of Hawaii were popping up on a daily basis now.

She looked up from the stack of legal contracts which buried her and out the 12 foot long east windows of her new office. The Hawaii State Capitol building across the plaza stood stately in the tropical sun, the American and Hawaii State flags standing proudly on 20 foot poles opposite one another, their colors gently flapping in the breeze. Just as it should be, she thought inwardly.

On the other hand, her orders, less than thirty minutes ago, called for the Iolani Palace to draw down its flag and replace it with another. At this very moment, the flag of the historical Royal Coat of Arms of the Kingdom of Hawaii was being hoisted.

Its quartered shield contained red, white and blue stripes representing the original eight inhabited Hawaiian islands as well as two emblems of taboo *(pulo'ulo'u)* on yellow; a central escutcheon depicted crossed spears. The shield was capped by the Crown of Hawaii. Two warriors, decked in ancient Hawaiian war costume, stood on either side. Inscribed below was the state motto: "Ua mau ke ea o ka āina i ka pono" translated as "The life of the land is perpetuated in righteousness."

Kay had always loved that phrase and she had no intentions of abandoning it; both the State of Hawaii and the Kingdom could share that, could they not?

A sudden roar from the crowd outside told Kay that the flag had been raised to its apex. She smiled; an expression, she realized, which had not graced her face in quite some time now.

Chapter Thirty Six

"You know the evangelical Christians are going to have a fit with this one," counseled Yunis, placing the document before her, the brightly colored sticky notes with arrows pointing to the lines which required her signature; multiple lines which seemed to shout *Sign Here*.

"It's not a religious building, Yunis. It's a cultural thing. I'm not having a church built in her honor, for God's sake. It's a historical and cultural center," she shouted, scribbling her name absentmindedly on the various lines and pages.

"That's not the way they're going to see it and you know it. You know they're going to claim you're re-instating the old ways, the ancient ways, building a new heiau to the goddess Pele and…"

"That's rubbish," she replied. "Today marks a brand new chapter in Hawaii's history, Yunis. And I intend for it to be the final chapter, a chapter that ushers in a lasting peace, a peace on behalf of everyone, not just some."

"The land has borne witness to too much strife, too much fighting, too much bloodshed. And I intend for all that strife to end. Hawaii will be one place, even if it's the only place on the face of this earth, where all are free to worship and honor any god they wish to. All, and each, shall have their place and be honored."

"I'll sign off on and lend my support to any Christian Church that wants to build; and the same goes for any Buddhist temple, Hindu temple, Jewish synagogue, or heiau to the ancient Hawaiian gods, for that matter. But if I hear a single note from any one of those groups, seeking to diminish, belittle, destroy, or conquer the sacred sites of the faith of their fellows, so help me God, I'll shut them down, once and for all."

Yunis was prepared to walk out, signed documents in hands; but Kay was on her soapbox and Yunis knew, one did not walk out on Kay until Kay was ready to climb off that soapbox.

"Why can't people learn to let it be, Yunis? Worship need not be a mutually exclusive thing. Those who wish to worship Pele – so be it! Let them worship her. Those who wish to worship Jehovah – so be it; let them worship him. Those who wish to worship Jesus, or Buddha, or Krishna, so be it; let them be worshipped. And those who desire to worship each or all of them… why must they be forced to pick one and forsake the others? Let the people worship whom they wish and let us all live together in harmony. Don't you think that sounds like…truth?"

Without answering, Yunis touched her elbow, signaling that it was time for her to make the entrance.

"Be a dear and bring me that koa bead necklace," she said, straightening her skirt as she stood.

"This cheap old thing?" he replied, flexing the tiny beaded necklace between his fingers, dangling it before her. "You know, Kay, these things are a dime a dozen; cheapest trinket to be found on the streets of Honolulu…"

"Oh my dear Yunis. If you only knew," she replied, bending her neck ever so slightly, signaling him to drape it around her. The history of this centuries-old necklace would remain unspoken; at least for now.

"There you are," he said, standing back to get a better view.

"Well? How do I look?" she asked.

He had to admit it…she was a striking woman, even if she was many years his senior. He had never quite looked at her in that way before, but now; he was a little amused for feeling what he felt…perhaps ashamed, as well, but…at the same time, honestly admitting, forever silently, of course, that he was attracted to this woman.

She read the blush in his cheeks – and allowed him to drown in his own embarrassment for only a moment before she gave him a reprieve.

"Well?" she asked again.

"Fantastic. You look like a _____.

"Don't say it!" she ordered, her index finger pressed against his lips.

The announcer at the microphone tried desperately to hush the crowd with his hands, in anticipation of his momentous announcement. As soon as the crowd noise had dimmed to an adequate level, which felt as if it took forever, he swallowed hard once, leaned into the microphone, and repeated his oft-practiced line, in the most somber voice he could muster.

"Ladies and Gentleman…her Royal Highness, the Queen of Hawaii!"

Kay Kuahuula stepped forth onto the veranda of the upper deck of the Iolani Palace. Her bright white pant suit glimmered in the brilliant sun, adding an aura about her that had not been planned.

Instantly, the crowd exploded in celebration, joyous shouts, shrieks, and yells mingling with drum beats and blowing conch shells. Every ship in harbor set off its massive steam horns and fireworks exploded from all directions. The cacophony of sound and delirious celebration continued, unabated, for a full thirty minutes before Queen Kaila could finally address her subjects for the first time.

Always one to memorize her speeches, Congresswoman, Senator, and now, Queen Kaila, leaned into the microphone. Cameras and video feeds buzzed, flashed, and clicked around her in a frenzied orgy of paparazzi style news coverage. She began:

"The Kingdom of Hawaii is restored…" It was all she could manage before the roar of the exultant crowd exploded once again, the sheer volume drowning out any hope that she could continue beyond those first six words. She stepped back a half a step and smiled… and smiled, and smiled, every bit of it genuine. And Yunis smiled with her.

Chapter Thirty Seven

Her first day as a Royal had exhausted her, beyond even her own legendary reputation for stamina. Kay found herself a quiet alcove, a smaller balcony just off the Palace's second-story library room. She had always loved to read, ever since she was a small child, but this time she sought solace there, not for the books, but for the isolation she figured she would find there at 11:00 at night – she was right; the room was empty.

Keeping the lights off, she made her way to a lounging couch, within inches of the balcony doors. Opening them, she welcomed the cool night breeze into the room. She plopped down on the couch, slowly kicking off her heels, one at a time, letting them drop from off her feet unceremoniously. Starlight filled the room with just enough illumination to perceive her surroundings.

She closed her eyes, bringing her delicate fingers over her forehead for a slow rub of her temples, then opened them again…and that is when she noticed someone standing in the main doorway, poised in-between the hall and the Library.

"Come on in," she said, the tiredness in her voice evident.

"I brought you some wine. You'll like it," he replied, his face brimming, hands filled with a bottle and two glasses. "It's my own private vintage. I make it myself, you know."

He poured her a glass, then one for himself, setting the bottle on the table next to them.

She sat upright, offering the space beside her on the small antique couch to him. Silence filled the room, punctuated only by the occasional sound of one or the other of them sipping their wine. She stared at him in the shadowy darkness for some moments, her eyes taking in the shape of him, his distinctive Middle Eastern features; the eyes, the hair, the slope of his nose…

"How come a young man like you is not out on a date at this time of the evening? No girlfriend?" she asked, her questions more small-talk than genuine curiosity.

She had known Yunis for years now, had originally hired him on staff when he was still in high-school, as was common amongst the Senate Pages. Looking back across the years now, she could not recall much of his résumé, nor how it had come to be that a young man like him wound up on the short list for service as a U.S. Senate Page in Washington, D.C. – nor how, in fact, he had ended up on her staff.

He was good, of that there was no doubt. He knew his way around people, had a gift for making others feel comfortable, spoke multiple languages, and was a consummate politician. Skills that would carry him far in life, yet…

"My father was Lebanese; my mother, Hawaiian," he offered, deftly avoiding her original question while simultaneously answering the one that was on her mind, as if somehow he knew what she was thinking.

"What kind of name is Yunis? God, you've worked for me for years now and I don't even know your history, your background…what kind of name is that, anyway?" she asked, her voice softening, almost seductive.

"It is Arabic, in origin," he replied.

"What does it mean?" she continued.

"I don't truly know what my name means; I do know how it translates into English, though," he said, a slight grin spreading across his face.

"Well?" she responded.

He answered, "It translates as Jonah. Yunis is Arabic for Jonah."

AUTHOR'S NOTES

LAVA, much like my first novel WIND IN THE PASS, is a work of fiction but…one which is closely based on actual events and real-life characters from history. Below are some (but not all) of the historically accurate examples of characters or events from the ancient past of the Azores, Brazil, and Hawaii, which show up in the text of the novel:

FACT: for many years there was a Catholic Jesuit Monastery on the Azore island of Faial, near the city of Horta; the existence of this facility is referenced by a number of historical documents. The last remaining edifice of this centuries-old institution is a parish church, Igreja Matriz São Salvador, which still stands today. In 1680, construction of this church began upon the former foundation of the old Jesuit Monastery. Today, this church also houses the Town Hall and the Museum of Horta. It is historically accurate that Jesuit monks were often the most educated persons within a community. During an era in which the vast majority of persons were illiterate, often including royalty and military officers, it was Jesuit monks who were multi-lingual, multi-literate, and who studied and understood advanced science, mathematics, and astronomy in addition to theology. There is no evidence whatsoever of Chinese monks being exiled from the temple of Shaolin and ending up in the Jesuit monasteries of Europe, teaching the art of kung-fu; that portion of the story is purely the work of this author's imagination.

FACT: the eruption of Cabeço Gordo on the Azore island of Faial. The Cabeço Gordo Volcano did erupt in 1672; this catastrophic event led to a mass migration of young Portuguese men away from Faial to destinations abroad, principally Brazil. I have taken the liberty of moving this event forward into time, more than a hundred years, to lend continuity and ambience to the fictional story I have created.

FACT: For a greater part of the 16th, 17th, and 18th centuries, the Azore islands were a ready supply for sailing ships needing to fill their crew with seamen. More often than not, a ship pulling into port on any of the Azore islands often left said port with a number of local men, mostly younger, seeking adventure, travel across the seas, or respite from the drudgery of a life devoted to the agricultural pursuits endemic to a small island out in the middle of the Atlantic Ocean. Over time, the Azore islands came to have a reputation among sea captains worldwide as a primary location for the recruitment of hard-working and able seamen.

FACT: the *Fair American* was actually a ship that did sail the oceans and was overtaken by local Hawaiians on or about 1790. It was a schooner of American registry, not a British warship, as I have portrayed it in my fictional account; it was deployed in pursuit of the lucrative fur trade between China and the Pacific Northwest. It was, however, truly captained by one Thomas Metcalf, the 19-year old son of Captain Simon Metcalf who was scheduled to rendezvous with his son's vessel in Hawaii. While awaiting said rendezvous, the *Fair American* was indeed attacked by native Hawaiians and every man aboard was killed, except one Isaac Davis. Muskets and cannon were scavenged off the *Fair American* and put to use by Kamehemeha's armies.

FACT: Captain James Cook was killed at Kealakekua Bay on the Big Island of Hawaii in 1779. His ship was the *Resolution* and it had docked there one month earlier, to a very hospitable reception by the local Hawaiians. Within a month, he returned to that site to repair a broken main mast and received a radically different reception. Records which remain from his voyage tell of a small party going ashore and encountering a kahuna whom they called the lizard-man. He is described as bloody-eyed and scaly-skinned, a condition credited by some as being the result of a life-long consumption of awa. Captain Cook's sailing master aboard the *Resolution* was, in fact, William Bligh, a man who would later go on to infamy of his own as the captain of the Bounty, and villain of the historically accurate *Mutiny On The Bounty*. Kamehameha (although not yet a King at that time) is believed to have been present at the death of Captain Cook and during this battle, his face was indeed scarred, a mark he carried for life. According to most accounts, Captain Cook's men, who by then had shot and killed locals, were fleeing back to their small dinghies when they were overcome by a Hawaiian fighting force; as Cook turned his back to help launch the boats, he was struck on the head by the Hawaiian soldiers and then stabbed to death as he fell on his face in the surf. His corpse was dragged back onto the beach. Still held in esteem by the Hawaiians, his body was protected by war chiefs and elders. Following the local practice of the time, Cook's body underwent funerary rituals similar to those reserved for the highest ranking Hawaiian chiefs. The body was disemboweled,

baked in fire to remove the flesh, and then the bones were carefully cleaned for preservation.
The site where Cook was killed is still visible to this day, off the Kona side of the Big Island, off State Highway 160, within the Kealakekua Bay State Historic Park. The location is marked by a white obelisk, named the Captain Cook monument, built around 1874; approximately 25 square feet of land around it is chained off. This land, though in Hawaii, has been granted to the United Kingdom; thus, the site is officially a part of the British empire. A small community, officially named Captain Cook, Hawaii, is found 45 minutes south of Kailua-Kona, near the Kealakekua Bay.

FACT: the isle of Fernando Noronha, otherwise known as Hole-In-The-Wall, is a tropical archipelago located 220 miles offshore from the Brazilian coast. By the 18th century, after having been claimed and occupied by first the Portuguese, then English, French, and Dutch sovereigns, it found itself under the control of a free and independent Brazil. The Brazilians made the island a prison, incarcerating their political and civil dissidents there. It remained as such until 1957.

FACT: Kamehameha I (or Kamehameha the Great) was the first sovereign to rule over the Kingdom of Hawaii. He fought and conquered the kings of the other islands and was the first Monarch to exercise rule over all of the individual islands of Hawaii, as a unified realm. Among his opponents was King Keoua, a cousin, who retained control over the west side of the Big Island Hawaii (including the districts of Hilo, Puna, and Kau) long after Kamehameha, who ruled from the east side of the island, had conquered both the islands of Maui and Oahu. Kamehameha was known as "the Lonely

One" due to his exile to the barren Kohala coast as a young boy, the present King of Hawaii being fearful of the young child and prophecies which accompanied his birth, among them one that the child would grow up to become a "Killer of Kings."
Eventually, Kamehameha defeated his cousin Keoau at a battle in Hilo, although King Keoua would not be killed at that time. The fictional account I have provided of his death is of my own making and varies from the known facts of the historical account.

The fictional story I have created paints King Kamehameha in a somewhat negative light while simultaneously painting King Keoua in a somewhat positive light – this is nothing but the work of this author's imagination and, in fact, strays from the historical perspective on these two monarchs. King Keoua was just as guilty as any other Hawaiian monarch of lusting for power and resorting to brutal warfare to achieve his own desires. There is nothing factual which indicates that King Keoua was a peace-seeker and, in fact, he warred against Kamehameha at every opportunity.

Kamehameha's legacy, on the other hand, has secured for itself a place of great respect among the Hawaiian people and the world at large. He has been nick-named the Napoleon of the Pacific for his military exploits and successful unification of all the Hawaiian Islands. He is remembered for the "Law of the Splintered Paddle" which protects the human rights of non-combatants in times of war; this edict alone is estimated to have saved thousands of lives during Kamehameha's various campaigns of conquest. It became the first written law of the Kingdom of Hawaii and was included in the State Constitution.

Near the end of his reign, Kamehameha ultimately ended the practice of human sacrifice, although he continued to follow native Hawaiian religion, traditions, and culture, including Lua, until the time of his death. Multiple statues exist of the first King of Hawaii including one at the northern tip of the Kohala Coast of the Big Island; one in Honolulu, across from the Royal Iolani Palace; one in Hilo (facing the Hilo bay); and one in the National Statutory Hall Collection at the U.S. Capitol in Washington D.C. Likenesses of King Kamehameha appear on the State quarter coin of Hawaii as well as on Hawaiian license plates. Kamehameha died on May 8, 1819; his body was subsequently hidden by trusted friends. To this day, his final resting place remains unknown.

FACT: a kapu system was in effect throughout most of Hawaii's history, including at the time of first contact with Europeans. This system enforced a strict hierarchy, or caste system, in which persons were codified as either royalty (ali'i), or among the chiefly class (subordinate rulers over others, including kahunas and landowners) or commoners (the working class). Under kapu, commoners were forbidden from eating together (men and women), could not eat certain fruits (among them banana) and, should the sun happen to cast even so much as their shadow upon one of the ali'i?...they were promptly executed.

FACT: the episode, wherein Princess Lilena claims a past life, is closely based on the factual story of Perpetua, a first century Christian martyr. Still extant are historical texts, undisputed in their veracity by scholars, in which she gives a first-hand account of her last days, followed by others who witnessed the manner of her death. Perpetua was a young woman of Tunisian noble birth who converted to Christianity during the first century A.D. She was a new mother, who was still nursing an infant child; nothing is known of the father of her child. She was imprisoned for her faith by the Roman government but refused to recant, a simple gesture that would have set her free. Scheduled for death in the coliseum, her last night in jail was spent nursing her child, a kindness which the Roman jailers allowed. The next morning she, and her Christian companions, were given a final opportunity to recant their faith by burning a pinch of incense, in honor of the Roman Emperor; they refused and were brought before a packed coliseum crowd for entertainment. Wild animals, including a bull and a leopard, were set loose and promptly tore the Christian martyrs to pieces, except Perpetua. Although severely injured by the beast's biting and scratching, her wounds were not fatal and the animals refused to proceed any further. A Roman gladiator was forced to finish her off by the sword; multiple historical texts tell of how this young Roman gladiator's hand wavered, the sword shaking, as it was fearfully placed to Perpetua's body. The reason for his apprehension remains unstated but many have proffered that the young gladiator saw something within Perpetua that caused him to greatly fear being the one responsible for her death. She reached out with her own hands and drew the positioned blade into herself, thus releasing the gladiator from his guilt-filled task and herself from this life. Veneration for Perpetua includes saint-hood from both the Roman Catholic Church and the Eastern Orthodox Church. The Lutheran Church, the Episcopal Church, and the Anglican Church of Canada all honor Perpetua through calendar commemoration and inclusion in the Book of Common Prayer.

FACT: First century Christians, often forced to conceal their beliefs upon the pangs of death, resorted to secret communication techniques; among these was the symbol of the fish, a graphical homage to the miracle performed by Jesus of Nazareth. According to accounts found in all four canonical Gospels, Jesus fed thousands of his followers by inexplicably multiplying just five loaves of bread and two fish into a quantity sufficient to satisfy the hunger of over 4,000 persons. Early Christians, wary of being identified as such, upon introductions to strangers claiming to share the faith, would often draw the half arc  then await their companion to finish the symbol by drawing the other half, connecting the apex of one end to form the shape of a fish!  Completion of this graphic icon assured both parties that they were indeed fellow believers. Failure to complete the icon typically led to suspicion that the un-initiated was not a fellow believer and was to be avoided, characteristic of an infiltrator seeking to ferret out Christians for submission to the Roman government for punishment.

FACT: Isaac Davis was a Welshman who served aboard the *Fair American*; in fact, he was the only sailor to survive a massacre by the native Hawaiians, who were allowed on board under the guise of trade, as the ship anchored off the Kealakekua Bay. He managed to live by jumping off into a canoe floating along side, after he had fought valiantly to save the ship. He was promptly clubbed senseless by the Hawaiian manning that canoe and believed dead. When he subsequently manifested life, his attackers were impressed by his spirit (*mana)* and brought him to the attention of King Kamehameha. The King maximized the opportunity by accepting Davis into the royal family while requiring of him certain duties; among these were instruction in the English tongue, instruction in the use of muskets and cannon (scavenged off the *Fair American*) and teaching Kamehameha's warriors European-styled war techniques. Davis was given a Hawaiian name and assisted the King with his military conquests of the islands, eventually becoming one of the Kamehameha's closest friends and adviser. He was ultimately appointed Governor of Oahu, and owned estates on Oahu, Maui, Molokai, and the Big Island. He died suddenly on April 1810 and was buried in Honolulu in the "Cemetery for Foreigners." Today, the exact location of this cemetery is a mystery and has been lost to antiquity.

FACT: The prophecy of Kapihe – the history and lore of the Hawaiian Kingdom includes a well known prophetic utterance given by a shaman by the name of Kapihe in the presence of King Kamehameha. This prophecy, recited verbatim in Chapter 28, states that, "The ancient kapu will be overthrown, the heiau and lele altars will be overthrown, and the images will fall down. God will be in the heavens; the islands will unite, the chiefs will fall, and those of the earth will rise." Initially capitalized upon by Christian missionaries, especially in view of the latter's claim to the land of the islands and the democratization of Hawaiian society that would eventually follow, the prophecy yet remains an enigma. Even the casual student of Hawaiian history will agree that the islands were united, for the first time, under Kamehameha I. It is true that, within one generation of Kamehameha's line, under the rule of his son Liholiho, the kapu system *began* to deteriorate but full dissolution of the kapu system remained years beyond the reign of King Kamehameha. Under Christian missionaries, idols were eventually torn down and yet…a literal fulfillment of this prophecy remains elusive…the phrase "those of the earth will rise" defies interpretation to this day and, given the modern resurgence of native Hawaiian deity worship, one could argue the prophecy has come full circle?

FACT: The Kilauea Crater did explode in 1790. At that time, Keoua's army, locked in a losing battle against Kamehameha, had divided itself and sent 1/3 of its soldiers, along with their wives and children, to Kau, fleeing around the path which encircles Kilauea Crater. At that exact moment, the crater erupted in a massive volcanic gush of fire, stones, hot ash, and poisonous gas, instantly killing over 100 souls.
King Kamehameha, upon learning of this cataclysm, promptly announced the support of the goddess Pele on behalf of his endeavors. For decades afterward, locals continued to tell of the ash-entombed effigies which remained in that area, whole bodied statues of soldiers, women, and children still frozen to the spot, their every feature still distinguishable through the grey-white coating of hot ash which had instantly calcified them. Today, the only remaining evidence of this event are the fossilized footprints still visible in the lava; these footprints can be found in the Hawaii Volcanoes National Park, accessed via the Kau Desert Trailhead adjacent to Highway 11 or via the Kau Desert Trail from Crater Rim Drive.

FACT: Human sacrifice was a common religious rite among ancient Hawaiians. During time of war, the act of taking one's enemy alive, and subsequently burning that enemy (still alive) upon an altar to a god or deity, was especially propitious.

FACT: The secretive island of Niihau, known as the forbidden isle, is the last place on earth where there still exists a concentration of pure native Hawaiians, approximately 130 permanent inhabitants. It is the westernmost island in the chain and is a very tiny atoll, consisting of no more than 69 square miles; it lies 17 miles southwest of Kauai, across the Kaulakahi Channel. Privately owned, and dedicated to the preservation of the native Hawaiian population, the island is generally off-limits to all but relatives of the island's owners, U.S. Navy personnel, government officials and invited guests. All residents live there rent-free. There is no telephone service, no internet service, and no automobiles. Horses are the main form of transportation; bicycles are also used. There are no power lines; solar power provides all electricity. Water comes from rainwater catchment devices. There is no hotel or general store; barges deliver groceries from the island of Kauai. All residents speak the Hawaiian language; other language use is discouraged. Residents have radio and television, although limited reception effectively limits the latter to watching VHS tapes and DVDs. In the past, the residents were not allowed to have newspapers, and most books were banned by the island's owners although that practice has been relaxed in recent years. In short, Niihau strives to be a microcosm of what ancient Hawaiian language, culture, practice, and way of life would have been, had it never been subject to influences outside of Hawaii. An ethno-social experiment of sorts, the results of which may never be made known or shared, as utmost privacy on the island, and to its inhabitants, remains paramount… as well as its secrets.

FACT: The Apology Resolution, U.S. Public Law 103-150, is a Joint Resolution of the U.S. Congress adopted in 1993 that "acknowledges that the overthrow of the Kingdom of Hawaii occurred with the active participation of agents and citizens of the United States and further acknowledges that the Native Hawaiian people never directly relinquished to the United States their claims to their inherent sovereignty as a people over their national lands, either through the Kingdom of Hawaii or through a plebiscite or referendum." The resolution has served as a major impetus for the Hawaiian sovereignty movement.

The legal effect of the Apology Resolution was addressed in the decision of the U.S. Supreme Court of March 31, 2009, which held that the 37 "whereas" clauses of the Apology Resolution have no binding legal effect, nor does it convey any rights or make any legal findings for native Hawaiian claims. The Court concluded that the Resolution does not change or modify the "absolute" title to the public lands of the State of Hawai'i. The decision also affirmed that federal legislation cannot retroactively cloud title given as a part of statehood in general.

The Resolution was adopted by both houses of the U.S. Congress on November 23, 1993. It passed in the Senate by a vote of 65-34 and, in the House of Representatives, it was passed by a two-thirds voice vote. A Joint Resolution, it was signed by President Bill Clinton on the same day.

The full affects of this landmark legislation are yet to be determined. Questioning on the floor of the Senate was intense and the debate sometimes heated. But in Hawaii, most of the residents celebrated the Joint Resolution as a "first step" towards sovereignty and, ultimately, the restoration of the Kingdom of Hawaii.

FACT: Iolani Palace – to enhance the prestige of Hawaii overseas and to mark her status as a modern nation, the government of the Kingdom of Hawaii appropriated funds to build a modern palace. The cornerstone for the Iolani Palace was laid on December 31, 1879 with full Masonic rites. In December of 1882, King Kalakaua and Queen Kapi`olani took up residence in their new royal home. The new Iolani Palace was outfitted with the most up-to-date amenities of that era, including indoor plumbing. Gas chandeliers installed when the Palace was first built were replaced by electric lighting five years later (less than seven years after Edison invented the first practical incandescent bulb). The King also installed a modern communications system that included the recently invented telephone. Iolani Palace became the official residence where Hawaiian royalty performed official functions, received dignitaries and luminaries from around the world, and entertained. It was the center of social and political life for the Kingdom of Hawaii until the monarchy was overthrown in 1893. Under the threat of violence, on January 17, 1893, Queen Lili`uokalani yielded her authority to Sanford B. Dole, writing the following:

". . . Now to avoid any collision of armed forces, and perhaps the loss of life, I do this under protest and impelled by said force yield my authority until such time as the Government of the United States shall, upon facts being presented to it, undo the action of its representatives and reinstate me in the authority which I claim as the Constitutional Sovereign of the Hawaiian Islands."

Two years later, a futile attempt by some Hawaiian royalists to restore Queen Liliuokalani to power resulted in her arrest. She was forced to sign a document of abdication that relinquished all her future claims to the throne. Following this, she endured a humiliating public trial before a military tribunal in her own former throne room, within Iolani Palace. The Kingdom of Hawaii was abolished.

Convicted of having knowledge of a royalist plot, the Queen was fined $5000 and sentenced to five years in prison at hard labor. The sentence was commuted to imprisonment in an upstairs bedroom of the Iolani Palace. During her imprisonment, the queen was denied any visitors other than one lady in waiting. She began each day with her daily devotions followed by reading, quilting, crochet-work, or musical composition. After her release from Iolani Palace, the Queen remained under house arrest for five months at her private home and was forbidden to travel away from Oahu for a number of years.

Today, the Iolani Palace, in Honolulu, Hawaii, has been meticulously restored to its original grandeur; it is available to the public for tours as well as special events. It remains the only royal palace in the United States used as an official residence by a reigning

Monarch and is a National Historic Landmark listed on the National Register of Historic Places.

FACT: The Sovereignty Movement - the islands of Hawaii occupy a unique place in the history of U.S. expansionism. Today, one of 50 United States, it enjoys a benefit not yet extended to other U.S. possessions and protectorates, such as the Virgin Islands, Guam, or Puerto Rico. Despite this, a strong sovereignty movement exists, with a number of native Hawaiians, and non-native or mixed-race residents of Hawaii, clamoring for dissolution from the United States and a return to full and independent sovereignty, as the Kingdom of Hawaii. The will of many, to see a full restoration of their rights to all property, and in some cases, reparations, based on Hawaiian ancestry or lineage, continues to abut the reality of modern-day economic and cultural dynamics, proffered by any number of non-Hawaiians or non-residents who claim that one simply cannot go back in time and un-do the reality of history. The fight for possession of the land, a battle which has claimed many lives, has spanned centuries of time, and enveloped populations of both native Hawaiians and outsiders, persists…the struggle continues.

FACT: A Spiritual Battlefield - a tiny collection of islands, out in the middle of the Pacific ocean, would appear to be an odd arena for a spiritual drama of this magnitude to unfold; yet Hawaii remains exactly that, and has been since before white Christian missionaries set foot on its volcanic soil. Three years before the presence of any biblical literature on the islands, and before the presence of any Christian missionaries, the Hawaiian culture and religion was already undergoing a revolutionary upheaval. Its creation myths, parallel in so many ways to the Genesis story, its construct for Cities of Refuge (directly out of the Old Testament), and its practice of male circumcision, among other factors, seems to have prepared the Hawaiian people for what was to come. Yet ancient deities do not give up their worshippers so lightly and, for a number of years after the arrival of missionaries, violence broke out among competing faiths. Worshippers of the ancient gods (Ku, Lono, Pele, among others) found their beliefs in conflict with the insistence of the Christian faith upon a single Deity. Spiritual struggles led to interpersonal battles, as royal Hawaiian lineages converted, sometimes back and forth, between the old ways (with its gods) and the new ways (with its One God) and the result was often bloodshed. Today, although bloodshed is no longer common, island dwellers are still spiritually conflicted, some fiercely Christian while others are fiercely devoted to the ancient Hawaiian deities – unfortunately, leaving a majority of spiritual seekers irrevocably caught in-between, as they seek to assimilate both ways of belief into their life…the struggle continues.

FACT: the Big Island of Hawaii ***is*** haunted. Too many reputable stories abound, from reliable first hand sources of multiple sightings of Pele (often glimpsed late at night, shuffling alone down the Volcano Highway, commonly in the form of an old bent over crone, a long mane of shocking white frizzled hair cascading down her back…I would know; I saw her!), to sightings of the night-marchers, to reports from those who have been attacked by the choking ghosts (another phenomena which I have been personally subjected to), to the haunted caves of the Puna District (where I experienced a horrific paranormal experience), to the ancient Hawaiian heiaus which dot the landscape; many of which still hold the spirits of those who were tragically sacrificed there, their horrendous and ghastly deaths forever imprinted upon the soil, the rocks, and the waters – and wreaking havoc with those among the living foolish enough to tread lightly into their domain…a lesson learned, yet again, through first-hand experience, an episode so shocking, so profound, and so life-altering that I cannot bring myself to describe it for you yet, although it has been 28 years since it occurred!

The History Channel's television series "Haunted History" has done an exposé on the hauntings occurring in Hawaii as the record of paranormal incidents from reputable sources continue to multiply – shocking, frightening, and (in some rare cases, including my own) actually harming those who have tread where they should not have gone – where no one of us (among the living) should ever go.

Look for David Allee's next novel, coming out soon…!

THE GOOD SERPENT ORPHANAGE

Never listed in public directories and located at the end of a desolate road, it remains one of the worst cases of child abuse ever recorded in American history.

At the turn of the century, children of the Good Servant Orphanage and Continuation School hailed from all over the world, including the infamous Appalachian Experiment children. Twelve year old Luther, a third degree burn victim and the reluctant head of the children, leads small groups of his deformed peers as they sneak out at night to find food, completely oblivious to how unforgiving a community can be of those who are "different."

So hideous looking are the small night-foragers that the locals soon change the name of the institution from its given moniker, "Good Servant" (referring to Christ) to "Good Serpent" (referring to the Devil). A deliberately set fire puts a violent end to the sufferings and horrors that were perpetuated upon these young innocents whom society abandoned to the custody of a wicked headmaster.

This historically accurate novel also serves to explain much of the paranormal occurrences in the old Borges Ranch area of Vallejo. To this day, the violent young souls of the Good *Serpent* Orphanage are often seen in this area at night; terrorizing anyone unfortunate enough to cross their paths after dark...making it one of the most haunted locales in northern California.